When Playas Play

by Da'Author Raymone

Publisher: Life After Death Publicationz

Editor: Katrina Breier

DEDICATIONS

I dedicate this book to all the playa's and playette's.

ACKNOWLEDGEMENTS

I would like to acknowledge my fans nationwide, thank you all for supporting my career. To my loyal supporters on social media websites and book groups, you fuel my drive to be the best writer I can possibly be. Thanks to Katrina and Charles at Life After Death Publicationz for signing me and giving me a chance. Thanks to Justin for designing my cover and MzHollywoodStacks for being my cover model. Fitzgerald, Georgia is representing. I would like to thank my wife and mom for staying down in the trenches with me because I can be tough to deal with at times. I love you two. Also, big ups to Chris at Pine City barbershop in Southern Pines, North Carolina for selling my books. I really appreciate it bro'.

DEAVIN

The past six months of my life had been filled with grief and pain on one end and continuous female drama on the other. As for the continuous female drama, it's been going on in my life for years. However, last November, my great grandmother passed away unexpectedly and it devastated me. With me being her favorite grandchild, she had always pampered me and in her eyes I could do no wrong. I lived with her, on and off, until my mid-twenties. Throughout those years she raised me to be a good, caring, respectable gentlemen; at least that's what she thought.

After moving from her home on Emory Smith Street in Taylortown, to Fayetteville, five years ago, I became what most people called a 'womanizer'. I had women blowing up my phone daily, trying to spark arguments or cuss me out over bullshit. The reasons being was that I'd either stood them up on a date or they'd claimed one of their friends saw me creeping around with another woman. I was the kind of guy who would tell a woman damn near whatever she wanted to hear when we were together, just to get what I wanted, or to have my way with her.

I stepped out of my apartment one afternoon about a month ago and discovered that someone had spray painted obscene words on the outside of my door. *'Whoorish Dog Motherfucker'* is what it read. Two days later someone slit all four tires on my Escalade, while it was parked directly in front of my apartment. To make matters worse, it was the second time my tires had been slit in a two-month span.

"It's time for me to move on," I told my pops after the last incident.

My decision to move didn't have a thing to do with the city of Fayetteville, it was my hometown and I loved it. I was just sick and tired of being hounded and harassed by the women I no longer associated with. I was also trying to get away from something that I had once vowed would never happen to me.

My Grandma Ada had left me $75,000 in her will and I had plans of starting my own business, once I relocated to another city. For four years I'd been busting my ass doing janitorial work for Ratcliff Cleaning Service. I did everything from buffing and waxing floors, to vacuuming and washing windows. I was dedicated to my job because it was easy work and paid the bills. I knew that since I stayed dedicated to Ratcliff for four years, I wouldn't have any problem working hard for myself.

"Mark!" I shouted across the room over the loud buffer, trying to get his attention.

This was my last night working for Ratcliff and I wanted to know if he was still interested in leaving town with me.

"Yeah Dee, what's up?" He answered, shutting off the buffer.

Dee was my nickname. The majority of my friends called me that.

"What are you planning to do?" I asked, walking up to him with a bottle of brass cleaner in my hand. "You moving down to the ATL with me or what?"

"Damn right," he replied, giving me some dap. "There's no way in this world I can see passing on a golden opportunity to move to the new Black Hollywood of the south."

"I'm glad you finally made up your mind. Shit, for the past week I been thinking that you were going to stay here."

"Nooo, man. It wasn't like that. It's not easy for a guy like me to just up and go. My finances haven't been straight lately."

"Your financial problems disappeared over the course of seven days?"

"You know it," he responded, grinning. "I got my income tax money back yesterday and I don't owe a living soul shit."

"What about your girl Lynda, she's coming with you, right?"

"Lynda?" He said as if her name left a nasty taste in his mouth. "I can't wait to get away from that controlling ass woman. All she wanna do is go shopping and out to eat every time I get paid. I got a trick for her gold digging ass this time around. She done dug the last dime out of me."

"Damn Mark, I thought you and Lynda had that Beyoncé and Jay Z kind of love going on."

"I thought we did too. That is until I realized she was the reason I stayed so damn broke. Hell," he chuckled. "That's what I get for being naive about everything."

Mark and I had been boys for years and I had no idea he'd been letting Lynda milk him for his money. I didn't want to talk about it and decided to change the subject. "I'm pulling up outta here Monday morning. When are you gonna be ready?"

"At least two weeks from now. I haven't even put in my two weeks' notice yet. Then I gotta go online and see if I can find an apartment and a half decent job in the Atlanta area."

"There's no need for you to worry about finding a job or an apartment before you leave. I already have a spacious two-bedroom condo lined up for me and I'll be more than happy to split the rent with you. Now as for a job, I'm gonna start my own business once I get down there. You can work for me."

"Work for you? Who in the hell you suppose be, Nino Brown?"

"Come on man, you know my motto. Work for it or let the ladies pay for it. I'll never attempt the drug trade, I value my freedom too much. To hell with going to jail, I can't even imagine living in that kind of world without women. I gotta have me a piece of pussy on the regular."

"I feel you on that."

"Here's the deal Mark. I'm going to start my own janitorial service in Atlanta. That city is booming right now and I know I'll be able to make plenty of money. There's countless office buildings and stores that need cleaning. So when I get there I'm gonna make it happen."

"That's a damn good idea Dee," he agreed, nodding his head. "ATL here I come."

Driving down All American Freeway, heading home from work that early morning, I felt good knowing I had worked my last night at Radcliff. I knew my boss, Mr. Temp hated to see me go since I was such a good dependable worker. But like the game of life itself, time goes on and things change.

"Take good care of yourself son," Mr. Temp had said, giving me a strong handshake and hug when I got off work.

I was really going to miss that man. He'd been like a father figure to me over the years. However, I couldn't dwell on the past. I had to move forward.

As I turned off the Bragg Boulevard exit my phone rang. I checked the number to see who it was. To my surprise I wasn't familiar with the number and quickly answered, just in case it was an emergency. "Hello."

"Hey Boo."

I immediately recognized the voice. It was Tracy, she was the only woman who called me Boo.

"What's up?" I asked, wondering why she was calling me from a foreign number at four o'clock in the morning.

"Come by my Cousin Rhonda's house and pick me up after you get off work?"

"I'm already off and I'm about a mile from the crib. I'm tired as hell right now and I'm not trying to drive all the way out to Tiffany Pines this late."

"Come on, Boo --"

"Where your car at?"

"I let Rhonda drive it to work. She don't get off until seven."

"Where's her car?"

"In the shop."

"I'm telling you Tracy, I'm not driving out there."

"You know I wanna spend time with you before you leave."

"I'm tired Tracy. I'm about to fall asleep now."

"Unh-hunh," she murmured. "It's like that. I was thinking about letting you have it your way. You know what that means."

I knew exactly what that meant. Tracy was nice built with a big booty, like K Michelle. She very seldom allowed me to hit it from the back. Her complaint was that it was too painful, but she knew I loved it. This was an opportunity I couldn't pass up.

"Alright, I'm on my way. Be looking out for my headlights."

"Okay Boo, I'll be ready."

I hung up the phone and turned right on Old Shaw Road with thoughts of Tracy heavily weighing on my mind. I'd always been turned on by her thick thighs and big booty. Her chocolate body was well proportioned from top to bottom and front to back. Of all the women I'd dated, I actually cared for Tracy the most. It didn't have a thing to do with her looks. Come to think of it, she was probably the least attractive of all the previous women I'd ever dated; at least facially. However, she was far from being an ugly duckling. On my dime piece scale of 1 to 20, I gave Tracy a 9 on her body and a 6 on her face. As far as I was concerned, a 15 wasn't bad in my book. Especially since I had yet to meet a 20.

I'd met Tracy eighteen months ago while picking up my clothes from the dry cleaners. I'd been standing in line when I felt someone tap me on the shoulder. When I turned around she immediately asked me how tall I was and since that day she and I had been seeing each other.

I got the, 'how tall are you' question asked to me almost daily. I stood six-feet-six, 220 pounds, dark skinned, kept my hair cut in a low skin fade and wore a well-trimmed goatee. Most of the women I dated said their first attraction to me was my dimples, but my thoughts differed. I believed that most women wanted to get with me because of my height. They thought all tall men were well endowed. I didn't know about the other tall men, but God had definitely blessed me below the belt.

Prior to my late Grandma Ada's death, she and Tracy had established a close relationship together. On weekends she would make the forty-five minute drive to my grandmother's house to attend church with her, or to just sit around the house, listening to the childhood stories my grandmother told her about me. Tracy had taken my grandmother's death almost as hard as I did. During our mourning period, our relationship shot up to a level I had never expected.

Little did she know, she had the hook in my mouth, but I was bucking on letting her reel me in. I wasn't ready for the committed relationship thing. I enjoyed playing the field and knew my position well. I was the star PLAYA.

"Boo, we need to talk," Tracy said in her soft voice when I came out of the bathroom and climbed back in bed.

It was nearly six-thirty in the morning and she and I hadn't long ago finished getting our groove on. With most women I just straight up fucked to bust a nut. But with Tracy, there was something about her. I always made love to her.

"What in the hell you wanna talk about this early in the morning?" I responded jokingly. "You know I had to pull a double last night."

"You lying. You know you didn't have to pull no double," she smiled, playfully nudging me with her elbow as we both sat up.

"Hell if I didn't. I busted my ass at work last night. Then I put the dick down on you off and on for two hours when we got in early this morning."

She smiled again, showing her pretty teeth. Damn she had a beautiful smile.

"Awww boy, cut it out. You didn't do all that. I wear your butt out most of the time anyway."

"Yeah, you're right. That's when I'm already tired from pulling one of my famous doubles."

My famous double consisted of working an eight hour shift and having sex with two women during the same day.

"Don't tell me nothing like that, Deavin." She shook her head with hurt in her eyes. "You know how I feel about you. I've invested over a year and a half of my life with you already. You know I'm looking forward to you settling down with me."

Her stiff statement actually caught me off guard. Honestly, I thought she understood my lifestyle of wanting to remain single. Being straight up about the whole situation, I had absolutely no intentions of settling down with Tracy, or any other woman as far as that was concerned. I already had planned to make myself a new playa card once I arrived in Atlanta.

"Dam baby," I spoke, trying to avoid eye contact. "You know I'm not trying to be tied down in a steady relationship right now."

"Mmm-hmm," she mumbled, folding her arms at her naked breast. "I know when you and I first started talking you told me you wasn't a one woman kind of guy, but I thought I could somehow change you and I thought I had. Especially by the way you and I have bonded lately," she said, staring at me as if I had betrayed her as tears formed in her eyes.

"Listen babe." I gently wrapped my arms around her warm body and pulled her to my chest. She looked up into my eyes. "You know how much I care about you and only God knows how thankful I am to have had you in my corner when Grandma Ada passed. I don't think I would've been able to make it through it all without you." I kissed her forehead. "You already know I'm leaving town next week. Once I get things situated I'm gonna send for you. Okay?"

No sooner than the last word left my mouth, I had to have her thick lips. They looked tasty with the teardrops rolling off them. I gave her a long wet kiss that eased the tension in the room.

"Boo. I don't know how I allowed myself to do it, but it happened. I've fallen in love with you."

I was at a loss for words when *'fallen in love with you'* rolled off her tongue. I wasn't use to women telling me that because I never really allowed them to get that close to me. Tracy had gotten close to me, too close. I realized it was my fault for allowing it to happen.

She continued, "You don't have to look at me all crazy because I told you I'm in love with you." She caressed the back of my neck. "How long will it be before you send back for me?"

"Four to six weeks tops," I replied, causing an instant smile to appear on her face. She pulled my face to hers and we locked lips again.

RRRIINNNNGG! RRRIINNNNGG! RRRIINNNNGG!

As Tracy laid comfortably in my arms, my phone began ringing. I cursed silently to myself for forgetting to turn off the ringer after we'd gotten in. My mind had been so focused on hitting Tracy's plump booty from the back, that it slipped my thoughts. I didn't want to answer it in front of her because I was 99.9% sure the caller was one of my long list of booty calls. I had to hurry up and do something.

Tracy was staring at me with a hateful glare in her eyes. More drama, I thought as I reached for the phone. "Hello!" I answered, trying to sound agitated.

"Hi, how ya doing? Is everything okay?" Tarica asked.

Damn..., I knew it.

SHANTE

It was early spring and things were going pretty good for a diva like myself. My birthday was only days away and I had recently become the manager of Dolly's, which was an upscale soul food restaurant located downtown, off Marietta Street.

Managing Dolly's wasn't as hard as I initially thought, before I was promoted to the position a few months ago. With the staff being so professional at doing their job, things were pretty easy for me. My $40,000 yearly salary wasn't all that, but when you're pampered by men like I was, $40,000 was plenty.

I shared a spacious two bedroom apartment with my best friend, Monica. She and I got along as if we were sisters, even though our personalities were a lot different than each other's. Monica went club hopping every chance she got. She had absolutely no idea how to handle men and dressed like she was competing against Lil Kim in a 'Who Can Wear the Skimpiest Outfit Contest'. I constantly stayed on her about her little mishaps because she was four years younger than me and had yet to begin taking life seriously.

I grew up in the suburban community of Ellenwood, Georgia with my mother and stepfather. Growing up as an only child had its advantages and disadvantages for me. I was lonely a lot because I didn't have brothers, sisters or cousins to play with. It was also very seldom my parents allowed me to mingle with the other neighborhood kids. On the other hand, my parents made sure I had all the baby dolls, toys and clothes I desired.

Besides the extra attention and gifts I was showered with while growing up, my mother had also taught me a lot about the opposite sex and how to deal with them. I felt that most of the men I dated were very much intimidated by me because of my beauty and the way I carried myself. I was the kind of woman who always stood up to meet the challenge. I was also strong minded and determined to succeed in life. Not meaning to brag or anything, but my presence alone was a real attention getter to the men who saw me out and about in public. I'd even caught women and gay men staring at me with lust in their eyes.

So I knew without a shadow of a doubt that I had it going on. I stood five-feet-eight, light skinned, with slanted hazel eyes. I wore my hair cut in a short bob and had a petite hour glass figure. I had juicy breasts that didn't sag and a perfectly round ass that made men's tongues hang when I walked by.

"What time is it?" I yelled from the bathroom, asking Monica as I was getting ready for work.

"Time for your sad, wannabe Halle Berry, ass to get a watch!"

"I know you didn't go there on me this early in the morning girl," I shot back. "With your Whoopi Goldberg looking ass!"

"See, I was giving you a compliment by calling you Halle Berry! Now I'm changing my mind, Kim Parker! Kimmie, dumb ass, Parker from The Parkers!"

I couldn't help but laugh. Monica knew she could be a comedian at times. Even though she'd gotten a laugh out of me, I wasn't in a playful mood and had to cut her bullshit short before she got on a roll and got carried away.

"Alright, Monica. You win this morning. All I want to know is the time." I said while touching up my hair with the curling iron.

"It's five-thirty, Kimmie."

"Thanks Miss Smart Ass. I might bring your silly ass a doggie bag full of rice back, geechie!"

That word immediately silenced her. I knew she didn't like being called a geechie, but it was the only thing I could say to shut her up.

Her mother was originally from Beaufort, South Carolina, which was supposed to be the home of the geecheis. Monica once told me her mother was geechie, so that automatically makes her one too. She was my girl and all and I knew she hated being called a geechie. However, it was my only defense mechanism to use against her when she started getting on my nerves. Personally, I didn't know why she took offense to being called a geechie. She was cute, with pretty coco brown skin and she had a nice slim figure. She definitely had the Afrocentric, Lauren Hill look going for her, but didn't know how to use it to get ahead.

I was expecting a long busy day at work. I had two young college girls starting their first day and I knew that it was going to be hectic for my staff and I to train them during our busy brunch meal. Dolly's was known all over the city for its tasty menu and it attracted a great deal of business. So without a doubt I knew my staff and I had our work cut out for us.

I stepped out of my apartment at 5:45am, early in the morning, heading to work. After an eighteen minute drive I was parking my champagne colored BMW in my reserved parking space.

They day didn't go so bad but was hectic, the girls were fast learners. After a grueling and long day at work I headed home.

"Hello," I said as I answered my phone, moments after entering my apartment.

"How are you, baby?" Tim asked, trying to sound sexy. "What would you like to get into this evening?"

"What did I tell you about calling me baby?" I snapped at him. "You haven't done enough for me to earn the right to call me that. I would very much appreciate it if you'd just call me by my name."

"Damn ba-- I mean Shante. You don't have to be so hard on a brother."

"You haven't seen my hard side and you best watch your mouth before I introduce you to Mister Dial Tone."

I loved being in control of things when it came to dealing with men. They all knew it, but were too afraid to say anything to me about it.

"What would you like to do this evening?" He asked politely.

"The Sun Dial would be nice."

"Sun Dial?" He repeated as if he was surprised.

"Oh, you have a problem taking me out to a four star restaurant? I can't stand a cheap ass."

"No, no, Shante. I didn't mean it like that. The Sun Dial is fine."

"Thought so. I'll be ready at seven-thirty."

"But I have to --"

"Hold up little man!" I cut him short because I didn't want to hear it. "If you're not here by seven-thirty you might as well not come at all and lose my number. Do I make myself clear, Tim?"

"I'll be there."

"Bye."

I hung up thinking about how stupid most men were. Especially the ones like Tim. He wanted to get between my legs so bad that he would do almost anything I asked of him. So when you have a brotha's nose wide open like I had Tim's, you gotta take full advantage of him. Trust me, I played the game the way it was supposed to be played.

Wanting to look nice for the evening dinner date, I went into my closet to pick out an outfit. While contemplating what I was going to wear, I started thinking about the two college girls my staff and I trained earlier. Both Sabrina and Deshundria were fast learners and appeared to be good workers. At least that was the first impression I perceived of them. I was glad they'd finally started because we needed the help.

Just as he was instructed, dressed in a silk Grecian dress, Via Spiga leather sandals and Pat's USA chandelier earrings, I was being escorted out the door at 7:35 by Tim. He was about my height, slim build, brown skinned, kept his head clean shaved and was good looking.

He and I made small talk all the way to the Westin Peachtree Plaza and I enjoyed the long ride up the elevator, eyeing the city's magnificent skyline in awe. Once we made it to the Sun Dial, which was atop the 70 story building, I gave Tim a peck on the cheek before the Maître D' seated us.

Tim and I ordered a steak dinner for the main course and a couple of side dishes that were too tasty for my own good. Tim nibbled on his dinner like he was too shy to eat in front of me. As for me, I was the total opposite, I ate and enjoyed my meal without shame and drank one too many glasses of red wine in the process.

Though Tim might've been shy about eating in my presence, he wasn't when it came to making good conversation. He talked about everything from the law firm he was partners at, to the senseless mass killing at the Pulse night club in Orlando. I really had a nice time and decided to let him know how much I appreciated it.

"Thanks for dinner tonight," I told him when we pulled up in front of my apartment in his late model Porsche.

"You're welcome. I guess I'll call you sometime later this week."

"You are so rude, Tim!" I spat, clutching the $900 Coach bag he'd bought me only weeks earlier.

"What did I do wrong this time?" He threw up his hands looking confused.

"Are you going to at least walk a sista to the door?" I smiled, looking into his eyes with my irresistible seductive stare. "Better yet, turn off the car and come inside." I reached over and grabbed his hand to let him know I was serious.

"Oh..., okay," he stuttered.

It was easy to see how surprised he was when I invited him inside. He and I had only kissed on our previous dates. Never had I invited him into my place after a late evening date.

The apartment was silent when we entered and I assumed that Monica was out with her boyfriend, since there was no TV on and all the lights were off.

Tim and I had been going out for nearly six months and I was finally ready to allow him to round second base. I grabbed his tie and led him into my room, locking the door behind us. He stood leaning against the dresser, loosening his tie while I slipped out of my clothes and laid back in the middle of my bed, butt booty naked. I parted my legs and motioned for him to come taste my Nana.

For close to an hour, Tim gave me the best oral pleasure my body had ever experienced. From the tip of my toes, thighs, navel, neck, pussy lips, nipples and even the deepest part of my ass crack, he licked and sucked it all. He literally had my entire body shivering in ecstasy as he brought me to multiple orgasms. When the action stopped, I opened my eyes and saw him taking off the rest of his clothes. Without a moment of hesitation I jumped up and told him I wasn't quite ready to take our relationship to THAT level.

After a few minutes of his unsuccessful pleas for me to give him some, he stormed out of the apartment mumbling under his breath with a frown on his face.

"Damn you too! You should be satisfied, I even let you take that trip down south with your good pussy eating ass!" I yelled, slamming the door behind him.

When I locked the door and turned around, I was stunned to see Monica standing behind me with her hands up over her mouth as if she was in shock.

" ... I thought you was...,"

"Yeah, I know. You thought I wasn't home, right?" She slowly shook her head at me. "Why do you be treating that man like that girl? You're gonna mess around and get your feelings hurt and heart broke by somebody one of these days."

"Heart broke!" I spat, passing her as I headed back to my room. "I don't think so. I'm the one who do the heart breaking in my relationships." I stopped and looked back at her. "And who you supposed to be, Miss Cleo or Doctor Phil? You seeing the future now?"

DEAVIN

I arrived in Atlanta a few days later than I had first anticipated. Things were delayed due to the fact that the utilities at my new condo had yet to be turned on. I used those extra days to talk with Mr. Temp every moment I could. I asked him question after question about what I needed to do to be successful at running my own business and each time, he gave me some good advice. By the time I rolled into Atlanta I was feeling good about my new start.

Driving a U-Haul truck, with my Escalade attached to it, down Peachtree Street that early Thursday afternoon, I was surprised that the traffic wasn't too bad. I'd heard how terrible the traffic problems were, which manhandled the city on a daily basis.

"Whoooowee!" I shouted out the window as I passed the famous Fox Theater. "I'm gonna love it here!"

Since I wasn't familiar with the city, I made my share of wrong turns before I finally found my condo off Monroe Drive, in Ansley Park.

Two hours later, I had unloaded the U-Haul with the help of my new friendly neighbor, Scott. I'd been struggling to get a heavy piece of furniture on the hand truck when he walked up asking if I needed any help. I had always heard stories about people being extra friendly in the Deep South and figured Scott was one of those people. Though he didn't want to accept it, I paid him for helping me out.

Soon after he left, I set up my bedroom and unpacked most of my clothes. By then I was tired, but my being tired didn't stop me from wanting to go out on the town. When I got out of the shower I quickly got dressed, slapped on a dab of Higher Dior cologne and brushed my wavy hair while standing in front of the bathroom mirror.

"Watch out Atlanta, a new playa is on the loose," I said to myself, stepping out of the condo, looking down at my black Clarks.

I jumped in my Escalade and pulled off, listening to Anthony Hamilton. As I cruised down Marietta Street, my stomach started roaring. I hadn't eaten anything since I left Fayetteville that morning and I was starving. I didn't want to stop by a fast food joint for burgers and fries. I wanted to eat something that would stick to my stomach, like a good home cooked meal.

Moments after spotting a small crowd walking through the door of a restaurant called Dolly's, I immediately turned into the parking lot.

"Reservations sir?"

"No ma'am," I answered the young hostess as I stood in front of a short line. "This is my first night in town. I'm only looking for a nice place to dine."

"Well you've come to the right place," she said with a smile, eyeing me from head to toe. "Table for one or two?" She asked, looking past me.

"One, ma'am."

She escorted me to a corner table and handed me a menu. While scanning over it, I couldn't help thinking about how sexy the tall, brown skinned hostess was. *"Damn, I'd like to hit that,"* I thought.

"Would you like to order now sir?" A waitress asked, interrupting me from my lustful thoughts.

I looked up at the waitress and was stunned by her beauty and Coke bottle figure. "Would I," I replied, staring into her eyes. "Only if you come along with the dish."

"I'm afraid I don't," she said, blushing.

I was barely able to keep my eyes off her while I was undecided about my order. She was light skinned, bowlegged and stacked in all the right places. Her short auburn colored hair was styled in soft finger waves and her thick glossy lips were screaming out to be kissed.

"I'll take the fish platter with a sweat tea, no lemon," I finally said.

"Will that be all sir?"

"For now, yes."

When she walked away from the table it was easy for me to see that she had way more back than the hostess. I knew then that I would have to have her.

Forty-five minutes or so later, I was full and in the process of leaving a tip when the waitress approached my table smiling. She'd been giving me flirtatious looks each time she checked up on me during dinner.

"My friend tells me that you're new in town."

"Your friend? Who is your friend?"

"Deshundria. She's the hostess that seated you."

"Ohhh," I said, catching on and remembering what I'd told the hostess earlier. "I just moved here and this is my first night out in the city. What's your name?"

"Sabrina," she answered, blushing.

"Well Sabrina," I leaned back in the chair rubbing my stomach. "I had been on the brink of starving to death before I luckily stumbled up on this place. Whoever the cook is back there, they can really burn. I haven't tasted fish this good in years."

"This is only my second night working this shift and I've already fallen in love with the Smith's cooking."

"You're new around here too?"

"I'm new to this job, but not the city. I'm a born and raised Georgia Peach."

"You don't say," I said smoothly, stroking my goatee. "Maybe you can show a brotha around town? That's if you don't mind."

"I probably wouldn't mind being your personal tour guide, but it would be nice if I knew your name first."

"Deavin."

"Oh, you have one of them pretty boy names."

I smiled, showing off my dimples. "I'm a handsome man, you know. I gotta have a nice name to go along with the looks."

"You saying it's all that?"

"Yeah Sabrina, it's all that and some."

"Okay, Mister Deavin and Some, just leave me your number. I have a few more tables I need to get to."

"I broke my phone earlier today while unloading my furniture. I gotta get another one."

Of course my phone wasn't broke. I just wasn't about to start passing my number out so soon. I didn't need or want a thousand and one women ringing my phone off the hook every day.

"Well here's my number," she said, scribbling it down on a napkin. "Call me tonight. I'll be home by ten-thirty."

"Alright cool," I pocketed the number as I stood up. "Take good care of that peach for me. I don't want it to rot before I get the chance to taste it."

She winked at me. "It won't."

Soon as I stepped back in my condo I thought about Tracy and the big argument she and I had gotten into after Tarica called.

****

"Who was that?" Tracy had asked immediately after I hung up the phone.

"Oh nobody," I lied, with a straight face. "They had the wrong number."

"Wrong number huh," she sighed. "Pass me the phone Deavin. I'm calling a cab."

"Why you tripping girl? I told you the caller had the wrong number."

"Wrong number my ass! I wasn't born yesterday. Now pass me the damn phone!"

I snatched the phone off the nightstand, tossed it to her, got up out of the bed and went to the kitchen to get something to snack on. I heated up a strawberry Danish in the microwave and got a bottle of water. I munched on the tasty Danish as I headed back into the bedroom.

"You tall, black, sorry fucker!" She spat at me the moment I entered the room. "I knew your ass was lying!"

"About what?" I replied, holding my cool.

"Aaauugghh!" She screamed, balling up her fist. "I knew that was one of your bitches who called. And you had the nerves to tell me they had the wrong number!"

I stood fast near the doorway, finishing up my snack while she continued on with her shouting tirade. Then I finally decided to speak up in my defense. "But Tracy, it wasn't...,"

"I don't wanna hear nothing your lying ass got to say 'cause you're bout to tell another lie! You thought you was smart by erasing the bitch's number off the caller ID, but I hit star 69 to see who the bitch was. Me and that bitch Tarica even had a short conversation," she said while putting on her shoes. "I'm gonna drag her red prissy ass when she get over here."

"What do you mean?"

"I'm gonna show you and that red bitch what I mean! She told me she was gonna kick my ass if I was still here when she gets here. I'm praying the bitch shows up. I can't wait to get on her ass."

"Now Tracy, you know damn well that I don't fuck around with her no more. And I don't know why she threatened you. She's not coming over here to do shit, but get her feelings hurt."

"If you wasn't still messing around with the bitch Deavin," she said with watery eyes. "You wouldn't have lied to me when she called."

"No, it ain't like that baby." I sat on the bed beside her and put my arm around her. "You know Tarica ain't nothing but a shit starter. So baby," I kissed her teary cheek. "Let that shit go."

"Why Deavin? Why do you continue taking me through all these changes time and time again?"

I couldn't tell her the real reason why I did things to deceive her, especially during the past few months. The truth was at the tip of my tongue, but I stayed strong and kept it to myself.

When Tarica pulled up in front of my apartment blowing her horn like a mad New York taxi driver, I told Tracy to stay in the room while I went outside to talk to her, but she wasn't trying to hear that shit. I ended up staying in the room holding her back until Tarica got tired of blowing the horn and pounding on my front door.

Now with Tracy not being able to get her hands on Tarica, she tried fighting me instead. I didn't even attempt to hit her back. I just wrestled her down on the bed and held her there until she eventually stopped.

Shortly after Tarica left, Tracy and I got naked and made up. That makeup sex was the most satisfying sex I'd ever had and I didn't even hit it from the back. My entire body shook like I was having a seizure as I exploded deep inside her.

****

I had a business lunch meeting with Mr. Davis, who was Mr. Temp's old army buddy. When I'd told Mr. Temp of my plans to start my own cleaning service in Atlanta, he immediately knew that his old friend would be more than happy to do him a favor by helping me get things up and running with my business.

I'd called Mr. Davis only a couple minutes ago. To my surprise, he didn't hesitate to set up the meeting. He wanted me to meet him at Dolly's at 12:30, Monday afternoon. I was anxious to meet with him because I was ready to start building the foundation of my new business to be.

While driving to the restaurant to meet Mr. Davis, I thought about the fine waitress, Sabrina. I still had her number, but I had yet to call her. I knew from years of experience that the longer I put off calling her, the easier it would be for me to hit it when I did decide to call. Without a doubt, it was very tempting for me to call her over that weekend, especially after I thought about how fine and fat her ass was. However, being the playa I was, I fought off the temptations and played my Xbox all weekend.

I entered Dolly's at 12:24 pm and Mr. Davis was already sitting at a table with food ordered, waiting for me.

SHANTE

I lazily rolled over in bed and thought about calling in sick. I had to second guess that notion because I didn't want to start setting bad examples for myself or the employees that worked under me.

Last week I started celebrating my birthday. Monica had come home from school and told me she wanted to take me out for an early birthday present. I had asked her several times where were we going, but her only response was, "wait and see." I eventually killed the questions and got ready. I slipped on some hip hugging Der'eon jeans, a Dsquared2 halter wrap top that showed off my cleavage and put on my crystal wedge sandals.

After I was dressed and ready, Monica took me out to a club in Decatur. When we got there I was a little hesitant about going inside, since I didn't care much for the club scene, but Monica convinced me to. There was a strange atmosphere about the club crowd when we entered. I didn't figure it out until Monica and I sat at a table near the stage. The place was filled with women and they were still coming through the door in packs.

"Girl, I know you didn't bring me to a strip club?"

"No, it's not a strip club," she replied sternly. "It's a regular club that's having a male review tonight."

"Oh my God!" I blurted, putting my hands up to my face, eyeing the stage. "I know them guys up there aren't strippers?"

"No, birthday girl," she giggled. "They're exotic dancers. Who you thought they were, The Village People?"

"That wasn't funny girl," I stood up holding my purse. "I'm about to go. I'm not about to sit up in here and watch no sleazy strip show."

Monica jumped up and grabbed my arm. "Don't take everything so damn serious. Sit your butt back down, loosen up and relax a little."

I did what she said, but I couldn't really relax. A stud seated at a table across from us kept licking her long tongue out at me like I had interest in her tongue ring. Just as I was about to get up and check her ass, she stopped. Seconds later, Monica called a waitress to our table and we ordered Long Island Ice Tea's. Once the drinks arrived, I sipped on mine and tried to enjoy the show.

"Ooohhh yes," she groaned like she was having an orgasm. "There he is girl!"

"There who is?" I asked, looking around in the crowd of screaming ladies.

"Dance Machine!" She shouted. "He's the finest dancer in the city."

"Well I can't tell."

"Just wait 'til he strips down and you'll see why all these women up in here are about to lose their minds."

As Dance Machine did his routine, my eyes became glued to his toned bronzed body. I couldn't help seeing that he had a lot of loving to offer a woman. The brotha had to have at least 12 to 14 inches of prime beef, swinging between his legs. King Dingling is the new name I thought up for him when he left the stage. At that point I had seen more than enough; Miss Tongue Ring included. I got up to leave.

"I'm outta here Monica."

"Come on Shante," she pleaded. "The show is just beginning to get good. I brought you here as my birthday present to you. Sit back down and relax. The drinks are on me, remember?"

"I wouldn't care if the drinks were on the house, I'm gone. Give me the keys. I'll wait out in the car."

Monica didn't attempt to stop me this time. She got up and left with me.

"What in this world gave you the idea to take me out to a strip club?" I asked as she and I turned out of the club parking lot onto Gleenwood Road.

"I thought it would be something new to you and figured you'd like it," she shrugged her shoulders. "But I guess not."

"I did enjoy watching Dance Machine's performance. That brotha definitely got it going on. I probably would've been able to relax and enjoy myself if it hadn't been for all the yelling and screaming. I swear to God I didn't think women could get that loud and indignant over some dick. To make matters worse, the light skinned sista who had the blonde dyed, short hair, which was sitting across from us, kept licking her nasty ass tongue out at me like she wanted to eat me alive. But when she started sliding her finger in and out of her mouth and winked at me in the process, I knew I had to get up outta there then."

"Why didn't you tell me that shit before we left? You know I would've got on that dyke bitch ass!"

"I know. I could've got on her ass too. It's good neither one of us had to go there. The last thing them women in that club needed to see was the South side Chicago ghetto side of you."

"Ghetto is exactly what I would've got up in that bitch! I just hate it when those dyke hoes be trying to sweat me on the sly --"

"Let's not start with the gay bashing. You know my cousin Valarie came out last year, but she don't be all out in the public trying to flaunt it. It is what it is. The problem is that a handful of gays make all gays look bad in the eyes of most people. But who are we to judge."

I checked my voicemail when Monica and I got back in from the club. I had four messages. One from my mother, one from Julian and two from Tim. He'd been calling and leaving messages since the night he stormed out of the apartment with my juices on his magical tongue. Damn he could give some serious head. I didn't return any of his calls. I wanted him to suffer awhile longer.

As for Julian, he was my unofficial boyfriend and I cared more than dearly for him. He had a six figure a year job, owned a $400,000 home in Cascade, drove a Lincoln Navigator and had the looks to embrace the cover of GQ magazine. He stood about six feet even, with a medium muscular build. His cinnamon colored skin, along with his shoulder length dreads, gave him that bad boy appeal. It would appear that he'd be the perfect catch for any woman. However, I wasn't satisfied with all the baggage that came along with him. Julian was married with children and he and I normally spent time together whenever his wife was out of town on business. She was a pharmaceutical sales rep and she was out of town a lot.

I sat on my bed and called him, hoping his wife was away.

"How you doing baby? I've missed you."

Hearing Julian's deep sexy voice instantly put a smile on my face.

"I'm doing fine as always and you know I've missed you too. Why has it been almost three weeks since you last called?"

"Joyce has really been riding my ass about you since one of her friends spotted us strolling through Centennial Park holding hands last month."

I sighed. "How did her friend know who I was?"

"She didn't have to know. Once she described what you looked like, Joyce knew it had to be you. When I got back home later that night the scent of my clothes smelled like the Portfolio body spray you usually wear. I didn't even have time to shower or change clothes. The moment I stepped through the door, Joyce was standing there looking pissed, holding a copy of our marriage certificate. She didn't say a word and mugged me in the face with the certificate. That's when all hell broke loose." He took a deep breath, blowing heavily into the phone. "Sorry, baby. It's taken me this long to iron things out with her."

I had met Joyce at a Zumba class that she and I were taking together a couple years earlier. Shortly after, she and I befriended each other and started hanging out together from time to time. The worst mistake girlfriend made was when she introduced me to her husband.

Initially, I never planned on sleeping with Julian, but the attraction between the two of us was too strong. He and I began messing around behind Joyce's back only a week after we'd met. The first ten months of our secret relationship, Joyce didn't have the slightest clue of what was going on. That is, until she walked in on us making love in their bed. Julian and I both thought Joyce would be out of town for an entire weekend. Apparently something got cancelled and she returned home a day early, catching me riding Julian's dick. After that shocking incident, she dropped out of Zumba and I haven't seen or spoken to her since.

"That's still not a good excuse for you to stop calling me. I've already told you once before to make a decision. I mean it, Julian."

"But she's my wife --"

"And I'm your girlfriend!" I added, cutting him off. I was sick and tired of hearing that same old my wife shit. "But I won't be much longer. You told me well over a year ago, how things wasn't working out between you two and you promised me you was going to file for divorce. I guess that was all a lie too."

"No, it wasn't a lie. I just can't up and file for divorce right now baby. Joyce's lawyers would trounce me in the courtroom. I have way too much at stake to lose and I think that filing for a divorce right now wouldn't be in my best interest."

"You know when I turned my phone on and saw your message, it made me smile. I had even got a little excited when I heard your voice. But right now, I'm far from being excited. You just told me you had a lot at stake to lose if you filed for divorce. Well, you still have a lot to lose if you don't. You're about to lose me too."

"Come on baby."

"No, Julian. I look too damn good and have too much going for myself to continue playing second fiddle to any woman. Especially your tired looking ass wife."

"Just give me a little more time baby? You know how much I love you."

"Like I said, Julian. I'm not going to continue playing second fiddle --"

"What exactly is it you're trying to tell me?"

"You don't seem to comprehend things well, do you?" I said, catching an attitude. "It's not what I'm trying to tell you, Julian. It's what I'm telling you. Our secret booty calls are over as of now. Call me when you get your life straightened out and if you wait too long you might end up being replaced. Bye, Julian."

I hung up without giving him time to respond. There was really nothing he could say that I wanted to hear. Don't get me wrong, I had developed some strong emotional feelings for him over the past two years. I wanted to love him so bad, but my heart wouldn't allow me to fall in love with a married man. I wasn't the type of woman who allowed men to dominate me or our relationship. At times I felt Julian was trying to do just that and I wasn't going for it. Sometimes a sista has to put her foot down. That's exactly what I had to do with Julian.

****

"Hap-py birth-day to you! Hap-py birth-day to you! Hap-py birth-day to Shan-tay! Hap-py birth-day to you!" Monica sang to me the moment I came through the front door. "Where you been all day, birthday girl?" She asked, closing the door behind me.

"Out getting my shopping on."

"That's obvious. I know it didn't take you all day."

"You know how I do it, girl. I shop 'til I drop."

She followed me to my room. "You tried to buy the whole damn store," she said as I sat my half dozen bags on the bed. "What all did you buy?"

"I haven't bought anything. Tim bought it."

"You know you need to cut your shit out and stop playing that man. You kicked him out with a hard dick last week. Today you used him to buy you all this stuff."

"Yep, that's what suckers are for. I didn't ask that nigga to spend a single dime on me. He bought all this shit on his own freewill. I picked it out and he paid for it."

"Neiman Marcus, Saks and Parisians," she called out the names of the shopping bags. "Damn, girl! How much did he spend?"

I shrugged my shoulders. "A couple stacks I guess. He used his Platinum card. He won't miss it."

"God gonna make you burn in hell for your ugly ways. I bet you still didn't give him no booty?"

"I wish I hadn't."

"It's about damn time. You made him wait long enough."

"I should've made him wait six more months. He didn't last five minutes."

"Oh my God!" She blurted, unable to control her laughter. "He'll probably last longer the next time girl. He might've been backed up."

"It won't be a next time, unless I'm hard up and desperate. And I don't think I'll be either one of the two anytime soon," I said, snapping my fingers and rolling my neck.

"What are you getting into tonight?"

"I don't know what you're getting into, but I'm getting into my bed."

"I'm going out to LA Mansion with Sherry. I'm gonna drag your Halle Berry looking ass out with us too. Now try me," she replied.

"Is that a threat or a promise?" I asked.

"A threat ... For real though, come on out with us tonight. You'll be able to party out your birthday instead of laying around here watching Netflix doing nothing."

She had a point. I really didn't want to spend the rest of my twenty-sixth birthday at home, alone.

"Okay Monica, I'll go," I pointed my finger at her. "But if I see any men dancing around in hot pink leather thongs, I'm outta there."

"Girl, you gonna be glad you went."

Monica, Sherry and I ended up staying at the club until it closed. We all had a good time. LA Mansion was TURNT! I danced to Beyoncé's "Drunk in Love" both times the deejay played it. That was my song and it played in my head until I hit the bed early that morning.

As I lay there falling asleep, I thought about being at work, sick as a dog the day before. This tall brotha had introduced himself to me and gave me his phone number. He was handsome as hell, well dressed, but looked like the broke type to me. I wasn't into dating broke men and usually found out what kind of money they earned on our first date. If his salary wasn't in the six figure neighborhood, there was never a second date. I was very high maintenance and it cost a grip to keep me up. A man had to have much more than a pair of Jordan's on his feet and twenty-sixes on his ride to get with me. I wasn't a hood rat.

DEAVIN

Three weeks had passed since I'd moved to Atlanta and it seemed like things were shaping up for me. After my first meeting with Mr. Davis, I went ahead and took care of all the proper paperwork involving the legal issues of starting my own business. From getting my LLC, opening a business account, to getting a business license, it was all taken care of. I had also gone out and purchased buffers and other accessories that I needed to run my business.

I was glad Mr. Temp had linked me up with Mr. Davis. Had it not been for the hookup, it would have more than likely taken me two months to get to where Mr. Davis had gotten me in weeks. He'd been running his own janitorial service in the Atlanta area for over 25 years and knew all the ups and downs to the business. Over the course of the past two weeks I had to call him a number of times to seek out advice concerning different matters. Every time I called, he gave me the exact information I was looking for. 'It felt good having connections in a city like this,' I thought, after hanging up with Mr. Davis that afternoon.

"Come on, Dee!" Mark complained while he stood in my bedroom doorway with his gym bag on his shoulder.

"I'm coming," I replied, stuffing my sneakers into my gym bag.

We were heading out to Bedford Pines Park off Boulevard to shoot some hoops. I loved playing basketball and should have made it to the pros. Back in my high school days I was a McDonalds All-American power forward at Pinecrest High school, in Southern Pines. I led the team to three straight Mid-Southeastern Conference titles and a state title. I was the biggest North Carolina high school star since James Worthy and Dominique Wilkins. I was heavily recruited by all the big powerhouse basketball schools, such as Duke, UNC, Kentucky, Kansas, Indiana and NC State, just to name a few. With my ability to dominate in the post with my six-foot-six frame, the college coaches and NBA scouts started comparing me to the likes of Charles Barkley and Larry Johnson. Not only did I average 28 points, 14 rebounds, 6 blocks and 4 assist during my senior year, I also had a 3.8 grade point average and scored over 1200 on my S.A.T exam.

During a playoff game against Seventy-First High School, I was having the game of my life. There were a host of coaches and NBA scouts sitting in the stands watching me because I hadn't signed a letter of intent or verbally committed to any college, even though I was leaning towards signing with the Tar Heels of North Carolina.

By the end of the third quarter of that intense playoff game, I had already scored 56 points (a school record), pulled down 17 rebounds, dished out 4 assist and blocked 7 shots. During the first minute of the fourth quarter, as the Patriot cheerleaders chanted, 'Deavin! Deavin! Deavin!' it happened.

I had just stole the ball and was dribbling the length of the court to attempt a windmill dunk when I jumped up, was undercut by an opposing player and wasn't able to break my fall. My body slammed hard onto the floor, knee first. That's where I laid, screaming in pain until I was placed on a stretcher and rushed to the hospital. I had a fractured kneecap and lots of ligament damage.

Months after I graduated high school and rehabilitated my knee, I was ready to play big time college hoops. However, the big time college programs were no longer interested in me. My childhood dreams of playing at UNC had faded. But that didn't stop me from playing the game I had grown to love and once dominated.

"Pass the rock!" One of my teammates yelled as I drove the lane for a reverse dunk.

"Strong move, Dee!" Mark said as he and I hustled back down the court to play defense.

We had won five straight games at the Bedford Pines Park late that afternoon. I had practically put on a basketball clinic for the guys I was playing against.

"Who you play for?" A tall lanky kid asked while I was sitting on the bench, digging in my gym bag for my towel.

"Nobody. I just run pickup games from time to time."

"Your game is tight man. You should be down at the Run-N-Shoot balling against the big boys."

"Run-N-Shoot?" I repeated, a bit confused. "What's that?"

"You can't be from 'round here man. Everybody knows about the Run-N-Shoot. It's like a big oversized gym with seven full courts, a track, weight room and aerobic classes. It be turnt!" He exclaimed, getting excited. "You need to go check it out sometimes."

"Alright. Where's it located?"

"Metropolitan Parkway."

"Alright, bet."

"You ready to roll?" Mark asked, getting up and rubbing his bad knees.

"Yeah, let's ride." I got up and we headed to my truck.

Mark and I left the park and went straight back to the condo. He and I had a double date set up and didn't want to be late. When Mark arrived in town the day before, I decided to call Sabrina for the first time. It was almost eleven o'clock at night when I dialed her number.

"Sabrina?" I asked, after a soft voice answered.

"Yes, this is she."

"The beautiful Georgia peach. I hope it's still sweet," I joked, remembering the first conversation she and I had at Dolly's.

"Deavin?"

"The one and only."

"When I didn't hear from you the first week I assumed you'd lost my number. Anyway, how's things been going since I last saw you?"

"I've been busy, but things have been good. What about yourself?"

"I'm good. I have nothing to complain about. By the way, where you from?"

"Fayetteville."

"Oh, Fayette County?"

"No. Fayetteville, North Carolina."

"North Carolina. I have family in Raeford. Have you ever been there?"

"Plenty of times. That's around my way in Home County. When will you be able to let me take you up on your offer?"

"What offer?"

"To be my personal tour guide."

"Oh, yeah. I thought you had forgotten all about that."

"I don't forget much," I assured her.

"I see. I'm off on weekends, so I'll be free tomorrow. Where would you like to go?"

"I'm not sure. Recommend a place, you're my tour guide."

"Have you been to the Underground yet?"

"The Under-what?"

She giggled. "Underground Atlanta."

"No. What's that?"

"I'll show you tomorrow."

"What time will you be ready to hookup?"

"Six-thirty tomorrow evening will be fine with me."

"That'll be okay with me too," I said, thinking about Mark. "My homeboy just moved here from Fayetteville too. You know I'd hate to leave him cooped up in the crib while you and I are out having a good time. Do you have a friend or cousin you can bring along with you?"

"My roommate Deshundria. She'll go out with me if I ask her."

"You mean the hostess from the restaurant?"

"Yep."

"She seem to be pretty cool."

"She is. That's my girl... Speaking of girl, did you bring yours down with you?"

"No," I stated firmly. "Don't have one."

"Wife?"

"Don't have one of those either."

"You mean you're single?"

"As single as they come."

"Coming from a good looking guy like you...," she sighed. "That's hard to believe. But since you say you are, I have no choice but to believe you."

"You look kind of young. I hope you're old enough to buy alcohol."

"Are you trying to ask me my age on sly?"

I chuckled. "I guess I'm busted."

"Yes, I'm old enough to buy alcohol. I'm a junior at Clark-Atlanta."

"College girl, huh. I know you have a boyfriend stashed in the cut somewhere?"

"No, I'm afraid not handsome. I've been single for over a year and a half now."

"Damn! Why so long?"

"Haven't found the right man yet, even though I haven't been looking. There's a lot of doggish men out there. There's also a lot of down low guys out there too. Atlanta is full of them. So a sista these days gotta watch who she sleeps with. HIV is spreading like crazy, especially among young black women. We all must be cautious and think twice before getting sexually involved with someone."

"I definitely feel you on that," I replied, responding to the HIV issue. As for the doggish men she was talking about, I wasn't about to reveal my trump card to her. She was going to have to find out on her own. "Where do you want me to pick you up at tomorrow?"

"I'll call and let you know?"

"Call?" I questioned, puzzled. "How?"

"Your number is in my phone."

DAMN! I thought I had it blocked when I called. "Let me get Mark on the phone so you can hook him up with your friend, alright. Guess you and I will be seeing each other tomorrow."

That night, as I was getting ready for my date with Sabrina, I couldn't help thinking about the super gorgeous, hazel eyed sista, I'd seen the other day. The sista was beyond gorgeous, God must've put her together with his bare hands. I know I said I wasn't going to start giving out my number, but the sista was too fine for me to bypass. The short conversation I had with her was all one sided. However, since she stood there and listened, I assumed she was feeling what I was saying and before I knew it I was handing her my home and cell phone numbers. It had been a couple weeks since then and she hadn't called yet. Forget her, I thought as Mark and I headed out the door. If God had made her, then he had made another like her.

SHANTE

"Thank God it's Friday," I said to my co-workers as I left the restaurant.

I called Cool D when I got in my car and stayed on the phone with him until I pulled up in front of my apartment. Cool D was an old college classmate of mine who had his own recording studio. I had bumped into him earlier in the week at Krispy Kreme, on Ponce de Leon. He remembered how good I use to sing when we were in school and offered me a 70% discount on studio time for the following weekend. I immediately jumped on it of course.

One of my dreams growing up was to become a famous singer. Throughout those years I'd made dozens of CD's on my karaoke machine and still had most of the CD's buried in my closet. Though I hadn't become the famous singer I dreamt of as a child, I didn't want to manage a restaurant for the rest of my life.

I packed a few bags and headed down I-85. Cool D's studio was located off Victory Drive in Columbus. I decided it would be better off for me to stay the weekend in Columbus rather than make the three and a half hour, round trip drive several times. I checked into a hotel when I got there and turned up the heat in my room. I wanted my voice to be ready when it was time for me to hit a high note. I went to bed early to make sure I was rested.

After beating my way through traffic, I parked beside the studio that following morning with butterflies in my stomach. I thought to myself, 'Thank God I made it here safely. Now it's time for me to go in there and get my Patti Labelle on.'

Being inside a recording studio for the first time, I was nervous and didn't know what to expect. However, after an hour into the session I began to relax a little, but I still had the jitters. The second day of the session, I entered the studio with a new attitude. I was rested, relaxed and feeling great.

While I stood in the soundproof booth waiting to take it from the top, I thought about the talent show I had won back in high school with my classmate Melvin. He and I sung Keith Sweat and Jacci McGhee's 80's hit "Make It Last Forever." With that on my mind, I knew I could do well and I did just that. From the high notes to the low ones, I was able to hit them all and stayed on key.

I left Columbus with my demo and high hopes. I had recorded two, four minute songs and felt damn good about them. My next move was to get copies made and start sending them out to record labels. Since I was a big fan of Diddy and JD, I planned to send them copies first.

I made it back to Atlanta early in the evening. The hour and forty-five minute back up on I-85 had me exhausted. I was more than relieved when I entered my apartment.

"How was your trip?" Monica asked, greeting me at the door with a hug.

"Fine...Oh, how you doing Trey?" I spoke when I saw him sitting on the sofa. He was Monica's boyfriend. They both attended classes at Atlanta Area Tech.

"I'm good," he answered. "Did you get your CD made?"

"Yes," I said with a smile. "I'm gonna let you and Monica hear what this diva did when she had a microphone put in front of her."

"Yeah right, Miss Mary J Tired," Monica interjected. "You probably sound like the real Milli Vanilli."

"I see you got jokes Gee --" I stopped myself from saying it before cutting my eyes at her. "You're gonna feel real shitty when you hear me blowing on this CD."

Not waiting around to hear a reply, I went to my room, dropped my overnight bags, closed the door, kicked off my heels and laid down on my bed. For the past couple of weeks and for some strange reason, I couldn't understand why, I'd been thinking about the tall handsome brotha who'd given me his phone number. I got offered dozens of numbers weekly. Some I accepted, some I didn't. It was also seldom that I would hold on to any of the numbers longer than a day. However, I held on to his.

Let me call this man and see what's up with him. I do need to start scouting for another sucker anyway. And please don't let him be BorB. (Broke or Bisexual)

"Hello."

"Dee?"

"Yeah. What's up?"

"Am I calling at a bad time?"

He sighed as if he was agitated. "Depending on whose calling."

"Since you literally forced your number on me, it shouldn't matter what time I call you, right?"

"Hazel Eyes?"

I could tell he was surprised that I called. I heard the excitement in his voice. "Pretty hazel eyes I do have, but my name is Shante."

"Since you didn't tell me your name the day I politely introduced myself to you at that restaurant, I'm calling you Hazel Eyes whether you like it or not. Now tell me what took you so long to call."

"You have a smart ass mouth," I said with much attitude. "I didn't call you no sooner than I did because you wasn't on my list of things to do."

"Why did you call tonight?"

"I was bored and extremely desperate, so don't feel lucky."

"Don't flatter yourself lil' mama," he shot back sharply. "It's gonna take a lot more than a phone call from you to have me feeling lucky. Believe that."

"Yeah right," I said, not believing he had the nerve to call me lil' mama. "Anyway, I called to check you out. If you don't wanna talk I'll be more than happy to hang up and let you be."

He chuckled. "Let's cut through the chase and get acquainted. Now tell me, why was a gorgeous lady such as yourself at a restaurant alone?"

"I wasn't there dining, I work there. Let me get something straight with you before you get it twisted. I am an independent woman. I don't need no man trampling behind me everywhere I go."

"I see you caught that disease too."

"What disease?"

"The Independent Woman Disease. Ever since Destiny's Child made that song you women think y'all can do without a man."

"First of all, don't you ever compare me to another woman. I'm unlike any woman you've ever met in your life."

"Do you have a man?"

"If I did, would it matter?"

"No, not really. I just wanted to know so I won't have to worry about him running in on us pulling an OJ."

"What makes you think I'll allow you to get that close to me?"

"I'm a confident guy, Hazel Eyes. Plus you called me. That gotta mean something."

"Alright, Smiling Bob, I hear you talking," I said, referring to the smiling confident white man on the old

Enzyte commercials. "No Dee, I don't have a man. I have friends. What about yourself?"

"I'm single."

"Stop lying. Keep it real with a sista."

"I'm keeping it real. I just moved here about a month ago. I haven't met nobody yet."

"Where you from?"

"The great state of North Carolina."

"What's so great about the state of North Carolina?"

"Michael Jordan, Nick Cannon, Jodeci, Fantasia, Anthony Hamilton, Steph Curry, J. Cole, me. Want me to keep going?"

"No, please stop. They're famous, you're not. What makes you think you're in the same category with them?"

"You'll find out one day."

"You probably won't admit it, but I'm sure you left a woman or two back home."

"Yeah, I did. My mom and sister."

"You know, you're full of it," I said, knowing he had to be lying. I was also thinking he might not be the sucker I thought he'd be.

"Being truthful with you, I was involved with someone, but things didn't work out between us. When I moved here, I forgot all about her and the problems she and I had."

"Yeah right, tell me anything."

"I'm serious."

Sure you are I thought to myself. "So what brings a single man like yourself to the ATL?"

"A change of scenery," he answered without hesitation.

"I thought you said the state of North Carolina was so great?"

"It is. My reason for moving here was the new scenery and the fact that I wanted to open up my own business."

Finally the conversation had gotten down to his occupation. I hope he's not broke. "What kind of business?"

"Janitorial service. That's why I was at Dolly's that afternoon. I had a business meeting with someone."

"Is it up and running yet?"

"Not quite. I'm only about a week away. Furthermore, I'm in no rush to start back working. I've worked my ass off for years. This break is well deserved."

"Do you live in the city or out in the suburbs?" I asked, trying to figure out his class of living.

"Midtown, Ansley Park."

It cost a grip to live out there. He just might not be broke after all. "You do maintenance work?"

"I do a little bit of it all."

"Well I hope you do. I be in need of a fix sometimes," I said, giggling.

"Straight up. I know I have the perfect tool for you."

"You know I was only kidding around with you, right. Anyway, how tall are you?"

"Six-six and a half, to be precise."

Ooooooooh, yesss! I know it's long, thick and black. "Well, Dee," I sighed, as if I was tired. "I'll call you back. No better yet, now that you have my number, you can call me whenever you like. It was good talking to you."

"It was good talking to you as well. Take care."

I hung up, laid back and exhaled, thinking about Dee. I wasn't sure if he'd lied to me when he said he didn't have any lady friends, but it really didn't matter to me. He was a man, so I expected him to lie. I couldn't front though, deep down inside I was hoping Dee could be the man who replaced Julian. That was if he qualified. The jury was still out on him and I wasn't sure of the verdict it would return.

I wasn't looking for love or emotional attachment to anyone. All I wanted was a qualified brotha who could tighten my bolts when they got loose and to lick my worries away whenever I desired it. Of course he had to have money, which was a must in my book. I loved reeling in paymasters, especially the big spending ones like Tim, who was the biggest paymaster I'd caught by far.

He'd called me the morning of my birthday apologizing about the night he stormed out on me and told me he wanted to take me shopping. Hearing the word *shopping* come out of his mouth was like music to my ears. However, I let him boo-hoo for a while about how sorry he was before accepting his offer.

Tim wasn't married, didn't have any kids and was partners at one of the top law firms in the city. He would have been a great catch for any woman, but he wasn't all that to me. He was too short and timid for my liking. I also wasn't attracted to weak men. My only attraction to Tim was his hefty six figure yearly salary.

The morning he'd took me shopping, he got us a suite at the Hilton. The moment he and I entered the room, he cuffed my butt and pulled me into his arms. He kicked the door closed and pent me up against it aggressively, before laying a kiss on me that caused my insides to tingle. Never had he taken charge with me like that and I found myself turned on by it. He even slipped off my blouse and bra and started sucking on my nipples before carrying me over to the bed.

Never the one to be outdone, I began taking off his clothes as he continued showing my hard nipples all the attention they needed. Moments later, his tongue made a beeline down between my thighs where it began feasting on my nana.

"Oooooh, Goddd...Yessss!" I cried out in ecstasy as he sucked on my clit and fingered my G-spot at the same time. Damn this brotha can suck the hell out of some pussy, I thought after having my second orgasm. "Lay on your back," I instructed, then pulled off his silk Polo briefs.

He was already hard and ready. I opened a condom and rolled it on his thick penis, then straddled him. I eased the fat mushroom shaped head inside of me and began slow grinding. My hands rested on his sweaty chest as I stared into his eyes and gave him his treat. I had to admit, the dick was good if only for a few minutes.

Just as I started to get into a groove, his body caught the fucking Holy Ghost. He moaned and grunted uncontrollably as he thrust deeper into me with force, blasting off. Five short minutes was all it took. My nana was soaking wet and wanting to be fucked, but Tim's soft ass couldn't get it back up. Giving it mouth to mouth resuscitation was out of the question. Sucking dick wasn't one of my specialties. Still hoping to get mine with the dick instead of the tongue, I let him get in the shower with me. Again, he disappointed me.

I ended up settling for another round of tongue action because he couldn't keep it hard long enough for me to slip a raincoat on it. Later, when he and I was in his Porsche on our way to Buckhead, he actually had the nerve to ask me if it was good. I wanted to laugh in his face for asking such a stupid question, but I didn't want to rain on his little parade. I told him it was the best I'd ever had and he shot me a flirtatious smile, believing it.

After it was all said and done, I got the last laugh when we entered Neiman Marcus, Saks and Parisians.

"Shante! Shante!" Monica shouted, banging on my door, awakening me.

"Come in crazy!"

She stepped in and closed the door behind her. "How you feeling?" She asked, sitting on my bed. "I hope you ain't mad at me for trippin' on you about the demo?"

"How could I get mad at you, girl? You know you off the chain."

"Trey said he'll be back over tomorrow. He wants to hear your demo."

"When did he leave?"

"Bout ten minutes ago. I started wondering why it was so quiet back here when I didn't hear no music coming from your room. You know I had to check on you."

"Good. Girl I dozed off."

"Let me listen to the demo? I wanna hear how you put it down."

"Look in my Coach bag and get that black CD," I said, hoping she would like it. I knew she would be my biggest critic.

DEAVIN

All week long I'd been interviewing various people, trying to find three qualified and dependable workers to put on my staff. I'm sure it seemed like anyone could do janitorial work. However, when it came down to slow buffing, knowing which pads to use, stripping and waxing floors, especially in public establishments, a person had to know exactly what he or she was doing. I wanted to have at least a solid five man crew, including Mark and myself.

Earlier in the week I'd won two bids and signed both contracts to clean a grocery store and a small office complex. The two contracts weren't going to bring in a lot of money, but it was a start and I was satisfied for the moment.

"I still can't believe you hired ol' dad," Mark said to me shortly after I'd hired my last employee.

I was sitting at my desk in the den of the condo. "Who is ol' dad?" I replied.

"Chain-gang dad. The ex-con."

"Oh, Mister Willis. What's wrong with him?"

"I don't think you made good judgement in hiring an ex con. That man just got out of prison after serving twenty something years. You don't know if, or when, he might flip out again and go on another killing spree."

"Just chill man," I told him, holding back my laughter because he'd gotten himself all worked up. "Mister Willis is a pro at doing floors. For years he worked the nightshift as a prison floor orderly, buffing, waxing and stripping floors at Georgia State Prison. I believe he's going to be a perfect fit for our crew, so I gave him a chance."

"An ex con!" He spat in disbelief. "You shouldn't have hired him."

"You don't seem to understand the way life is Mark. That man is forty-seven years old and he's trying to start his life over again. By him being a poor, black, convicted felon alone, makes it that much harder for him to get a half decent job. Since I'm a brotha in a position to help him out, I did. I gave him something he's been trying to find for months now."

"What?"

"A job."

After I interviewed Mr. Willis, I hired him on the spot. He had explained to me why he'd spent so many years of his life in prison and how he was living in a cheap boardinghouse in East Atlanta. Hearing his story, I knew in my heart that I had to give him a chance.

He told me that he'd left his pregnant girlfriend at home one morning in hopes of finding a little side job to make some extra money to help out with the backed up bills. Roaming through the cold streets all day without any luck, he ended up frustrated and desperate for money. So when he spotted an elderly white man coming out the back door of a restaurant, carrying a moneybag, he didn't think twice before making the mistake that cost him to spend over half his life in prison.

Mr. Willis had crept up on the elderly man and tried snatching the moneybag, but the man didn't let go of the bag without putting up a fight. Seeing a Colt 45 bottle within reaching distance, Mr. Willis picked it up and beat the man in the head with it until he finally released the moneybag. As he attempted to make his getaway out of the dimly lit parking lot, a police patrolling the area, making his nightly rounds, saw Mr. Willis fleeing the scene and arrested him a block away after a short foot chase.

Days later, after sitting in jail, charged with armed robbery and aggravated assault, the elderly victim died from the head trauma he'd received during the robbery. Mr. Willis's charges were quickly upgraded to felony murder. Seven Months after the incident, he signed a plea bargain deal for life in prison, rather than to risk going before an all-white jury that he felt would have convicted and sentenced him to die in the Georgia electric chair.

He was so ashamed of what he'd done that he didn't tell his family or girlfriend he was in jail. With him being arrested and convicted under an alias name, he never worried about his family or anybody he knew finding out about his arrest. Over the years he had eventually made contact with his family, who lived in Mobile, Alabama. On the other hand, he was unable to locate his girlfriend and their child.

"I'm gonna find them one day," Mr. Willis had told me with tears forming in his eyes during the interview.

I felt for him and wanted to do more to help him out. I agreed to pick him up for work each night until he was able to get to the work site on his own. He gave me a firm handshake before leaving the condo, heading to the nearest bus stop.

RRRIINNNNGG...

"Hello," I answered, still sitting behind my desk, feeling like a real businessman.

"Dee! You are one sorry ass excuse of a man!"

"Tammy?"

"You got that right!" My sister spat with bitterness.

"Why you calling snapping on me like that?"

"Cause your lying ass been gone a whole month and ain't called Tracy to let her know how you doing. I don't even know why you told that girl you was going to send back for her once you get yourself situated down there. You know you wasn't."

"You right. I wasn't. I'm not even thinking about her no more. I'm on some new shit down here."

"You're my big brother and all and I love you 'til death, but you ain't hitting on shit. I can't believe you can be so cold hearted and treat women so bad. But don't worry about it playa. The same thing you're doing to these women is going to come back and bite you in the ass one day. I can't wait."

"I can't believe my own sister is playa-hating on me."

"You can call it what you want to!" She shot back. "I hate how you're treating Tracy. You need to call that girl and let her know what time it is with your sorry ass so she can get on with her life."

"Okay, I'll hit her up tonight." I lied.

"You better!" She barked and hung up.

Later on that evening I went to pick Sabrina up from work. She had plans to spend the night with me and I was glad, I didn't get a chance to hit it the day she and Deshundria double dated with me and Mark.

Sabrina had actually turned out to be a good personal tour guide for me. She took me to the King Center on Auburn Avenue, Underground Atlanta and she and I went for a stroll through Woodruff Park. I enjoyed myself with her, especially when she started grinding her ass up against me while I sat on the back of a park bench. You got to know that I was a little disappointed driving back home that night with my dick harder than times in '29.

I whipped into Dolly's parking lot, blasting Regina Belle's old school hit "Baby Come to Me." Before I was able to park, Sabrina and Deshundria came out the door with carryout trays in their hands.

"Hold up a minute," Sabrina said, holding up her finger as she went to her car. She popped the trunk and took out what I suspected was her booty-bag.

"How was your day?" I asked, kissing her luscious lips when she got in my truck.

"Fine. I brought you something to eat."

"Good looking out," I replied, cutting my eyes at the carryout tray that was smelling good.

"You might want to eat all this food before we get in bed together. You'll probably need the energy."

"You saying you got it going on like that?"

She looked at me and smiled. "Yes, I do."

This young girl just don't know what she's about to get herself into. She's about to find out though.

"You know I got class at nine o'clock. You gonna have to take me home early in the morning."

"No problem," I said, speeding down Marietta Street, thinking about the energy comment she'd made.

When we entered my condo about fifteen minutes later, I was itching to get her in bed. I hadn't had sex since I'd been in Atlanta and had a lot of pressure built up inside me.

"You have a nice place here," she complimented me as I led her through the living room.

"Thanks. You know a brotha like me wouldn't have it any other way."

I had a plush leather, cream colored, sectional sofa and a stained Oakwood coffee table with a tinted glass top, sitting in front of the sofa atop a gorgeous Italian rug. A large aquarium sat in the far right corner and a framed, 20 inch painted portrait of my Grandma Pearl hung on the wall. The highlight of my living room was the 80" screen Smart TV.

Sabrina showered while I demolished the mouthwatering Buffalo wings, string beans, mashed potatoes and cornbread she'd given me.

When she stepped out of the bathroom into my presence, butt-booty naked, my dick immediately jumped to attention.

"Goodness...," I said, eyeing her perky breast, slim waist, thick hips and thighs. "Is all that for me?"

"Mmm hmm," she muttered, turning down the light.

"Come to Daddy."

She slowly sashayed into my arms while I sat on the side of the bed. Without saying a word she began unbuttoning my shirt, her hard nipples gently brushed across my lips while doing so. Once she took my shirt off, I wrapped my big hands around her tiny waist and pulled her forward until one of her nipples rested between my lips. As I took turns sucking on her swollen nipples, she reached between my legs and started massaging my already enormous erection through the thin fabric of my Dockers.

"Hold up a minute," I told her, then pulled off my pants and boxers. Soon as I tossed the clothes to the side, she got on her knees, grabbed my penis and carefully took it into her warm mouth. She gave me a few minutes of oral action before stopping.

"Oooh wee, you got a big dick," she said, eyeing it after she'd pulled it out of her mouth. "You have any condoms?"

I reached under my pillow for a pack of Magnums. I handed them to her and she wasted no time putting one on me. I scooted back to the middle of my king size bed and she climbed on top, straddling me. She guided my throbbing head to her moist folds and lowered herself onto it until my penis rested deep inside her vagina walls.

"Ohhhh...shit!" She moaned, frowning as she slowly rocked her body back and forth.

The deeper I penetrated, the faster her pace got. Her tight, gripping walls, fitted my penis like a glove and the pleasure it was giving me was unbearable. Knowing I was on the brink of exploding, I grabbed her ass cheeks and started giving it to her harder. Her breasts bounced up and down as she panted and let out loud moans. Not being able to hold back any longer, I began cuming as her own white cream coated my thick, black shaft with every swift thrust.

Moments later she collapsed on my chest, almost out of breath. After she and I caught our breath, we engaged in a long sensual kiss that set our bodies on fire again. I rolled her over, slipped on another Magnum, placed her legs on my shoulder and plunged deep into her wetness. With me being in total control this time around I began feeding her long swift strokes. She moaned and screamed as I pounded into her, but was able to throw it back, matching me stroke for stroke. I continued pumping away with beads of sweat popping up on my forehead as I felt myself nearing another explosion.

'Damn she can take some dick,' I thought, after I came the second time. However, I wasn't finished. I had to hit that fat round ass from the back. She got on all fours and I entered her from behind. I parted her cheeks and watched as my shaft slowly eased in and out of her before I picked up the pace. I began slamming into her so hard that she tried to scoot forward, but she couldn't go any further, the headboard was stopping her.

With no room to run, she just buried her face in the pillow and started throwing it back. The feeling of her tight walls squeezing around my penis was sensational. I pounded into her with a vengeance until she brought me to my last satisfying orgasm. It had been a while since I'd went three continuous stimulated rounds of good skin smacking intense sex.

After we were spent and the room smelling of funky sex, she curled up in my arms and we fell asleep.

"My first Georgia Peach," I said as I drove her home the next morning.

"And last," Sabrina responded, giving me a serious look while she sat comfortably with her booty-bag in her lap.

I shot her an assuring smile as we continued down Northside Drive, listening to the RYAN AND WANDA MORNING SHOW on V-103. She looked restless, her eyes were drowsy, but you could easily tell she felt good and safe being in my company.

"I'm going to give you a call when I get off work tonight," she said, kissing me on the lips before getting out of my truck in front of her apartment.

I waited until she was safely inside before I pulled off, laughing at one of Wanda Smith jokes from the RYAN AND WANDA MORNING SHOW.

My first full month in Atlanta flew by faster than I could have ever imagined. Initially I knew I wasn't going to have any problems meeting beautiful women, but damn, I didn't expect to meet so many in such a short period of time. Mark and I had caught the Marta train to Lennox Square Mall earlier in the week. As he and I walked through Lenox Station, we were approached by two women who looked as if they were in their late 20's with corporate careers. While Mark and I conversed with the two women, we received unappreciative stares from the majority of the black women and white men that passed us. Mark ended up exchanging phone numbers with one of them before we stepped off. I declined on giving the other one my phone number because I didn't date outside my race.

"I love black women, even though I might mess around on them from time to time," I'd told Mark as he and I headed into the mall.

We strolled through the mall with our North Carolina swagger, for close to two hours. He and I bought a couple outfits and pocketed a handful of numbers before we left. It seemed like half the women in the mall tried flirting with us and I enjoyed every minute of it.

It was also easy to see that Mark did too. He wasn't a bad looking guy. He was brown skinned, stood about six-foot with a medium build, wore a sharp taped nappy fro' and was a casual dresser.

"Dee?" Mark called out when I got back in from dropping off Sabrina.

I stuck my head in his room.

"What's up?" I asked.

"Some girl name Shante called last night after you left to pick up Sabrina."

"Damn! I spat because I'd missed her call. "What did you tell her?"

"That you went to the store. Was that okay?"

"That's cool. I wonder why she didn't call my cellphone."

He sighed. "She wanted you to hit her back when you got in. I didn't get the chance to tell you last night because Sabrina was with you and I didn't wanna disrupt what y'all had going on."

"Don't trip it. Shit, I'll tell her that you was asleep when I got in and didn't get her message 'til this morning."

"Alright, cool," he replied, rolling over and grabbing his pillow.

I closed his door and went straight to my room to get some sleep. Though I was a little worn from sexing Sabrina, I knew I needed to get all the rest I could. I had a date with Shante later on that day. She didn't tell me where we were going. She just told me to bring some workout clothes and sneakers along with me.

The first time she'd called me I was on cloud nine, not believing my luck. From that conversation she and I had, I immediately realized she wasn't wet behind the ears and could tell by the aggression in her attitude that she wasn't to be taken lightly.

Her beauty was another thing altogether. Never in my thirty years of living had I ever saw a woman who looked as good as she did. She was Halle Berry, Beyoncé, Jessica Alba and Gabrielle Union, wrapped into one. The bad thing about it was the fact that she knew it and had that *'I'm the shit'* attitude to go with it. However, I was up for the challenge to break her and bring her back down to earth, like I'd done all the others before her.

At 6:15 pm, I called Shante. She told me to meet her at the Taco Bell on Lee Street in West End in forty-five minutes. "Don't forget to bring your workout clothes," she reminded me before hanging up.

SHANTE

Outside of working, I'd been spending a lot of time trying to shop my demo around to numerous record labels. I had also been giving Monica copies to pass out to some of the club deejays to play in hopes of getting discovered.

"Girl, I still can't believe that's you singing like this," Monica told me, for what seem like the twentieth time, as she and I lounged in the living room, listening to my demo. "Ashanti ain't got nothing on you."

"I know that," I replied with a smirk. "Tell me something I don't already know?"

"Oh yeah girl, I almost forgot to tell you. Julian called while you was in the shower. He wants you to hit him back ASAP."

"Damn Julian. Ever since he saw me and Dee together the other day, he's been bugging the shit outta me. I don't have no talk for him. Hell, he's married anyway."

Monica eyed me like she was crazy before she spoke. "What does his being married have to do with it? You knew he was married when you first started sleeping around with him."

"So! Regardless of the matter, I'm through with his ass now. I'm not looking back."

"I don't care what you say or how you front, I know you're in love with Julian. I didn't just fall off the turnip truck this morning. You can't tell me anything."

"Apparently you don't know this sista too well." I snapped my fingers. "I care for him and all, but being in love with him is a no, no. I'm a lot smarter than what you give me credit for."

"Yeah, right. Why you been creeping around with him for so long?"

"He's a good looking man who knows how to satisfy my sexual desires and he's been paying the note on that fifty-five thousand dollar Beamer I drive."

"What about Tim?"

I shrugged my shoulders. "What about him?" I shot back.

"You have feelings for him or are you using him too?"

"See Monica, there's a lot you don't understand about how I handle mine. Tim is my human puppet. I take him out of the box and use him for my convenience when I'm bored. I keep the box closed when I have no use for him."

"And you have the nerve to tell me, I'm off the chain. If anything, you're the one off the chain," she giggled.

"What's up with this new guy, Dee who's been calling you lately?"

"I'm not sure. The jury is still out deliberating and hasn't reached a verdict on him. So I don't know what I'm going to do with him yet."

"I've heard enough of your Betty Wright attitude for tonight," she said, getting up. "I'm going to bed."

I kicked off my house shoes and curled up on the sofa. My mind immediately drifted back to the date Dee and I went out on.

I had spotted him the moment I turned into the almost empty Taco Bell parking lot. He was leaning against a black Cadillac Escalade, drinking a bottle of water. "Follow me," I told him as I slowly cruised past him without stopping. He got in his truck and followed me to the Run-N-Shoot for our date.

Already dressed in my workout clothes, I sat on one of the Run-N-Shoot benches for well over five minutes fighting off men and women asking for my number, while Dee was in the locker room getting dressed. When he finally came out, I got up and led him to the exercise bikes. We rode them for nearly twenty minutes before we began working on our abs. My stomach was already flat and tight and so was his.

Normally when I worked on my abs I hated the workout because it was so tense, but doing it with Dee was sort of relaxing. It felt good having his strong hands on different parts of my body. Our workout ended with us jogging two, slow paced miles around the track. He and I then bought energy drinks, sat on the bench and talked about the senseless police killings of unarmed black men until he got a run on the basketball court.

I stayed seated and watched in amazement as he literally ran circles around the competition he was playing against. When he looked over and noticed that I was actually checking out his basketball skills, he started showing off. Chris Paul, no look passes and Lebron James type dunks. He was doing it with ease.

Nearing the end of the second game, something happened to me that very seldom happens, especially when it's concerning a man. I began to get a little jealous of Dee's newly formed fan club. There was a small crowd of women that was sitting about fifteen feet away from me and they would holler and cheer every time Dee scored a basket. The bitches were starting to get on my nerves. I even heard one of them talking about how fine she thought he was and how she wouldn't mind sucking the sweat off his lower head.

"Nasty bitch," I mumbled as I stood up, wanting to make my presence felt. I stepped on the edge of the basketball court, causing the play to stop. I called Dee up to me and told him I was going to the ladies room. I also put my hand on the back of his sweaty head and gave him a satisfying tongue kiss. "Yes, he's with me ladies!" I said loud enough for them to hear as I walked past them.

Moments after, I came out of the bathroom, I almost fainted when I spotted Julian and Joyce coming through the glass door entrance. Damn! I picked a bad time to come here, I thought, taking my seat back on the bench.

I had a very uncomfortable feeling in the pit of my stomach as my ex friend and lover strolled past me, hand in hand. I exhaled and felt a sigh of relief when I realized Joyce didn't see me, but Julian did. He was even bold enough to wink and blow a kiss at me. By then, it was time for me of get up out of there.

I called Dee off the court and told him I was ready to leave. He shot me a funny look before going to the locker room to get his bag. Minutes later he and I walked out with my arm draped around his waist. Once we got out in the parking lot, I told him I had to hurry home and left him standing beside his truck, looking lost.

"Why did Julian and his tired, horse face looking wife, have to show up and rain on my parade?" I mumbled as I made a left on Metropolitan Parkway.

I was almost positive that Dee was upset with me for leaving him hanging the way I did, but I figured he would get over it. I'd pulled some hella stunts on my dates over the years, what I did to Dee was really nothing compared to what I'd done to the others. Normally I could care less about how rude I treated a date, or how pissed off I'd left them. But with Dee, there was something about him that had me feeling bad for what I'd done, so without giving it much thought I called him.

"Yeah," he answered dryly.

"Where you at?" I asked because of the noisy background.

"I know damn well you ain't trying to check me. You got the game confused, Hazel Eyes. You put lames and squares in check. Not a brotha like me."

"Check you!" I spat with venom. "I have no reason to check something that's not mine. I only asked your simple ass a question. And who do you think you getting all sporty outta the mouth at anyway? I'm not your average woman. You better catch a grip and recognize."

"I can't tell you ain't average, but I'm not gonna dwell on it. I'm bigger than that. To answer your question, I came back inside to finish balling after you left. Where you at?"

"Still on my way home. Would you like to come join me when I get there?"

"No doubt, but I have no idea where you live."

"I'm sure you're smart enough to follow instructions."

"I'm all ears," he said with confidence. "How far is it from here?"

"I'm only joking with you. This was only our first date. I think it would be a little too premature for us to start spending time together at each other's places."

"So what was up with the kiss and hugging earlier?"

"Just marking my territory."

"Oh," he chuckled. "You play the game like that?"

"Yep."

"What makes you so sure I'll be your territory to claim? You must be a Real Estate Agent on the side?"

"Like I told you before, I'm unlike any woman you've ever dealt with in your life and I'm sure of everything I say. And as for being a Real Estate Agent, you'll find out soon enough."

"Be careful Hazel Eyes. I'm not one of them guys you're use to manhandling. You play with fire, you'll get burned."

"That same statement applies to you as well."

While Dee and I conversed, I had this strange feeling that Julian was watching him, trying to figure out who he was.

Four days had passed since the Run-N-Shoot incident, and Julian had been calling me nonstop. I purposely avoided all his calls. He'd left messages for me at work and at home. I didn't even answer my cellphone when I saw his number.

Early one morning, at 5:58am, as I was about to enter the back door of Dolly's, I heard footsteps behind me. When I turned around I saw a dark figure standing about ten yards away from me in a dimly lit area, I froze in fear. God please don't let nothing happen to me. I'm not ready to die.

"It's me baby," the dark figure said, just above a whisper, coming closer. "Why haven't you been returning my calls?"

A big sigh of relief immediately surged through my body when I realized who it was. "Don't be fucking sneaking up on me like this, Julian!" I shouted, placing my hand over my fast beating heart. "What are doing here anyway? I told you already that it was over."

"Don't be like that baby. You know I love you." He stepped closer, gently grabbing my hand. "Why are you handling me like this baby? I can't take you being out of my life."

I stared into his eyes and thought about how much I really cared for him and how bad I missed him. "I'm not enjoying this breakup either, but I'm not stupid." I yanked my hand away from him. "You're a happily married man, Julian. You have a wife and kids at home who love you. Isn't that enough for you to realize we're wrong for each other?"

"I'm not happy at home. It's just --"

"You looked mighty happy when I saw you two at the Run-N-Shoot together."

"That was just a front. You know --"

"I don't know nothing Julian and I don't want to hear another one of your lame ass excuses either. I've waited for you to commit to me for well over a year now, but I can see that's not happening. I gotta move on with my life."

"With who?" He spat, getting angry. "That tall guy I saw you with?"

"Maybe. Maybe not. Just because I told you I'm moving on, doesn't mean I'm getting involved with someone else right away."

"I hope not," he replied with a smirk.

"What is that supposed to mean?"

"That tall guy you was with came back in after you two left. I saw him kickin' it with another woman and they ended up leaving together too."

"I don't care about that Julian," I said, forcing a weak smile, as if I really didn't care. It did have me thinking if Dee did end up with one of those sistas who was sitting on the bench cheering for him. I closed my eyes and sighed. "Would you please excuse me? I have work to do."

"Okay. Call me later."

I agreed, trying to get rid of him. To my surprise he left without saying another word.

When I finally made it into my office, all I could think of was what Julian had said about Dee leaving with another woman. Oh, he thinks he's a playa. I'm going to show him how real playa's play.

DEAVIN

"Damn, this shit feels awkward Dee. I kind of like it though," Mark said as he waxed the floor. "Just a month ago I was up in North Carolina busting my butt for Mr. Temp. Now I'm down here in the ATL busting my butt for you."

"What you doing now ain't shit compared to what Mr. Temp had you doing. At least you don't have to worry about the stress of running that slow buffer every night."

"Yes." He smiled, nodding his head. "Thanks to Mr. Willis and Chuck's good buffing asses."

It was early Tuesday morning and I, along with my new crew, was at an office complex working. It was my first night of business and I was feeling good. I kept my fingers crossed in hopes that things would workout smoothly for me in the long run. Besides putting all my time and effort into the business, I'd been spending a lot of my spare time building up my new playa card.

The evening Hazel Eyes abandoned me in the parking lot, I ended up meeting an older brown skinned sista. She'd stepped up to me while I sat on the bench, waiting for my down on the basketball court.

"Would you like something to drink?" She asked, extending her hand to me with a bottle of water. "You look like you need it."

"I'm not really thirsty, but since you're offering it, I'd be more than happy to accept it." I took the bottle. "You can have a seat. I don't bite and thanks for the water."

"I don't know about that," she replied, shaking her head with both hands on her hips.

"You don't know about what?"

"Getting bit. I saw your girlfriend."

"Girlfriend?" I repeated, puzzled. "That word is foreign to me. I don't have one of those."

"Who was the woman you walked out and hugged up with?"

"Why the questions? I don't even know your name."

"I'm Toi with the O-I not the O-Y. I come here three days a week to exercise and get my jog on." She sat down beside me. "What's your name and who was the woman you left with?"

I started to tell her to get lost after she asked that same question again. But when I realized how fine she was, I figured I would continue making small talk with her.

She stood about 5'3, bowlegged and had a thick, toned body, with pretty brown eyes.

"I see Georgia women are pushy-pushy, I'm Dee and I'm single. I just recently moved here."

"Good to meet you Dee." She extended her hand to me and I kissed the back of it. "Mmm," she murmured. "I see you know how to greet a real woman when you meet one."

"All the time." I smiled. "But how am I supposed to know you're a real woman? This is Atlanta, you could be a transformer."

"Oh, I'm real baby," she said with arrogance as she stood up. "I can't believe you said that to me. I'm all woman." She turned around, slowly showing off her thick figure.

She had on a navy blue, skin tight, body workout suit and it fit her curvaceous body like a glove. My manhood began rising at the thought of seeing her naked.

"You definitely look stunning, but I still don't know if it's all real."

"Trust me." She batted her eyelashes, sitting back down. "Ain't nothing fake about me. I'm not one of them bitches you see on those reality shows that's pumped full of shots and silicone. I'm cornbread fed, for real baby."

"I'll have to inspect that for myself. That's if you don't mind."

She shot me a flirtatious smile. "I just might let you do all the inspecting you want if you tell me who that woman was."

"She was nobody, because if she was, you and I wouldn't be having this conversation right now."

"Yeah right, tell me anything."

"I have no reason to tell you a bold face lie. I just met you. The woman you saw me with was just a friend. Nothing more, nothing less."

"Yeah right, pretty boy. I was born at night, but not last night."

"Listen here Toi. I have no strings attached to any women, outside of my mom and sister. I go and come as I please and only answer to the good Lord above."

"Oh, I see." Her face lit up. "You're the playa type."

"I won't say that, but..."

"You don't have to explain it to me handsome. I like your type."

Toi and I sat there and conversed for over an hour. When my down came up on the court, I declined it and continued getting my mack on. I was surprised when she revealed her age to me. She was forty six, but didn't look a day over thirty. I had never dated a woman sixteen years my senior. However, I was intrigued by it.

The following day, Toi and I went to the Georgia Aquarium where she and I both had a great time. From there, we stopped by the Varsity and got a bite to eat before checking into a motel room, where I sexed her. Out with an older woman, I actually enjoyed spending the day with her. She voluntarily paid all the expenses, and in return, I tried to fuck her brains out. Toi was a nymphomaniac and rode my dick like it was the last one on earth. She'd even begged me to enter her backdoor.

"What the hell," I said, moments before I began pounding deep up into her gripping anal walls. She wasn't a virgin back there and took dick like she was Kapri Styles the porn star. The only thing she didn't do was give head. I didn't trip it though, she had satisfied me.

As I relaxed in the bed, feeling myself after I rocked her world, she surprised the hell out of me when she dug into her pocketbook and pulled out a box of cigars.

"What's them for?" I asked, assuming they belonged to one of her male friends.

"I smoke these." She held up the Black-N-Mild cigar box. "It's not often I do though." She smiled. "Only when I have good back breaking sex."

I immediately got dressed and told her that I was going out to the vending machine to get something to snack on. Instead, I jumped in my truck and bailed out.

I couldn't stand being around a woman that smoked. It was a total turnoff to me. So when she lit up the cigar, I knew our short fling was over. She called me five straight days in a row, but I never answered her calls. Finally, I guess she got the hint and lost my number.

Over a week had passed since the last time I'd spoken to Hazel Eyes. I hadn't heard from her since the day she'd left me alone in the parking lot. I was still trying to figure out why. I hated to admit it to myself, but I wanted to call her so bad. The only thing stopping me was my playa-pride.

"Fuck it," I said as I stepped in my room after getting home from work early one morning. I pulled out my phone and dialed her number.

"Hello," she answered.

"What's been up Hazel Eyes? I know it's early, but since you have to be at work by six, I'm sure you was about to get up anyway."

"No! I wasn't about to get up anyway!" She snapped.

"My bad then. I'll just hang up and forget you ever existed."

"If you think you can do it, fine. If not, hold on a minute."

I sat there on hold for nearly five minutes and was on the brink of hanging up when she finally picked the phone back up.

"Hello."

"I'm still here, but I almost hung up on your rude ass. Why haven't you called me?"

"The same reason your rude ass ain't called me."

"So you playing games now, right?"

"I'm not a playa, I don't play games. I'm also not the kind of woman who chase behind men. I let y'all do the chasing."

"Yeah, whatever," I said nonchalantly, as if her comment didn't bother me. It wasn't just bothering me, her slick ass comment was killing me. "Just hit me later on today, whenever you get off work. Maybe we can hookup and do a little something."

"You called me at four-forty-five in the morning, waking me out of my beauty sleep, now you want me to call back later. Boy please... I have fifteen minutes to burn before I normally get up for work anyway," she sighed.

"Whatever you called to talk to me about this early, spit it out."

"I'm gonna let that smart ass comment ride this time, but don't keep trying me like I'm some duck ass lame. Where did you get that sour ass attitude from this early in the morning anyway?"

"I don't have an attitude. I just put men in their place when I see fit."

"In other words, you're trying to handle me on the sly?"

"No comment," she replied, taking a long pause. "I know why you haven't been calling me either. It's all good though. You can search the whole city and you'll never find another woman of my caliber."

"What point are you trying to make? You've lost me."

"You're trying to play crazy now."

"Honestly, I have no idea what you're talking about."

"I left a set of eyes behind me at the Run-N-Shoot the evening you and I went there. So don't act. You know what I'm talking about."

"That was nothing," I said, feeling a little uneasy. "Why did you leave a spy on me? You told me playas played games. I guess that makes you a playa then."

"I didn't intentionally leave a spy on you, Dee. A friend of mine had seen us together and told me how he saw you kicking it with someone else after I left."

"Yeah, some sista pushed up on me. She wasn't my type though."

"Since you're so picky in deciding your women, do you dump them before or after they give you the booty?"

I giggled. "I plead the fifth to that question."

"I see what you're all about now. Trust and believe that I can break you if I wanted too."

"I feel the exact same way about you. You definitely need to be broke in."

"Hunh, that'll be the day. I don't think you or any other man is capable of accomplishing that with me."

"I can show you better than I can tell you."

She laughed. "Take your best shot playa."

She and I stayed on the phone a short while longer and I was able to sense some jealousy in her about Toi. However, Hazel Eyes had the kind of attitude that would destroy a weak minded man. With me being the kind of brotha who controlled my relationships, I knew for a fact that I wasn't going to have any problems standing my ground against her. I could easily tell she liked to dominate her relationships just like me, but little did she know that I wasn't the one to be dominated.

Later that afternoon, Mark was trying to convince me to go out on a double date with him, Christie and her friend Wendy. Going out with beautiful shapely women had always been my thing. On the other hand I was skeptical about accepting his offer to double date. Not only was Hazel Eyes planning on taking me out to a comedy club, Sabrina was also supposed to be spending some time with me as well. I had no idea why I continued to do it to myself, but I was always over scheduling myself with dates and knew that it was bound to catch up with me one day. I'd just deal with it, if and when it does.

"I need you to go out with her just this one time?" Mark pleaded to me for the umpteenth time. "Do this little favor for me and I'll never ask you for nothing else."

"You know I've already made plans for the night. I can't stand Hazel Eyes up like that."

"When did you start worrying about breaking promises you've made to women? This one night ain't going to change nothing."

I was in the living room playing NBA Live on my XBOX and was getting beat down while he continued bugging me about the date. I just couldn't concentrate on the damn game.

"I'm not worried about breaking no promises. It's just that Hazel Eyes seems to be a cut above all the other women I've ever dated. She's without a doubt, the baddest and I don't wanna mess up the opportunity to hit it."

"You know I would do it for you Dee." He dropped his head with a sympathetic look. "I did go out with Sabrina's friend Deshundria for you when I first got down here, remember?"

"You don't realize what you're asking of me, do you? You know I don't do white chicks."

"Put you're prejudice aside for this one night and take the girl out. Damn! It ain't like I'm asking you to sleep with her."

"Why is it you want me to go out with this white chick so bad?"

"Because Christine asked me if you would take Wendy out with us and I told her you would. So if you don't go with Wendy, Christine probably won't go out with me. And don't ask me why, it's probably a white thing."

"I surrender Mark. I'll go out with y'all tonight. Don't put me in no shit like this again. I'm gonna leave your ass hanging the next time."

"Alright man," he said, showing a weak smile.

I hated the thought of standing Hazel Eyes up for our date. However, in my own way, I felt that I owed her back for leaving me hanging in that parking lot. From the one date and phone conversations I'd had with her, I could easily tell she was used to having her way with the men she dated. I wasn't going to fall victim and allow her to have her way with me. My goal was to break her dominate cycle and I figured that standing her up would be a good start.

On the flip side, things with Sabrina and I were going alright. I was feeling her energetic company and positive attitude. School had let out for the summer which meant she had lots of extra time on her hands, but I wasn't about to start letting her burn all that time off on me. I wasn't tripping her attachment to me because I was used to women falling hard for me. My only worries were her and Hazel Eyes bumping heads.

"What's on the agenda for this evening?" I asked Wendy, making conversation as she and I rode in the backseat of Christine's late model Mercedes.

"House party."

"On a weekday?"

"Yep. Here in Atlanta we party and have fun when it's most convenient. This isn't really going to be a big house party like you're probably use to. We have some friends up from Miami so were just having a little get together before they head back to Florida."

"That's wassup," I said, checking out her thick legs. I couldn't front, she had it going on.

She and I continued making small talk until we arrived at the party.

When we all go out of the car and headed for the door, all we heard was Drake and Future's hit song "Grammy" blasting from one of the opened windows. 'Damn they jamming up in there,' I thought as Christine rang the doorbell.

Seconds later a gorgeous woman with curly red hair opened the door and let us in. Whatever race she was, I didn't know. She wasn't white or black. She might've been a combination of both. What I did know is that she was drop dead gorgeous. It was easy to see that she was into the Gothic look. She had several piercings in her face and had a tiny waist with the fat, roundest ass I'd ever seen. The short, sleeveless skirt she wore, revealed her countless tattoos and curvatious figure. I was stunned by her booty and beauty and couldn't believe my eyes. WOW!

Wendy had hit it on the head, it wasn't a big house party. There was about twenty of us in all. However, the house was huge. The large living room alone was almost as spacious as my entire condo. Whoever the homeowner was had to have plenty of money because the place was laid.

While eyeing the unfamiliar, but comfortable atmosphere, Mark got in the middle of the floor and turned into Chris Brown. I didn't know he had it in him, but he could dance his ass off. It wasn't long before everybody else followed his lead. Hey, I wasn't much of a dancer, but I could definitely two step. For the next few hours I partied and enjoyed myself. At the same time I found out all I could about the fine tatted, big booty, redhead.

Her name was KeKe and she was from Miami. She was also single and very down to earth to be so beautiful. When Wendy disappeared to the bathroom for a few minutes, I used that time to get KeKe's number. To my surprise she didn't give me her number and told me that she wasn't what I wanted. I didn't know what she meant by that, but that only made me want her more. She did give me her Instagram name and asked me to follow her.

"Krushink," I mumbled her IG name as I read it off the back of a Celebrity Seaborn Salon card she'd handed me.

Shortly after ten o'clock that evening, I was being driven home by Wendy. We'd left Mark and Christine behind, hugged up in the Jacuzzi like they were inseparable.

"It was good spending the evening with you Deavin. I had a wonderful time," she told me as I got out the car in front of my condo.

Don't be rude. Grandma taught you better than that. I sat back in the car and gave her a hug and peck on the cheek. "I had a nice time with you as well. Drive safe."

SHANTE

"Hi Mama. What is it, is something wrong?" I asked her over the phone.

"No darling, not really. There's something I do need to let you know though."

"What is it?"

"It's your father--"

"Is he sick again?" I asked with urgency. He'd been in and out of the hospital for prostate cancer treatment.

"Not Ricky honey," she sighed. "Your real father. He has surfaced after all these years."

I couldn't believe what I was hearing. I was in shock. "Surfaced where? Did you see him?"

"No, I haven't seen him and really don't care to see him. I wanted to let you know that he's trying to find us. I figured you needed to know what was going on before he popped up on your doorstep one of these days with some sad story to tell."

"How do you know all this going on way up there in Chicago?"

"I got a call from an old friend of mine who use to live next door to your father and I when I was carrying you. She'd gotten my number from Miss Wilson and called this morning telling me that your father was in their neighborhood, asking our whereabouts."

"Why do you think he's looking for us?"

"I haven't the slightest idea honey. When Sarah called, she told me that your father--"

"Hold up ma," I said, cutting her off. "Please stop referring to that man as my father. He's nothing to me as far as I'm concerned."

"OK honey, I understand. Getting back to what I was saying. Your fath..., I mean, Howard. Sarah told me that he didn't even know I'd been married all these years. Like I've told you time and time again over the years, Howard had all the love in the world for me, especially when I got pregnant with you." She sighed. "To this day I can't seem to understand why he abandoned us like he did. He just wasn't that kind of man."

"That was a long time ago Mama. He ran off and left you pregnant without saying a word. There's nothing else to be said about the loser. He's a deadbeat and I hate him!"

My mother was pissing me off. It sounded to me like she was having sympathetic feelings for him. All my life I'd grown up with my step daddy Ricky being my father. I wasn't about to make room or feel sorry for Howard's deadbeat ass.

"OK honey, I understand where you're coming from. I was just--"

"If it won't be a problem, Mama, can I call you back and discuss this with you tomorrow? I'm not up to it right now."

"That's fine honey."

"Love you Mama. Tell Daddy I love him too."

"We both love you too honey. Bye, bye."

It felt sort of funny after having that conversation with my mother. I wanted to be mad at her for having sympathetic feelings towards my long lost sperm donor of a father. Deep down inside I at least wanted to know what he looked like and why he abandoned us.

It wasn't a hot minute after I'd hung up with my mother that my phone started ringing again. A frown immediately appeared on my face when I saw who was calling.

"Hello," I answered dryly.

"How you doing, Hazel Eyes?"

"What in the hell you want with me?" I spat in a nasty tone.

"I'm calling to let you know something came up yesterday evening. I'm sorry for not letting you know sooner."

"You sorry?"

I was really pissed at his ass for standing me up, especially after I went out and spent money for comedy club tickets. The first time I'd ever spent my own money on a man. I was really more surprised than hurt by being stood up. It had never happened to me before. I always did the standing up.

"Yes Hazel Eyes, I'm sorry. Is there anything I can do to make it up to you? Cause like I said, something came up."

"Something like what? Whatever it was that came up, you could've at least called and let me know what was up."

"You're right. I can't argue with you about that one, but I can explain to you why I didn't. That's if it'll make you feel better."

"Whatever the reason is, it better be a good one or I'll be introducing you to Mr. Dial Tone."

"Listen Hazel Eyes," he said sounding pathetic. "My business associate, Mr. Davis called me around four o'clock yesterday, telling me how urgent it was that I meet him at his office off Cobb Parkway and that my meeting him could boost my business. I ended up meeting with him and this guy who owns several office buildings. To make a long story short, I spent the majority of the evening discussing business and riding around checking out the new office buildings my crew and I will be cleaning. I was so excited about signing the new contract that by the time I realized you and I had a date, I was on my way to pick up Mr. Willis for work."

"I guess I'll have to accept your explanation this time. But only because it had something to do with your business. Don't let it happen again."

"I won't."

Even though he apologized to me and everything, I still wanted to cuss his ass out. Luckily, I had Tim on standby and he took me out to the comedy club after I realized Dee was going to be a no show. Had it not been for Tim filling in, I wouldn't have let Dee's ass off the hook so easy. That's why I always kept a sucker like Tim on a short leash. I never knew when I might need him.

"So you would like to make it up to me?"

"Yeah, if you let me."

"I'll let you, but there's a catch to it."

"What kind of catch?"

"You'll find out if you slip again."

"You playing games now."

"I wouldn't call it game playing Dee. If you slip again it's over."

"Alright, Hazel Eyes. I've thrown in the towel."

"That's the best thing you could've done."

"I fully understand that I was wrong by the way I handled the date situation yesterday. I can also understand why you'd be upset with me. But I'm not feeling your nasty ass attitude right now."

"Whatever, Mr. Standup Man. My attitude has a lot to do with another problem."

"Can I be of any help? I'm pretty good at solving other people's problems."

'I'm sure you do solve a lot of problems with that dick of yours,' I thought. "I don't think I know you well enough to be discussing my personal problems with you yet. Thanks for the offer though."

"Anytime. Whenever you feel that you can confide in me with any of your personal problems, feel free. My shoulders are yours to cry on."

"That's so sweet of you, but how do you expect me to confide in you when you can't even pick me up for a simple date. To top that off you still haven't told me your age and last name."

"I'm thirty and my last name is James... It takes a special lady to get that kind of information out of me. I just wanted to let you know that."

"Now that's a start."

For the next hour or so he and I really got to know each other. When our conversation turned to being good parents, even though neither one of us had any children, I used that opportunity to vent about my long lost sperm donor. However, I played it off to Dee like Monica's father was the long sperm donor who was searching to find her, not me.

To my surprise, he really made me feel at ease about the situation. It seemed that he had a logical explanation for every negative question I threw at him about my, so-called, father.

After talking about my deadbeat sperm donor, he told me about the upcoming weekend date he was going to take me on to make up for standing me up. He said that it would begin at 9:00 Saturday morning and end at noon on Sunday.

"What are we planning to do for our twenty seven hour date?" I asked him.

"It wouldn't be a good surprise if I told you now. Just wait and see."

Since I had never been taken on a mysterious twenty seven hour date, I was excited. I just didn't let him know. I'd been taken on a six day cruise in the Caribbean, spent a week in Cancun and vacationed in Las Vegas on numerous occasions with my ex-boyfriend. I knew about all the previous date destinations weeks in advance. Never had a date held me in suspense about where we were going or what we were planning to do. Hopefully everything would turn out fine.

I had managed to avoid Julian up to that point. I had come in from work Friday afternoon and climbed my tired ass in bed. Hours later I was awakened by Monica, who had done the unthinkable, knocking on my room door. She told me I had company waiting in the living room. By the look on her face, the first person that popped in my mind was my long lost sperm donor. I put that thought to the back of my head after realizing Monica wouldn't be stupid enough to let an old stranger into our apartment.

I got out of the bed and went straight to the bathroom to get myself together. I slipped on my Black Lives Matter T-shirt and a pair of loose fitting jogging pants before going into the living room to see who awaited my company.

"What's been up baby?" Julian spoke, standing up in front of the sofa, holding a dozen red roses with a big smile on his face as I entered the room.

"Why, Julian?" I stopped in my tracks, putting my hands on my hips. "I told you not to come over here."

"Bu—But," he stuttered.

"But you're still married, living with your wife and kids."

"You're right baby. Why didn't you return my calls after you said that we could go out and discuss this over dinner?"

After hearing that question I knew it was time for me to set things straight with him for the last and final time. "Have a seat Julian."

He sat down, placing the flowers on the table in front of him. I took a seat right across from him. Something told me Monica's nosy ass had her head hanging outside her room door, trying to listen, but at the moment I really didn't care what she heard.

"What is it you want to talk about?" I asked him.

"Us, baby."

I sat there for nearly forty five minutes listening to the same old lame ass stories he'd told me many times before. The only time I said anything was when he tried to accuse me of wanting to leave him for Dee. Little did he know that I would've played him and Dee's ass at the same damn time. I had already played on him with Tim and with Charles before I cut him off.

At that period in my life I realized Julian would never be my man alone. I told him for the last time that it was over. Apparently he understood that I was through with his games and that I wasn't bullshitting. He took the flowers off the table and left without looking back.

"Bye Julian," I mumbled under my breath as I closed and locked the door behind him.

"Monica!" I shouted, heading down the hall to her room. "Why did you let Julian in here after I specifically told you not to?" I stood in her doorway while she had the phone to her ear trying to ignore me. "You might as well hang that damn phone up and face the music!"

She hung up, got off the bed and came up to me with her head down. "I'm sorry Shante. I let him in because I knew how you felt about him and the fact that I didn't like seeing you acting like a prisoner around here. I figured that if you stopped avoiding him and went on ahead and talked with him, you could finally get a piece of mind and start acting yourself again. I love you like the sister I never had and it was just killing me to see you acting so strange around here these past few weeks."

"Look at me Monica," I said, lifting her chin up so I could see her face. I was stunned to see she had tears in her eyes.

"I'm sorry."

"You don't have to be," I replied, giving her a strong hug. "I was mad with you at first, because I thought you let him in as one of your practical jokes. I see now, what you did for me was out of pure love and I'm happy to know you care so much for me." I stepped back a step or two after we released each other's embrace. "But don't you ever do nothing like that again! That man could've pulled a knife and did us both in."

"It'll never happen again," she said, showing her silly looking grin. "I know it's none of my business, but are you really kicking Julian to the curb for good?"

"Yep," I took a deep breath. "I'm through with married men."

"Good. Now does that mean you're gonna give Tim a fair chance or are you gonna get with that brotha Dee?"

"Tim is just Tim. He's too soft to get a fair chance with me. Now as for Dee, I haven't returned a verdict on him yet."

"You'll never change, Shante, but you'll always be my girl. Let's go eat some of that tasty German chocolate cake I made."

"Is there any strawberry ice cream left?"

"You know it."

"We'll it's on!"

We took off for the kitchen like two hyperactive ten year old kids.

****

Where are we headed to?" I asked Dee as we cruised down Moreland Avenue. He had picked me up at my apartment at 9:00, like he'd promised earlier during the week.

"Six Flags."

"Six Flags?" I repeated, a bit surprised. "Why didn't you let me know this ahead of time?"

"I do it like that."

I didn't respond. We rode on listening to Rihanna's "Bitch Better Have My Money." He had called me about an hour in advance and told me what I needed to bring along for our date. He put me in suspense when he said the date would consist of five stages and that I would need to bring three changes of clothes.

"Make one set some evening wear," he'd told me before hanging up.

When we arrived at Six Flags it appeared to me that Dee was more excited than I was. Though I had no idea he was taking me to the theme park when I got dressed that morning, I was glad I dressed for the occasion. I wore a pink tank top, black DKNY shorts and Louis Vuitton sandals.

I felt very comfortable and relaxed as Dee and I entered the theme park holding hands. Initially, I thought our date would go alright. Little did I know he would be the perfect gentlemen and crazy at the same time. He wasn't lunatic crazy, he was ride crazy. He and I rode the Ninja, Batman, Scream Machine, Georgia Cyclone, Superman and the Acrophobia.

After he kissed and sweet talked me into riding the Acrophobia for the second time, I was through with the rides for the rest of the day. We sat on one of the many benches and he and I fed each other ice cream and cotton candy. To top it off, he and I went into a room and made a music video. I really enjoyed making the video. We selected Diana Ross and Lionel Richie's "Endless Love." Even though Dee wasn't much of a singer and didn't know all the words to the song, I still enjoyed making the video with him.

We left Six Flags carrying all kinds of stuffed animals. Dee had won them all by shooting a basketball through a narrow rim. I had to literally pull him away from the game because it looked to me as if the theme park worker was getting angry. Dee had won eight stuffed animals in all.

As we pulled out of the parking lot, I closed my eyes as the mellow sounds of Adele played on the radio. What's next, I thought, after realizing I still had twenty one more hours left on the date. I was feeling a little exhausted and dozed off as we passed the Fulton Industrial exit.

"Wake up, Hazel Eyes," I heard Dee say as he shook me from my short nap.

I opened my eyes and immediately noticed we were at the Marriott Hotel. Before I could get a grip on what was going on, he was at my door, extending his hand to me while the bellboy took our luggage out of the back. The long day at Six Flags might've had me tired, but I wasn't tired enough to realize what he had on his mind by taking me to a hotel.

"What you think you're up to?" I asked, getting out of the Escalade.

He pulled me into his arms and followed up with a sensual kiss that caused my nana to tingle.

"Remember, Hazel Eyes," he whispered into my ear while he still held me in his arms. "This is a long twenty seven hour date, so let me handle things until noon tomorrow, alright?"

I looked up into his eyes for sincerity and agreed to follow his lead.

'God please help me to stay strong. This handsome, smooth taking man is trying to sweep me off my feet,' I thought as he and I walked through the lobby with his arm wrapped around my waist.

As I entered the room, well it wasn't a room, it was a spacious suite, I was surprised.

"Newlyweds?" The middle age bellboy asked while placing our luggage inside the suite.

The question startled me, but I didn't answer it since I felt it was directed more towards Dee than me.

"Yep," he answered with a smile, handing the bellboy a twenty dollar tip. "Isn't she beautiful?"

"Sure is. You're a very lucky man," the bellboy replied before Dee closed the door behind him.

"Why did you just tell that lie?"

"Because newlyweds always get good room service and much respect from hotel staff."

"How do you suppose to know what kind of treatment newlyweds receive if you've never been married?"

I was dead serious about that question. I had no intentions of getting involved with another married man again. Since I didn't know the skeletons he had in his closet, he could have been lying to me about not being married.

"I've had a few buddies who've gotten married. They have all told me about the royal treatment that was received from the hotel staff when they knew that they were dealing with newlyweds."

"Think your slick, don't you," I told him as I playfully punched him in the stomach.

He snatched me up over his shoulder and started slapping my butt as he carried me to the bed and dumped me on it. He straddled me. I tried my best to wrestle out from under him, but he was too big and strong. Just when I thought he was about to let me up, he began tickling me again.

"Plee--aa--se stopp Dee! I--gotta-pee!" I hollered out through my giggling.

Before letting me up, he started planting wet kisses all over my neck. I responded by pulling his lips to mine and we kissed until I felt moisture build up between my thighs. Not yet. I rolled away from him without any resistance and went to the bathroom.

Here I am in an expensive suite with one of the finest men God put on this earth. My nipples are hard and my pussy is wet, but I have got to stay strong and fight off my own sexual urges towards him. You know how it is sistas, you can't give up the goodies too quick. Most men will lose respect for you. Plus you won't be able to reel them in to pay your bills and take you on shopping sprees, like men have done for me in the past. So from now until the end of this date, I'm going to try my damnest to keep his fine ass at arm's length.

"Are you asleep in there?" Dee asked me from the other side of the door, shaking me from my thoughts.

"No... I'm OK."

When I stepped out of the bathroom minutes later, I had expected to see him standing outside the door, but he wasn't. I went into the other room and there he was, laid back on the bed watching Sports Center.

"Are you alright?"

"I'm fine," I replied, looking through my bags. "I'm about to shower."

"Don't keep me waiting. Stage two starts when you get out. I got something for you that's going to relax you."

"I bet you do."

"It's not what you're thinking, trust me."

I got what I needed out of my bags and headed back to the bathroom.

It was 6:00pm when I got out of the shower. I slipped on some shorts and a blouse before going back into the room where Dee was. He had a large beach towel spread out on the bed and a brown jar in his hand.

"What's up with that?" I asked, placing my cosmetics on the dresser.

"Hurry up and take off some of them clothes and you'll see what. We need to get this over with. I have more plans for us tonight."

I shot him a curious look. "What are you going to do?"

"Give you a full body massage. I'm very good at it."

"You want me to take off all my clothes and lay face down on that towel?"

"Exactly. You can cover your butt with that small towel that's folded on the dresser."

I stripped down to my black thong and laid comfortably on my stomach with the towel covering my booty. "You can turn back around now. I don't want you to get too excited and forget what you're supposed to be doing."

"I might get a little excited, but I'm not going to forget what I'm supposed to be doing. Trust me."

I exhaled, then closed my eyes as the smell of the coconut body oil filled my nostrils. When his soft, but strong hands touched my body, my mind wondered off to LaLa Land. He started at my shoulders and slowly worked his way down my back. His magical hands brought parts of my back to life that I never knew were there. His hands slipped under the towel and worked the lower part of my back, causing my entire body to tingle before he slid down to my upper thigh. He massaged me so good in that area I almost came on myself.

I was relieved when his busy hand finally got below my knees, but embarrassed at the same time. You see, when he was massaging the lower part of my buttocks the feeling was so good that before I realized it I was rolling my hips with the movement of his hands. It even felt good as he massaged the bottom of my feet. Out of all the guys I'd ever dated, Dee was the only one to give me a full body massage. His hands were so magical I'm sure he could have been a professional masseuse had he chosen that profession.

"How was that beautiful?" He asked, sitting beside me.

"Sooo good."

I pulled him down and gave him a kiss of appreciation. Not only did the kiss get me aroused. It aroused him too. When I felt his dick pressing against my stomach, the next thing I knew he was on my nipples and that's when I actually realized my bare breast was exposed.

"Damn, I almost got carried away," he said after pulling his lips away from my throbbing nipples. "We need to take a quick shower and get dressed. We got somewhere to be in about an hour and a half."

"Let's just shower together," I said without thinking.

He picked me up and carried me to the bathroom. I eased off my thong and got in the shower while he got undressed. When he finally got in the shower with me, my eyes instantly darted below his waist to his pole. It wasn't even fully erect, but it was by far the biggest I'd ever seen. I couldn't believe it, for the first time in my life I didn't feel like I had total control of the situation.

Dee was just too much of a take charge man and I couldn't control him like I'd done the others. He didn't even hesitate before lathering up the rag to bathe me. He lathered my breasts and butt with his soapy hand instead of the rag. When he finished with me I washed him. His body was fit and I took my time bathing him. I used both hands as I lathered up his balls and long thick shaft and by the time I was done cleaning it, he was rock hard. I gasped at the size of it when the water rinsed the soap off.

We got out of the shower and dried each other off. "Now get dressed," he said, slapping me across my naked ass.

I had absolutely no idea where he was taken me, but he told me to dress elegantly and that's exactly how I looked when I was done. I wore a Valentino, pink toga wrap dress, with Greek God dress and irregular hemline, tied with a string belt. After I touched up my hair with some Pantene oil, sheen spray, my bob looked like I had just left the beauty salon. Dee entered the room as I was putting on some lip gloss.

"Damn!" He looked me up and down shaking his head, "You look stunning in that dress. Come here and let me sample them lips before you put that gloss away."

"You wanna taste them?" I said, signaling him to me. "You come to me handsome."

He strolled over to me wearing a gray and black stripped, button down, Tom Ford shirt, Sean John slacks and a pair of black, Stacy Adam shoes. I almost missed the tiny diamond stud earring that was blinging in his left ear. The brotha was looking good.

I put my hands around the back of his freshly cut skin fade and pulled him down until our lips met. He kissed my lips until all the gloss was gone.

"You taste good," he told me after coming up for air. "Let's go. The show starts soon."

He grabbed his keys, I grabbed my handbag and we left.

The suspense was killing me as he drove down Peachtree Street, I had to find out where we were going.

"Where are you taking us?"

"To see the play you've always wanted to see."

"Oh no you didn't!" I blurted in disbelief.

"Oh yes I did," he replied with a smile, showing me the tickets.

The second phone conversation he and I ever had, I told him that I wanted to see "A Raisen in the Sun" play when it came to the Fox Theater. I had no idea he would remember it.

When he and I made it inside the theater, one of the ushers escorted us to the front row.

"Thanks for having an attentive ear." I gave him a peck on the cheek.

"A gentlemen always listens to what a woman has to say. Especially when he sees something in her."

I wasn't sure what he meant by that comment, but at the moment I didn't care. He had my nose wide open. He draped his arm around me and I laid comfortably in his embrace throughout the entire play, I loved it. All the actor's performances were breathtaking and it was the best play I'd seen by far.

I strutted out of the Fox Theater on a high, with Dee's arm around my waist. I was also about to starve to death. He must have been a mind reader because as soon as we got into the Escalade he called the hotel restaurant and ordered room service. I had to give it to him, the brotha was smooth and I was really digging his style.

The food was delivered to our suite minutes after we walked in. Dee showed no shame about eating in front of me. He and I both devoured the lamb chops with honey allioli and black bean lasagna, like we hadn't eaten in days. For desert we fed each other pecan pie with whip cream topping and followed that up by feeding each other grapes.

"Turn around and let me take that dress off you," he instructed me after putting the grape bowl back on the cart.

Without hesitating, I backed up to him and allowed him to undress me. When I was stripped down to my lace bra and thong, I began walking away from him.

"Where you going?" He asked.

"You thought it was going to be that easy," I stopped and looked back at him. "You gonna have to come get this." I took off and ran to the balcony.

The suite was way up on the eighteenth floor and the view of the city's skyline looked magnificent at night. The cool late night summer breeze had even made my nipples hard.

"I love it when you play hard to get," he said, nibbling on my ear as he ground his erection against my ass.

Seconds later he pulled my thong down and entered my wetness from behind. Immediately a red flag went up in my head and I reached back to see if he was wearing a condom. Thank God he was. Standing practically naked with my bra and heels on, I gripped the balcony railing, spreading my legs and poked my butt out. His hands were wrapped firmly around my hips as he slowly pushed deeper into me. I looked over my shoulder, giving him my best fuck face. "Fuck me Dee."

"No, Hazel Eyes," he said, pumping into me with long slow strokes. "I'm gonna make love to you."

He took off my bra and played with my nipples as he began pounding deeper into my tight pussy. "Aaaaahhh shiiiiit!" I cried out, gripping the rail tighter, cringing in ecstasy as I felt myself on the brink of a massive orgasm.

When the flood gates opened I came and came and came. I moaned and screamed loud enough for the whole city to hear. When he finally pulled his dick out of me, he picked me up and carried me to the bed where he entered me again. I stared into his eyes as he pumped away in my sweetness. It felt so good.

Before long he had me close to another orgasm. I couldn't deny it, he had it going on like no other. He brought me to four mind blowing orgasms, with the power of his dick alone, before I cuddled into his arms and fell asleep. He didn't only rock my world, I rocked his as well. I had him moaning, grunting and calling out my name too.

Being that I was so use to waking up early in the morning for work, I woke up at 5:00 AM. Dee was still in a deep sleep. I sat up and stared down at him, thinking about the great time he'd shown me. I was really surprised that I didn't have the next morning blues after sex. I felt like I belonged right there in bed with him and it scared me.

He looked so peaceful as he slept, that I didn't bother to wake him. I kissed him on the lips and got out of bed, heading for the bathroom. He'd already taken me through the first four stages of our date. Six Flags, the massage, the play and the love we made. Whatever stage five was, I didn't think I would be mentally ready for it. So without making any noise I texted Monica and told her to come pick me up. I packed up all my things, stuffed animals included. I wrote Dee a short note, gave him one last kiss and snuck out on him.

One of the bellboys took my things to the front entrance. By the time I made it down to the lobby, Monica came through the door.

"What is your sneaky ass up to this early in the morning?" She asked, giving me a hug. "And girl...," she looked me up and down. "You smell like you been knocking boots all night long."

"I have," I smiled without shame. "Now let's hurry up and get out of here before he wakes up."

TRACY

Two long, heart aching, months had passed since the morning Deavin promised he would send back for me once he'd gotten himself situated in Atlanta. I don't know why I believed him in the first place. However, the love I had for him was so strong that I made myself believe almost everything he told me.

I knew he had his new business up and running smoothly. I also knew that he had settled nicely in a two bedroom condo. His sister Tammy kept me updated on him. She had even told me to move on with my life and forget about him. Little did she know how complicated that really was for me.

A month after Deavin and I first met, I found out he had multiple women in his life. At the time, it didn't matter much to me. I was just happy to have a handsome man taking me out and showing me so much attention.

Coming up as a child, I was the butt end of a lot of jokes. My uncle had told some friends at our family reunion that I had the kind of looks only a mother could love. Things didn't get no easier for me at school either. My classmates often called me such names as Buck Teeth, African Booty Scratcher, Piglet and Tar Baby. The names went on and on. I was called everything in the book. Finally I decided to do something about it. At the start of my freshman year in high school, my mother took me to the dentist to get braces for my teeth. I started cutting back on what I was eating because, at the time, I weighed well over 260 pounds and it looked a hot mess on my five foot five frame.

My transformation was slow and it took some years to do. By the time I graduated high school, my braces were gone. I had ditched my ugly Catwoman glasses for contact lenses and my weight had dropped down to around 190. However, I still hadn't caught a boyfriend and was still a virgin.

When my eighteenth birthday came, I decided that I was going to lose more weight, but what I didn't realize was that I would become so obsessed in losing it. During my freshman year at Fayetteville State University, I walked the quarter mile track five days a week until the pounds started falling off. At the same time, I carried a half pound weight in each hand and swung them as I walked. My body started looking tighter and fitter, instead of loose and flabby. By the start of my sophomore year I was down to 150 pounds, feeling good about my appearance and had a half ass boyfriend who took advantage of my low self-esteem. I considered him a half ass boyfriend because he was only into me for the sex and the money I gave him every time he came begging.

I eventually got up the nerve to dump him, thanks in part to my friend Stephanie. She told me I could do much better, she was right. Guys started checking me out, thanks in part to my booming figure. I felt like a queen when I got down to 139 pounds and I was finally satisfied with my appearance. Going from ugly duckling to a cute swan in six years changed my life around. I began wearing French rolls and wore clothes that showed off my figure. My measurements were an astonishing 36 - 26 - 44 and I was getting way more attention than I ever wanted.

A couple years and two more half ass boyfriends later, I met Dee. He was so tall and handsome that I couldn't believe he asked for my number. It did take him a long time to call me, but when he did, he asked me out and I happily accepted. Our first date was to the movies. He wanted to see one of Ice Cube's comedy movies and I wanted to see Denzel. After a few minutes of our disagreement, he gave in and we watched the movie Denzel was starring in.

"We'll be back next weekend. You know I gotta see my boy Cube," he'd told me as he escorted me down the dark aisle with his big hand palming my juicy butt. I was more than happy to know that we would be going out again. That following week, after leaving the movies, he took me back to his place and put the dick down on me like it had never been put down before. Hey, what can I say, I fell head over heels in love with him that night. Even when I found out about his other women, I was too far gone and there was no turning back. He never paraded the other women around in my face so I didn't trip it.

Shortly after he and I started going out, he took me to Taylortown to meet his Great Grandmother Ms. Pearl and I instantly fell in love with her. When Grandma Pearl and I became closer, I told her that Deavin was cheating on me. She was more shocked than surprised to hear that Deavin wasn't being faithful to me. However, she told me that it was going take a strong minded woman to change his ways. She thought I was the woman who could do it. I wasn't so sure if I was the right woman or not, but I wasn't going to give up on him. Regardless of what he was doing in Atlanta, I still had all the love in the world for him. After all, he was my boo.

The day before, I had an appointment at the clinic and found out that I was almost ten weeks pregnant with Deavin's child. I hadn't told anyone yet, I wasn't sure if I was going to keep it. "God please give me the strength to carry this baby and help me make the right decisions," I prayed before I went to sleep with tears in my eyes.

DEAVIN

"I got 99 problems and a bitch is one," I sang along with Jay-Z's classic song, changing a few words.

It had been three weeks since the morning I woke up at the hotel and discovered Hazel Eyes had literally ran out on me. I was still trying to recoup from that heavy blow to my ego. I had went all out, trying to show her a good time and spent a lot of money in the process. I didn't normally go out on a limb and shell out money like I did on that date with Hazel Eyes, just to make her happy. For once in my life I tried to play the gentlemen role and the shit backfired on me.

She had me going, especially after we'd finished making love. I usually just fucked women and left it at that. If they decided to come back for seconds like most of them did, I would continue to hit the pussy to satisfy my sexual craving. With Hazel Eyes, things were different between her and I that night. We didn't just fuck each other, we made love until we were both exhausted. Not since Tracy, had I developed feelings for another woman.

I always thought Tracy had the prettiest naked body I'd ever seen. That is until I saw Hazel Eyes' naked body. She was too beautiful for her own good without the use of makeup and had the body of a Goddess to go along with her exotic beauty, feisty attitude and personality that reminded me of 'Girlfriends' sitcom character, Toni Child's and I loved everything about her. On my scale of 1 to 20, she was without a doubt the whole 20.

While she laid in my arms that night, I became fully aware that she was the woman who could convince me to turn in my playa card for a family wagon. What separated her from the others I'd dated was the fact that she didn't allow me to walk all over her and she wasn't afraid to speak her mind about things.

"Is everything squared away upstairs?" I asked Mr. Willis after reading a message Krusink had sent me on Instagram.

"Yes sir, Mr. James. Chuck is up there wrapping up the buffers as we speak. When he's done with that we can call it a night."

"Good job," I replied with my thoughts shifting back to Hazel Eyes.

"What's the matter, Mr. James? You haven't been yourself lately. You wanna talk about it?"

Talk about it. I've never had to discuss my relationship problems with anybody. Shit, this is the first time I've ever been locked up almost as long as I've been living. What can you possibly tell me about female trouble?

But then again I do need to talk to somebody. Talking to Mark about it was out of the question.

"You're old enough to be my pops Mr. Willis and I would prefer that you call me Dee or Deavin instead of Mr. James. Now back to what you were saying, we'll talk about it on the drive home."

"That'll be ok with me, Deavin."

Ten minutes or so later, I locked up the doors to the office building and said goodbye to the rest of the crew before Mr. Willis and I got in my truck. Mark didn't ride with us, he'd been driving his own car since he'd been spending a lot of his time with Christine lately.

"Yeah, Mr. Willis," I spoke as we pulled out of the office complex parking lot. "I been going through some hard times lately with this woman and I don't know what to do about it. See, I'm new to this territory and I'm not use to sitting around moping over no woman. It's usually the other way around with me." I chuckled, "I guess the chickens has finally come home to roost."

"You seem to be a pretty tough fella to me. This has got to be one helluva lady to have you feeling down in the dumps."

"One helluva lady she is."

"Lay it on me then. I can probably help you out."

I explained to him everything I knew about Hazel Eyes. I told him about the first date and how she left me in the parking lot. I told him how I stood her up on the second, but explained how I made it up to her.

"I woke up the next morning and she was gone," I said, finishing up the story about the twenty seven hour date.

"You mean to tell me, she snuck out on you after all that?"

"Yep," I replied dryly.

"That doesn't sound right. And you haven't heard from her since that night?"

"Nope. She did leave me a Dear John posted on the bathroom mirror."

"What did it say?"

I reached up in my sun visor and got the letter. I don't know why I continued to hold on to it. I'd read it at least thirty times and damn near knew what it said by heart. I began reading it for the thirty first time to Mr. Willis.

The quality time you and I spent together yesterday was one of the best days of my life, but what we did last night really complicated things. It frightens me because you brought out something in me I have never felt before. So before one of us gets hurt, I decided it would be best for me to bow out ahead of time. Atlanta is full of women and a man as handsome as you are shouldn't have any problems meeting that special someone. Sorry things had to end like this. Always, Shante.

"Let me see that letter if you don't mind," he said, soon as I finished reading it.

I handed it to him. I peeped at him every other second, trying to read his facial expression while he studied the letter. After a couple of minutes he passed it back to me.

"What do you think?"

"First of all, have you called her yet?"

"No. But--"

"That's part of the problem. There's probably another story behind the letter she left. I suggest you call her up and talk to her about it. From my understanding of the letter, she fell hard for you. I could be wrong about it, but it's up to you to find out. You never know, she's probably been waiting patiently for your call."

I immediately shook my head. "I don't think so Mr. Willis. She got way too much going on to be waiting around for my call."

He cracked a smile. "You'd be surprised young man."

"I just might do that. It won't be tonight though. Maybe sometime tomorrow."

"Whenever you and she do get it together let me know. I wanna do something special for you two."

"That won't be necessary. You don't need to spend your hard earned money on me."

"No, Deavin, you don't understand. I want to do something good for once in my life. I'm alone you know. I don't have anyone."

"Didn't you tell me a while back that you found out your old girlfriend had a daughter?"

"Yeah, I did," he sighed. "I haven't had much luck since then. It's like I just...," He shrugged his shoulders. "I ran into a roadblock."

When Playa's Play

"Why don't you check with the Vital Record Service and get a copy of your daughter's birth certificate? At least with that you'd be able to find her."

"That's a good idea. I didn't even think about that. Hold up, I might have a big problem with that."

"What kind of problem?"

"My ex-girlfriend got married. So I'm sure my daughter was probably adopted by the husband. She probably don't carry the same last name she was born with."

"Just keep searching. I'm sure you'll have some luck in the end."

"I will Deavin. I most certainly will," he said with a sad expression on his face.

It took me about fifteen minutes to get home after I dropped Mr. Willis off early that morning. I thought about calling Hazel Eyes as soon as I stepped through the door, but I pushed the thought to the back of my mind and took a hot shower before going to bed.

I woke up later to the smell of Mark's cooking. The boy could really burn. He could take a can of Spam and make it taste like steak when he was done with it.

"What's up master chef?" I said, entering the kitchen. "What you got on the stove smelling so good?"

"Spaghetti, meatballs and garlic bread."

"That's what I'm talking about." I patted my stomach. "I'm hungry as hell."

"It should be ready in about twenty more minutes," he said as he put the lid back on the pot. "Let me get back

127

over here and finish watching this tennis match." He rushed back over to the sofa and flopped down, eyeing the TV.

"Damn! When did you become such a big tennis fan?"

"When the two sistas started playing. And Dee," he said, rubbing his palms together, shaking his head in disbelief. "The youngest one got ass for days. K. Michelle's ass ain't got nothing on hers. Come check her out."

"I don't watch tennis."

"At least watch it to support the two sistas. Those girls have broken barriers in tennis. You gotta support that."

"I don't give a flying fuck about those two white cum drinking sisters. Althea Gibson, Zina Garrison and Arthur Ashe tore down the race barriers for blacks in tennis. I respect them. As for the two so-called black sisters, I lost all respect for them when they started dating white men."

"Man you tripping. What's wrong with you? I date white women. You still got respect for me don't you?"

"Of course I still got respect for you man. The point I'm trying to make is that when the sisters got rich and famous they chose to date and share their fame and wealth with the same race of men who raped our beautiful black sisters and enslaved our race for four hundred years, instead of dating men of their own race. If those two sisters didn't have the fame and wealth, the white men they fuck around with, wouldn't give them the time of day unless sex was involved. You probably wouldn't either. Hell, under the wigs, hair extensions and pounds of makeup they wear, they are both ugly and look like masculine men to me."

"You're just prejudice. Everything you see is black and white. You don't see people for who they really are."

"I call it the way I see it. Ain't no sense in sugar coating it."

"You still see things black and white."

"Believe me Mark, I see. I see everything for what it is. I also see all these black men and women who gain fame and wealth, run off and find a white man or white woman to share it with. Just off the top of your head, name me five black men and five black women who are famous that are currently dating or married to someone white?"

"Clearance Thomas, Ice T, Kobe Bryant, Terry Crews, John Legend and Montel Williams. Want me to keep going?"

"I know you can keep going. You named six instead. Now name some black women?"

"Tina Turner, Heather Headly, Keke Palmer, Kerry Washington, Zoe Saldana, Tatiana Ali...,"

"That's enough. You named six of them too."

"Ok," he said, holding out his hand. "What's your point?"

"We gonna get to the point. Name me five rich or famous white women that are currently married to or dating a black man and I'll give you five hundred dollars right now?"

"Oh, that's easy."

"Take off."

"Let me see." he closed his eyes as if he was in deep thought. "Kendra Wilkerson."

"Ok, keep going."

"Kloe and Kim Kardashian."

"That's three. I need two more."

"You gonna give me five hunded, right?"

"Yeah. You know I'm a man of my word."

For the next few minutes the only sound in the room came from the tennis players grunts on the TV.

"Can't think of no more, can you?"

"Yeah, I admit, you got a point, but it still don't give you the right to judge people."

"I also know that the Paris Hilton's, Courtney Love's and Lindsay Lohan's of the world aren't as naive as TMZ and the rest of the media make them out to be. They're not seen out in public or on the red carpet with no brotha on their arm. Why? Because they're taught better. But us black people, we don't know any better. We think that when we gain fame and wealth we gotta get somebody white to share it with, to solidify the white man's American dream, which is bullshit. I do respect and appreciate the rich and famous brothas and sistas who are out there keeping it real. Damn the fake so-called brothers and sisters."

"We boys and all, but you are a real racist."

"No I'm not. I'm a realist. I deal with reality."

"Holp up a minute with all that strong black brotha shit. The reason why we have all these beautiful black sistas running to the white man in the first place is because of brothas like you who dog them out every chance y'all get."

"I'm so sick and tired of hearing people use that as an excuse. Both white and black men cheat on their wives and girlfriends, so the grass don't get greener on the other side. I'll admit that I play around on women, but I've never been engaged or married either."

"You always got some slick comeback remark. The shit be sounding good too, but it don't mean you're always right."

"Listen, Mark. Women are always talking about how they want a good man with money and one whose gonna love and cater to their every need. That's a lie. Those kind of guys are classified as squares and too soft by most women. They run through men like that. Women want a challenge in their relationship. If you can manage to challenge her throughout the relationship she'll probably stay faithful to you a lot longer. But if you go into the relationship with that good guy image, she's gonna control you off the dribble and probably end up giving your brother or homeboy the pussy."

"See, there you go again with that playa philosophy crap. That shit don't work all the time. If it did you wouldn't have that long face you've had these past few weeks. I know you probably won't admit it, but that girl you call Hazel Eyes did something to you the last time y'all went out. You've had that droopy face since that morning you got back in from that long date with her. It's strange that you haven't been talking to her either. What's up with that, Mr. Lover man?"

"Nothing," I replied calmly, not wanting him to see the hurt I was really going through. "The playa don't always get a hit, but you best believe it's not often that I do strike out."

"So she dumped you, huh. We boys. You know you can talk to me about it."

"I don't need no coaching Mark. I am the coach and don't forget that. It's about time for that spaghetti and garlic bread. Let's eat."

He got up and went to the stove while I made my way to the cabinet to get a plate. For the rest of that afternoon he didn't bring up Hazel Eyes' name again.

When I picked Mr. Willis up for work that night, he surprised me by not asking any questions about Hazel Eyes and I was relieved. I didn't want to talk about her any more that day.

On the other hand, Sabrina had spent two nights with me those past three weeks. She wanted to stay a lot more than that, but I wasn't having it. She'd even noticed something was bugging me and tried to get me to talk about it. I shot her a quick lie, telling her that my sister was ill back home. I knew it was wrong to lie on my sister like that. I couldn't tell Sabrina that her boss had dumped me the morning after we made love. Sabrina was a good girl in and out of bed and I knew she deserved better than me. My feelings for her were minimal, but I could easily tell her feeling for me was love. When I realized it, I had to start distancing myself from her.

"Can I come over and stay the night? You know we haven't been spending much time together lately," she asked a couple of weeks back.

"I'm gonna be tied down for a while. At least until I get the business running the way I want it. I'm gonna be needing all the rest I can get."

"What about during the weekends? We can go catch a movie and then go back to your place and do the, you know what," she said with a light giggle.

"That's cool, but why don't we go back to your place after we leave the movie. Mark is supposedly having some out of town guest visiting this weekend and I don't want us to be in their way," I lied. I just didn't want her getting too comfortable laying up in my bed.

"That'll be fine with me. We can go back to my place, even though it's not as spacious as yours."

"I can care less about the size of your crib. As long as your bed got strong springs, I'm good to go."

"The mattress is new and the springs are certainly strong," she said, flirtatiously. "I'm hoping you have enough stamina to hang with me."

"You did try to fuck me to death the last time you spent the night, but it don't normally go down like that. I usually beat your back out and you know it. I hope you ain't piping those ecstasy pills."

"My stamina stays high. You know how I do. "That's why I want you tonight. But since I can't have you tonight, what day do you want to hook up?"

"Saturday night. I'm gonna come through and scoop you up around eight thirty, so be ready."

"Ok baby, miss you."

"I'm missing you too, bye."

I shook Sabrina from my thoughts as Mr. Willis and I continued our ride to work. He showed me two pictures of his ex-girlfriend. They had to be old because he was hugging her in one of the pictures and he'd told me he was nineteen when the Polaroid picture was taken. His ex-girlfriend was on the other picture by herself. She was beautiful, sporting big late 80's Jeri Curl. I knew there was no way I could have known the woman in the picture, but she looked so familiar to me. Instead of asking her name, I looked on the back of the pictures and it had the initials C.B in the corner. I didn't dare ask him what the initials stood for. I figured he would tell me when we got a little closer.

It had been nearly a month since Hazel Eyes told me her roommate's father was searching for her. As crazy as it might seem, Mr. Willis might be Monica's long lost daddy. If I ever get the chance to talk with Hazel Eyes again I'm gonna ask her about it.

SHANTE

The first time I laid eyes on you
I had to know your name
Didn't want you to think
That I was playing a game
I never met a man like you
As sexy as you boo
And boy you know you're beautiful too
That's why I gotta have you
I-I-I gotta have you in my life
I gotta have you
Gotta have you
In my life
Wanna make you my boo
Gotta have you in my
I gotta have you yeah
Gotta have you in my life
Wanna make you my boo...

"Girl, that was hot. When did you write that?" Monica asked after I finished singing.

I smiled. "Thanks. I stayed up half the night working on this song. I can't wait to get back into the studio to record it."

"As hot as the music industry is right now, you need to put forth more effort into shopping your demo around before the window of opportunity slams shut. Being straight up with you girl, you look and sound better than most of the sistas out there in the industry anyway. So you need to tighten up and handle your business."

"That, I will do. For the time being I need to hit the studio and lay down my vocals while I'm feeling this song."

"Who is the boo you're talking about in the new song?"

"Nobody. It's just a song."

"Stop lying. You wrote that song from the heart. Who's the boo? Is it Tim, Julian, Dee or that new brotha Anthony who has been calling you the past few weeks? Come clean with a sista," she begged.

"It's not about Tim, nosy. Are you satisfied?"

"Nope. You lying. I can see it in your eyes."

"OK then," I got up off the sofa. "Come watch my door close in your face since you can see so good."

I went to my room and slammed the door. I laid on the bed and thought about Dee. It had been a whole month since I walked out on him and I hadn't heard from him since. If I could have done it all over again, I wouldn't have walked out on him. I should have waited until he woke up and told him how I really felt about him. That long month had been hard on me, both physically and mentally. I wasn't able to get my proper beauty sleep and the date Dee had taken me on played through my mind constantly.

I went out to dinner with this guy Anthony earlier during the week. The only reason I went out was to get Dee off my mind. It didn't work, it ended up ruining the whole date.

"Is it the food or are you sick?" Anthony had asked while we were having dinner at Ruby Tuesdays.

"No, I'm fine," I sighed, showing a weak smile. "I'm just a little tired from working earlier."

"You haven't said much since we arrived here almost an hour ago. I've tried my best to make this evening worthwhile. It seems to me that your mind is a million miles away."

"I'm sorry Anthony," I reached across the table and grabbed his hands. "I shouldn't have met you here this evening. I don't believe I'm quite ready to get involved with this dating thing right now."

"I saw it in your face when you got out of your car. I did try my best to take your mind off him though."

"What makes you think it's a he?"

"It can't be a she...or is it?" He asked, looking confused.

"Nooo," I found myself laughing for the first time that evening. "I'm strictly dickly. How did you figure it out?"

"I've been there and done it before. Whoever dude is, he's a lucky man to even have a gorgeous woman such as yourself thinking about him."

"It isn't what you think. He and I only went out twice before I broke it off."

"That makes it that much worse. You fell in love with the dude in two dates. He must've captured your heart overnight."

"I think he did," I took a long pause. "I can't believe we're having this conversation. I am so sorry for dragging you into my problems."

"It's life Shante. But don't worry about it, I don't hate the game, I play the game. And I play by the rules. Give me a call when you get yourself together." He stood up, tidying up his clothes. "I'm outa here."

"Hold up Anthony," I got up and hugged him. "Thanks for understanding." I gave him a peck on the lips.

"Anytime. I'll handle the bill on my way out, you tip the waitress."

"That's fine with me."

Since he and I had been seated by a window, I sat back down and watched him get into his Range Rover and pull off.

I had met him inside Neiman Marcus at the Mall of Georgia while I was at the counter about to pay for a pair of $289 Prada jeans. "I'll take care of that miss," he told the cashier and handed her what appeared to be a Platinum card. What Anthony did for me wasn't shocking. That happened to me a few times before. He wasn't a good looking guy. However, he had that larger than life presence that was hard for women to ignore. He also wore an expensive suit and had a Rolex on his wrist with no wedding ring on his finger. After he purchased the jeans, he invited me to one of the mall eateries, where we ate ice cream and chatted for a while before exchanging numbers.

The only reason I'd given Anthony the time of day was because I was trying to get Dee out of my system. As you can see, it didn't work. I'd been thinking about him so much that I wrote the song "Gotta Have You" about him.

Over the course of that month's separation, I had called him twice but hung up before his phone started ringing. A girl gotta do what a girl gotta do if she wants to end this foolishness. I sat up on my bed, reaching for my phone, as Ruben Stoddard crooned about how sorry he was on the radio. My phone began ringing the moment I picked it up off the nightstand. I exhaled when I saw Dee's number.

"Hello."

"... Hazel Eyes. Damn I've missed you."

"I've missed you too, Boo-- I mean Dee," I said nervously.

This man had my mind so twisted I couldn't even think straight. It seemed to me like the sassy Shante Blackmon had disappeared out of my body and I was back to being a little twelve year old girl again.

"I might like being your Boo instead of Dee. You left Dee back at the Marriott, remember."

"I am really sorry for the way I handled that situation. Will you let me explain?"

"Please do... You fucked me up."

"God knows," I sighed. "I have so much to talk to you about that I don't even know where to start."

"Start back at the hotel before you abandoned me. No, better yet, you and I need to talk about this face to face."

"Ok. Where do you want to meet at?" I asked.

"Your place or mine, it really don't matter to me. You're the only thing that matters to me right now."

"Come on over."

"Just still be there when I get there," he laughed.

"I will," I assured him.

I had always found that talking face to face was a lot easier than talking on the phone. My aggressive attitude and beauty alone, intimidated the average guy. However, Dee was far from average. His good looks and overbearing manner, along with his height and intimidating presence, were going to make it that much harder for me to deal with him face to face. It would have been easier for me to shoot him a string of lies over the phone, but now I knew that I wasn't going to be able to slip too many lies past him face to face. I decided I would just suck it up, put my tough girl image to the side for once and be straight up with him.

Monica came to my room about twenty five minutes later, telling me there was a stranger knocking at the door. I jumped up to get the door, knowing it had to be Dee.

I almost melted when I opened the door and saw him standing there. He had on a clean baggy blue jumpsuit with the name Deavin James stenciled across the top of the pocket. James Janitorial Service was stenciled in larger letters above his name.

"Are you going to invite me in or stare me to death?"

"I'm sorry Boo, come in."

He stepped in. "Thanks."

I closed the door behind him, took his hand and led him straight to my room. I had to do it like that in order to keep Monica's nosy ass from hearing our conversation.

Soon as I shut my room door, he pulled me into his arms. We hugged for nearly a minute without saying a word to each other.

"I'm glad you invited me over, but I can't stay no longer than a half hour. I gotta leave by ten thirty so I can pick up Mr. Willis and head to work."

"That's fine with me," I got on my tip toes and kissed his sexy lips. "You can have a seat on the bed. I promise you that I'll never sneak out on you again."

"I'm still trying to figure out why you snuck out on me in the first place. I thought we were really feeling each other."

"I was, I mean, I am." I sat down beside him. "I woke up early that morning more than feeling you. What I was feeling scared me so bad that I had to get away from you to see if what I was feeling was actually real or a night of passion."

"Do you still feel the same way about me now? Or did your feelings for me disappear after the night of passion we shared faded out of your mind?"

"No..., my feelings for you have grown a lot deeper since then."

"Why didn't you call me and let me know how you felt? It's been over a month now. What if I wouldn't have called you tonight, would you have forgot about me?"

"I don't think I could ever forget about you. And believe this or not, I was about to call you, seconds before you called me."

"Yeah right. Oprah is my rich aunt too," he said with a smirk, which sort of pissed me off. "You've mentioned to me several times already about your feelings for me. Explain them to me? Show me how real they are?"

"I don't know how it happened so fast, but I felt love in my heart for you the morning I left. Since I wasn't sure if the love was real and instead of complicating things, I had to free the both of us. I left you, you came back and right now I couldn't be any happier. Most of all..., I love you."

"I love you too," he replied, looking into my eyes with sincerity.

"I know you don't have long before you go to work," I rubbed my hand between his legs. "Make love to me."

I didn't have to say it twice. He slipped off the jumpsuit and laid back in the bed with his hands clasp behind his head before I finished undressing.

"Hold up baby!" He startled me. "Don't take off the panties yet. Turn around and let me see how they're fitting from the back."

I pulled the silk bikini panties into the crease between my ass cheeks and slowly turned around in a circle, showing off my flawless 36-24-38 figure, to let him see what he'd been missing. I shook my ass for him like I was an exotic dancer from Magic City.

"How do you like that?" I asked, looking back at him while I continued making my ass jiggle.

"Oh my God!" He blurted, holding his monstrous erection. "Come here and let me eat them panties off you."

"If you insist Boo. I'm yours for the taking."

I got in the bed with him and it was on. Not only did he use his long tongue to pull the panties from between my ass crack, but he stuck it so deep up in my pussy that I almost screamed his name. Dee's lips and slithery tongue made love to my clitoris. He licked and sucked on it with intensity, sending my body into a frenzy, causing me to scream out his name as I creamed in his mouth.

When he came up for air, he kissed me deeply and I tasted my own sticky love on his tongue. I had never allowed that to happen before, but somehow it was arousing to me.

"Let me hit it from the back," he asked after our long sensual kiss.

I got in the doggy-style position and he entered me. "Ohhhh!" I moaned, the deeper he eased up into my moist vagina walls.

For the first few minutes he sexed me at a slow pace. His fat dick was stretching my walls and hypnotizing my entire body. When I creamed on his dick I got wetter and he picked up the pace. To muzzle out my loud moans and screams, I buried my face in the pillow as the sounds of my cheeks slapping up against his muscular thighs, echoed through the room.

If I had not muzzled out my screams, Monica probably would have called the police, thinking Dee was trying to kill me. When he started grunting, I felt his body jerking at the same time. I knew he was on the brink of cuming so I started throwing it back to him as hard as I could. The mixture of pleasure and pain had me on a sexual high until I felt him releasing his warm load inside me. That's when I realized he wasn't wearing a rubber.

OH SHIT! I know being in love don't make women stupid. I can't believe I let him stick his dick inside me without making sure he had on a condom first. Unprotected sex has always been a no, no for me ever since I made that big mistake when I was a teenager and I'm not about to start breaking my rules because I love this man. Hell, I don't know where his dick has been. Contracting HIV or the AIDS virus is about the only thing that scares the shit out of me. I'm not worried about catching something that's curable, even though I'm not trying to catch shit. AIDS is an incurable death sentence. That's something I'm not going to risk catching, regardless of how good the dick is.

"We need to talk Boo," I said, sitting up on the bed with teary eyes.

The tears were from the pounding he'd just put on me. It did hurt, but at the same time it felt so good that he'd brought me to multiple mesmerizing orgasms before he had his first.

"What's the matter Special?" He asked, holding my hand and looking me in the eyes.

"You came in me. I don't have unprotected sex Boo, it's too dangerous. You and I were moving way too fast and I didn't realize you wasn't wearing a rubber until it was too late."

"My bad. I didn't know you felt that way. I don't carry rubbers in my work clothes."

"All you had to do was ask me for one. I keep some in my dresser drawer. I'm not sure where we stand on the relationship level, but we need to get something straight if we're going to be sleeping together."

"I called you Special a few minutes ago because that's exactly what you are to me. I'm not gonna be shy to say it, you are the only woman that has ever made me want to slow down. That's the God honest truth. You might not be sure where we stand on the relationship level, but as of now you're Mrs. Deavin James. That's if you don't mind being my woman?"

"I don't mind you being Mr. Shante Blackmon," I said with a smile. "But right now you gonna have to tell all your other women that it's over and be committed to me. Me only. I mean it Dee."

"What makes you think I have all kinds of women? I've only been in Atlanta a few of months."

"Don't play that bimbo shit with me. I knew you were a playa after the first conversation we had. I continued to kick it with you because it was challenging. You never hesitated to tell me no when we would disagree on different things and you just took the cake the night you stood me up, even though you claimed to have had an unexpected business meeting, which I felt was a bunch of bullshit. I know a playa when I see one and there is no telling how many women you left back home in North Carolina with broken hearts. You and I both need to come clean with each other so there won't be no unexpected surprises popping up later."

"I was involved with this woman back home who I sort of cared about. I didn't want to take that relationship to the next level so I ended it. You are without a doubt the only woman who has ever made me think about the big house with the white picket fence and whole nine yards. I'm willing to stay committed in this relationship with you because I believe it's gonna turn out to be something special."

"I hope it does too. Now, what about here in Atlanta? I'm sure you have a late night booty call or two on the side. Don't try to lie to me either. This is the only chance I'm giving you to come clean. Be straight up with me Dee. I promise to be straight up with you."

"I started kicking it with this sista named Sabrina not long after I moved here. It was nothing serious and I really haven't spent much time with her lately."

"You need to call her up tonight and let her know that it's over. Also, you and I both need to schedule an appointment to get tested for AIDS."

"AIDS!" He spat, looking as if he was about to panic. "Please tell me you ain't got that shit!"

I started to joke with him by telling him I had already tested positive for HIV, but I quickly realized that lying about being sick wasn't a joking matter. "Calm down before you have a heart attack," I grabbed his limp penis and began to slow stroke it. "I'm clean..., unless you infected me tonight."

"Damn!" He exhaled. "You scared the shit out of me."

"I felt the same way when I felt you cum in me. At twelve o'clock tomorrow I want you to come by my job so we can go get tested together. This AIDS epidemic is real, especially here in Atlanta. I'm not taking any chances with that shit."

"I'll meet you at work tomorrow. I feel that getting tested is the perfect way to start off our relationship. In the meantime, what are you going to do to ease this hard on you gave me?"

I got a condom out of the drawer and put it on him. It was too small, it barely covered half of his long, thick shaft. "I guess it'll have to do for now. Only Magnums will be able to fit this plus sized dick," I said, then I straddled him, sticking his stiff pole up my throbbing hole and got my ride on. I rode that dick until we both came again.

While I laid comfortably on top of him with my face on his chest, his phone started ringing. I reached on the nightstand and passed him the phone.

"Damn it!" He spat, seconds after listening to the caller and then he hung up. "I'm late for work. That was Mr. Willis. I gotta go pick him up."

"If you're so late for work why are you still smiling?"

"Mr. Willis assumed you and I had made up. He said you was the only woman in the world who could possibly cause me to be late for work. He's right about that. He's my buddy and I look at him as a father figure away from home. I had even let him read the letter you left me and he basically told me that you had fallen in love with me. I didn't believe him though."

"Do you believe him now?"

"No doubt," he answered, getting out of the bed, putting his clothes back on.

"Do you want to bathe right quick? I know you don't wanna go to work smelling like my juices."

He licked his lips. "The taste of your sweet juices are still on my tongue. I don't mind taking that to work with me," he chuckled. "Real talk though, I'm already running late and don't have time to shower. I work around four rusty guys, so I don't mind carrying your scent to work with me."

I got up off the bed and gave him a hug and goodbye kiss. However, it almost turned into something else. I was still naked and he massaged my ass cheeks while our tongues danced around in each other's mouth.

"If you mess around and hit the wrong button you won't make it to work tonight."

"I'll see you at noon tomorrow." He grabbed the door knob. "Don't think I forgot either, it's your time to come clean tomorrow."

"I haven't forgot."

I put on my nightgown and went to lock the door behind him. On my way back to the room, Monica stepped out her door.

"What are you smiling for?" I asked.

"You're my sister and I'm glad to know you're alright."

"What gave you the impression something was wrong with me?"

"The way I heard him blowing your back out in there I'm surprised you're able to walk straight," she said, busting into laughter.

"Oh bitch, don't act. I've heard you hollering and screaming many of nights when Trey be over here."

"Yeah, I know I'm a screamer. But damn, I ain't never heard you putting on like that."

"Turn your radio up louder so your nosy ass won't hear it the next time!" I spat, going into my room and slamming the door.

DEAVIN

When I got in from work I took a long shower, washing Hazel Eye's dried up juices off me. I set my alarm clock for 11:15 a.m. then got into bed.

While at work earlier that night, we had all worked our butts off. Mr. Willis black padded the floor with the slow buffer, while Tony came behind him, red padding with the other slow buffer and Chuck followed up Tony, white padding the floor with the fast buffer. Mark brought up the rear, dust moping and waxing while I vacuumed and polished the brass and stainless steel in the ten small offices. The four man crew and I had been knocking out a lot of work and doing a good job.

It seemed like every week a new business would call and request my services. Some of the jobs I accepted, some I didn't. The only reason I turned down some offers was because I didn't have the man power to handle the jobs. Despite that, two months of running my business was going a lot better than I could have ever imagined. I had payroll checks made up and paid my workers every Friday morning before they left the job site.

"I see you and Shante have finally got it together," Mr. Willis had said as I took him home early that morning.

"Yeah man," I found myself smiling. "I've never been in love like this before."

"It's a good feeling son and you need to cherish every moment of it. Love is a beautiful thing. Don't forget that."

"The few times I've spent with my Special are already cherishable moments to me. She's one helluva woman."

"You've already given her a pet name so I know she has to be special. You wouldn't happen to have any pictures of her would you?"

"I got a picture that we took together at Six Flags," I took the picture out of the console and handed it to him. "She's beautiful isn't she?"

He didn't respond right away. He eyed the picture as if he was in a trance.

"I know her from somewhere. I just can't remember where."

"She works at Dolly's. You know, the soul food restaurant downtown on Marietta Street."

"Maybe that's why she looks so familiar. I been there once. They serve the best pork chops, fish and greens in town."

"I know. I ate there the first day I moved here."

"What are your plans for today?" He asked as he passed my picture back. "You know I would like to do something for you and Shante."

"We're going to the clinic or somewhere to get tested for AIDS this afternoon. I'm not sure what she and I will be getting into later."

"Her idea or your idea about getting tested?"

"Hers of course. I do understand why it needs to be done."

"It's good y'all are getting tested. AIDS is deadly son and it's not to be taken lightly. I've seen guys in prison die of it. Some were heterosexuals who brought the disease into the prison system with them. Some caught it from using tattoo needles that weren't sanitized properly. Others caught it by engaging in homosexual activities. Whooow!" He said loudly, shaking his head. "I never want to see the inside of another jail or prison again. Well as for you and Shante, if you two haven't made plans by six o'clock this evening, give me a call. There's a place I'd like to take y'all to."

"I'm gonna call you up by four o'clock and let you know what's up."

"Deal," he said as I dropped him off.

****

I was awakened by the sound of my alarm clock and the ringing of the phone at the same time.

"Hel-lo," I answered, drowsily.

"Why you playing games with me? Ever since the night after we went to the movies you been acting funny towards me. What have I done to you to deserve to be treated like this?" Sabrina asked, catching me off guard.

"We never committed to each other Sabrina. We were just kicking it."

"Just kicking it! What you mean just kicking it! You gave me the impression that you was my man!"

"First of all you need to stop hollering in my ear," I told her as I took a deep breath. "We kicked it a few months and I enjoyed the good times we spent together. I never told you that I was in a committed relationship with you, but I did respect you every time we were together. What I'm telling you Sabrina is that we can't kick it no more. It's over."

"Oh hell fucking no! This can't be happening! You played me! You fucking played me! Please Deavin, please." She lowered her voice, "Tell me this is all a joke. Please Deavin?"

"I'm not joking Sabrina. I'm pressed for time. I gotta go. Bye."

I hung up before she had a chance to respond and it actually made me feel like shit. Sabrina was wife material for any man, even me. She just wasn't comparable to Hazel Eyes and Hazel Eyes is who I wanted.

"Why is it so hard for you to be on time, Boo?" Hazel Eyes asked when I parked beside her BMW in the Dolly's parking lot, fifteen minutes late. She was sitting in the passenger seat of her car with the window down. "Lock up your truck. You're driving my car."

"Whatever you say Miss Daisy."

"Why are you still dressing like a teenager?" She asked after I got into her car.

I had on a Cam Newton Carolina Panthers jersey. Baggy denim jeans. Tarheel fitted cap and a pair of blue and white, patent leather, retro Grant Hill's. She kissed me on the lips before I slid the seat back as far as it could go.

"I'm not dressed like a teenager, I'm rocking my Carolina gear because I'm representing where I'm from."

"You better watch how you dress down here, wearing all that blue. These ignorant Negroids might mistake you for being in a gang and try to start some shit."

"I'm not worried about it. I'll deal with them young punks if they ever step to me about what I'm wearing. Which way are we headed?"

"Make a right. We're going to the West End Mall."

"We going shopping?"

"Shopping," she repeated, laughing. "I wouldn't get caught buying chewing gum out of that mall."

"What's wrong with that mall?"

"Everything they sell in that place can be found at the flea market downtown."

"Oh, it's a hood mall?"

"Exactly. Today they're having HIV testing in the mall parking lot and we'll be able to get our results before we leave."

"Th-that's straight."

"What's wrong with you? I hope you ain't scared of taken this test?"

"I'm scared to death. I hope God is on my side when the result come back," I said, thinking about all the countless women I'd hit without wearing a rubber over the years.

I'm gonna lose my fucking mind if these people tell me I'm positive. If my test comes back negative I'm promising God that my sleeping around with woman after woman, is over.

"Ain't no reason to get scared now, big time playa. You should've thought about the risk of catching AIDS when you was out there sticking your unwrapped pickle in all those contaminated holes, playa."

"I'm clean. I know I'm clean. God is with me."

"Why is it that when people get scared, the first name they call on is God? You should've thought about God before you did all that dirt you was doing."

"I'm not gonna let you keep trying to spook me. I'm alright," I told her as I turned up the radio."

"I don't like that song. I think the lyrics are degrading." J. Cole's "Wet Dream" was playing.

"You just hating now. First it was my North Carolina jersey and fitted cap. Now it's a North Carolina rapper. I guess you don't like Fantasia either?"

"I was only joking with you about the J. Cole song, I like J. Cole. You seem to be touchy about anything having to do with North Carolina. I didn't know you was that sensitive Boo."

"Don't let the smooth taste fool you," I shot her my playa look. "The only sensitive part of me is hanging low. You're gonna find out soon enough."

She licked her lips. "I just might. You had my sensitive spot in your mouth last night. Did it taste good?" She asked, giggling.

"You got down on me then. You best believe that I'm gonna have the last laugh. Since you find it so funny you need to come clean to me right now."

"I don't have anything to hide."

"Let's hear it then."

"Around the time you and I met, I had just broken up with my part-time boyfriend, Julian. I haven't seen or spoken to him in over a month now. He's my past and that's where I intend to leave him."

"Fill me in, Special. What's a part-time boyfriend?"

"Don't cut me off. I'm gonna explain everything to you. Again, Julian is married and he's my past."

"You was kicking it with a married man?"

"Save it Deavin. I don't want to hear it. That's my past. There's also someone else, his name is Tim, he's a wimp. I called him while I was at work and told him to take a hike. When he started whining I hung up on him. I do want you to know that I wasn't in love with either one of them. You're the first man to earn that title."

She kissed me as I pulled into the West End Mall parking lot.

"I know you left a few skeletons in your closet. I'm gonna find out about them one day."

"The same goes for you too. I know you left all kinds of skeletons hanging in your closet back in North Carolina. When they end up hunting you down I'm hoping we'll be able to handle them."

"That's something neither of us will ever have to worry about. Trust me."

"You see all those people standing over there around that bus. That's a clinic on wheels. They do free HIV testing and have the results ready pretty fast."

"After we get this over with, what are your plans for later?"

"Nothing really, what's up?"

"Mr. Willis wants to take us out this evening."

"Where to?"

"I don't have a clue. He told me that he wanted to do something nice for us once we made up and got back together."

"It's fine with me," she said, opening the car door. "I wouldn't mind meeting him."

She and I got out of the car and stood in line. I couldn't tell if Hazel Eyes was nervous about getting tested or not. If she was she didn't show it. I was the total opposite, I was a nervous wreck and couldn't hide it.

Thirty minutes or so later, Hazel Eyes and I were waiting for our results. While waiting for our names to be called, I saw people walking away with smiles on their faces. I saw one dude who apparently tested positive, he just lost it. He kicked over the two long tables that had the AIDS and HIV prevention pamphlets on them and threatened to physically harm one of the nurses if they didn't retest him.

"Mr. James! Miss Black!" An old freckled face nurse called out our names.

God please don't let me be the one who kicks over the next table. I'm not ready to die.

SABRINA

When Deshundria and I left the house that morning, headed to work, I was pissed off at Deavin from the phone conversation he and I had earlier. I still couldn't believe he'd broken up with me out of the blue. I drove to work teary eyed.

"Don't be crying over that sorry ass nigga, girl," Deshundria said as I drove down Northside Drive. "He wasn't all that anyway."

"I'm not crying over him. I'm hurt by what he did to me. I know I shouldn't have fallen for his good looks and smooth talking.

"You didn't fall for nothing. You was only being the good woman you've always been and got involved with a piece of shit. There's a million good men out there, so you need to get over his ass and move on."

"I'm going to try my best to. It's not going to be as easy as you think."

I'd went eighteen months being celibate and without a boyfriend before Deavin and I became romantically involved. When I first laid eyes on him, I thought he was the most handsome guy I had ever seen. I wasn't only nervous while I waited his table, I had goose bumps all over my body. After I'd gotten home from work that night, I stayed up until one o'clock in the morning expecting his call. Every time my phone rang for two straight weeks, I was hoping it was him. However, when he did finally call three weeks later I couldn't have been any happier. I had given up on him.

Our first phone conversation had me on an emotional high and I started feeling him after the first time he and I went out together. But after the first time we made love, I was whipped. He had me feeling like a queen that night as he held me in his arms, caressing me to sleep. He had it going on, in and out of the bedroom. At times, it seemed as if I couldn't get enough of him. I wasn't sure if it was love or if I was just infatuated with him.

I was only twenty-one years old. Prior to getting involved with Deavin, I had always dated guys my age. Even though Deavin was nine years older than me, the age gap didn't make much of a difference in our relationship. He'd always treated me with the utmost respect and showed me the kind of attention that I had never received from any man before. He and I never sat down and discussed the status of our relationship, but I considered him my man. I thought he'd felt the same way about me. In spite of that, I couldn't understand why he had up and dumped me. I planned to find out though.

A year and a half before Deavin and I hooked up, I'd broken up with my ex-boyfriend Allen. He and I had been together for over a year before I caught him and my then roommate, in our dormitory room fucking. I was supposed to have been spending the whole week in Washington D.C. with my Aunt Tina. That is until she and I got into a big argument that caused me to pack my bags and fly back home three days early. I didn't call Allen before I left. I wanted to surprise him. However, I was the one who was surprised. When I opened my dormitory room door they didn't hear me enter because they were listening to one of Chris Brown's love songs, which was blasting from the radio.

"What the fuck!" I'd shouted, charging them with my fist balled.

They'd been going at it in the doggy style position with their backs to me. By the time they looked back and saw me, it was too late for them to react. I hit him in his temple as hard as I could and he fell on his back with his dick sticking straight up in the air. I grabbed it and tried my best to twist it off.

While he screamed in agony, pleading for me to let it go, my roommate Wanda was trying to put her panties back on. I immediately let Allen's dick go and grabbed a handful of Wanda's long micro braids.

"Don't get scared now you backstabbing bitch!" I hollered as I commenced to beating her in the face until my hand felt numb. "I'll be back tomorrow for the rest of my shit!" I spat, kicking her in the face before grabbing my bags and heading back out the door.

I crashed at Deshundria's apartment that night and moved in with her a few days later. Allen called me at least five times a day after the incident. I disregarded his calls, I wasn't trying to hear a word he had to say. On the other hand, Wanda had written me a letter the day after I whipped her ass. She'd left the letter on my bed. I found it the day I went back to pick up the rest of my things.

I had called ahead of time and told her that she better not be in the room when I got there. I had easily spotted the letter because she'd wrote it on bright yellow typing paper. I sat on the bed and read it.

I'm sorry Sabrina. I didn't intentionally try to hurt you. Allen had been trying to get at me for months, but I never said anything to you about it because I didn't want you thinking that I was trying to start some shit to break you two up. He had spent the night in your bed the day before you walked in and caught us. He laid down his charm and sweet talked me almost that entire night before I eventually fell weak.

Looking back at the situation now, I realize that I should have told you about Allen when he first tried me. You and I were like sisters and I know we'll never be that close again. I do hope that you can find it in your heart to forgive me.

Sincerely, Wanda.

I had thought about her letter as I drove down Marietta Street. I did eventually forgive her, only because I started feeling guilty about the ass whipping I'd put on her. As for Allen's cheating ass, I didn't take him back, but I gave in and let him explain himself to me a month after the incident. He had the nerve to shed some tears as he pleaded with me about how sorry he was and how bad he wanted me to give him a second chance. I wasn't about to fall for his teary eyed sob story and told him point blank that I would mace his ass if he ever stepped to me again.

For the next eighteen months I didn't give out my phone number to guys, even when some of them literally begged me for it. Throughout that time, I was mad at men in general. That is, until I met Deavin. I let my guard down and opened up my heart to him. Getting involved with him might have been one of the worst mistakes I've ever made in my life, I thought as I turned into Dolly's parking lot, immediately spotting his Cadillac Escalade. I knew it had to be his truck because of the 'First in Flight' North Carolina tag.

"Look," Deshundria pointed at the truck. "Isn't that Deavin's Escalade?"

"Yep, that's it. I wonder why he came by the job. He could've called and talked to me."

"Maybe his sorry ass came by to apologize."

"I don't know what he's here for and I really don't care," I said, trying not to let her know how happy I really was. All the bad thoughts I had about him disappeared as I got out of my car. I damn near tripped and fell flat on my face while trying to get inside the restaurant to see him.

"Slow down girl," Deshundria had said, catching me. "That man ain't going nowhere. What other reason would he be here for?"

"You're right," I replied giggling, feeling a little embarrassed.

Moments after I got inside, I went out to the large dining area, looking for Deavin. When I didn't see him, I went back outside to see if his truck was still there. To my surprise it was. I even took a peek inside it to make sure it was his truck. When I saw the small picture of his grandmother pasted to the dashboard I knew without a doubt it was his truck.

"Where in the hell could he be?" I mumbled before going back into the restaurant.

Wherever he was, I intended on seeing him before his truck left the parking lot. If I flatten his tires he would have no choice but to come ask me for help whenever he got back.

SHANTE

After getting our negative HIV results back, Dee and I cruised around the city before we ended up at his condo. It was my idea to stop by there, I wanted to see what the inside of his place looked like.

"Make yourself at home Special. I gotta get to this bathroom before my bladder busts," he told me and rushed down the hall.

I had to give him some credit, his living room was laid. The large fish aquarium is what really caught my eye. It was beautiful and had different kinds of tropical fish in it.

"I see you've taken a liking to my goldfish already," he said, coming up from behind, kissing me on the back of my neck.

"I don't care for the goldfish. It's the tropical ones that look so exotic to me."

"Have you seen the water moccasin in there yet?"

"Moccasin!" I blurted, almost knocking him down as I quickly backed away from the aquarium. "I know you don't have a poisonous snake in here!"

"Yeah, I got one in the aquarium. I also got a python crawling around in here somewhere. It got loose yesterday and I haven't been able to find him yet."

"Let's go! I'm scared to death of snakes. I ain't trying to be in the same room with one whether it's caged or on the loose."

"I was just kidding with you. Shit, I'm scared of snakes too."

"You were only kidding?" I pushed him away. "Snakes and rats are something I don't joke about."

"Come here," he grabbed my hand and pulled me into his arms. "I'm sorry," he apologized before slipping his tongue in my mouth. "Can I make it up to you?"

"You already have. Let me see what your bedroom looks like. And none of that hanky-panky stuff either. You know we have to meet Mr. Willis in a couple more hours, remember."

"Of course I remember. But the only reason why I'm letting you off the hook is because I don't wanna mess up your hair."

"Yeah right," I eyed him with a smirk. "You might've ran the show at the hotel that night, but don't get it twisted. I'm running the show now. No hanky-panky."

"I'm gonna be a gentlemen today and let you have your way."

"Just like I thought. Let's go see your room."

He held my hand and led me down the hallway to his room. I had always thought it was important to see what a man lived like. Some guys looked clean in their appearance, but kept a filthy home. Dee wasn't one of them guys. His room was clean, bed neatly made and it appeared to me that he had nothing laying out of place. That alone told me a lot about him.

I checked his hairbrush to see if I could find any strings of women's hair. I even looked through his bathroom to see if I could find any signs of a woman having been there. Eyebrow pencil, lip stick, curling iron, bobby pin, perfume. I found none of it. Even the toilet seat was up. He'd passed my personal inspection so far. I was only hoping he didn't have any major skeletons in his closet. I had fallen hard for him and I wanted to make sure the coast was clear before I decided to give my all to the relationship.

We left his condo and went straight to my apartment. I wanted to freshen up before we picked up Mr. Willis. I winked at Monica when Dee and I stepped through the door. She was about to leave for class.

"How are you doing?" She spoke to Dee as he held the door open for her to step out. "I hope you take care of my sister."

"Monica," he said, extending his hand to her. "That's my Special. She's in good hands with me."

"Your Special?" She replied, cutting her eyes at me. "You two got it going on like that?"

"Bye Monica!" I interjected before Dee could answer. "You're gonna be late for class."

She caught the hint and stepped on out the door.

"Your roommate seems to be protective of you."

"She's not protective. She's just nosy as hell. I still love her like a sister though."

"Has she had the chance to meet her father yet?"

'Her father? Monica talks to both her parents at least one a week. Why would you ask a stupid question like that?' I thought, before realizing that I had lied to him about my own long lost sperm donor.

"Ohhh," I smiled, trying to play it off. "She met up with him about two weeks ago."

"That's good. Let me call Mr. Willis back and see what's up."

"Alright. Make yourself comfortable while I go back here and get myself together."

Forty minutes later, I strutted back into the living room, ready to go. I had on my brand new Norma Kamali white swimsuit dress, Cesare Paciotti peep-toe sandals, with matching bracelets and ring. I could see that Dee had got more than comfortable, he had made himself at home. He was laid back on the sofa watching the new web series "Damaged Goods" starring Wanda Hunter as Patrice. He had a glass of orange juice in one hand and my glazed doughnut in the other.

"Who gave you permission to watch my TV, drink up my juice and eat my last doughnut?"

"Damn! You looking good girl."

I put my hands on my hips. "That much I know. But what I don't know is who told you that you was at home?"

"When you told me to make myself comfortable, I did just that." He put the rest of the doughnut in his mouth.

"I love this series. Patrice got it going on, she's the new Pam Grier." He smiled at me. "But you got it going on in my world."

"That compliment ain't gonna replace my last doughnut," I sat in his lap putting my arm around his neck and kissed his sweet lips. "What did Mr. Willis say?"

"He wants us to meet him at Uptown Comedy Club. I hope you know where that's at?"

"Yeah, it's off Courtland Street," I answered, thinking back to the night he stood me up.

"Let's go get my truck." He patted my butt. "Your little car is killing my knees."

"If you don't like it buy me something roomier. That GL 450 Mercedes would be nice."

"I know it would, but my Escalade will do the job for now."

"Do you wanna follow me to Uptown or are we going to bring my car back here?"

"We'll leave your car here and catch a cab to my truck. We'll head on out from there."

"Sounds good to me."

He pulled his phone out and called a cab.

"Where you going?" Dee asked, moments after he and I had gotten out of the taxicab. "We don't have much time to waste."

"Come on in with me, Boo? We'll only be a few minutes. It's kind of hard for me to be in this parking lot and not go inside to check on things."

"Go ahead on. I'll he waiting in the truck."

The first person I saw when I entered the restaurant was the young college girl Sabrina. She didn't look like she was doing too well.

"What's the matter, are you sick?"

"No, I'm not sick. I'm having some men problems right now."

"We all have those kind of problems sometimes," I said nonchalantly before taking a good look at her. It then appeared to me that she was having a major crisis. "I'm sort of in a rush right now, but you can give me a call this weekend and we'll talk about it. That's if you don't mind."

"I do need to vent a little bit," she sighed, closing her eyes. "I can't talk to Deshundria about it. She doesn't have no kind of understanding."

I used her pen and jotted down my number. "Call me girl. I'll be more than happy to discuss male issues with you. That's my favorite subject."

"Thanks Miss Blackmon," she said with a smile.

"It's my pleasure. Talk to you later."

"I walked on through the restaurant, speaking to the rest of the employees before I headed back out to the parking lot.

"Why are you sitting in the passenger seat?"

"I chauffeured you around all day like I was Morgan Freeman, in Driving Miss Daisy. It's your turn to drive now."

"I don't like driving SUV's."

"That's the same way I felt when I squeezed into your tiny BMW, but I did it."

"Oh, you challenging me?" I went around the truck and got into the driver's seat. "Let's ride Hoke," I called him, Morgan Freeman's character name from the movie, Driving Miss Daisy.

It felt funny for me driving an SUV because I was so use to driving my sports car. However, it didn't take me long to get used to it. We were locked into V103, listening to Greg Street and we rode out.

Being in a relationship with a brotha like Dee was actually new territory for me. All my life I held the men I dated at bay. I basically controlled what went on between us. I was always like the dictator in all my previous relationships, but with Dee, he wasn't going for it. He was a take charge man and didn't hesitate to put me in my place when I over stepped my boundaries as his woman.

"There's Mr. Willis," Dee said, getting my attention as I turned into Uptown Comedy Club parking lot.

I was a little excited about meeting Mr. Willis since Dee had spoken so highly of him. "I know that's not him in the black shirt standing in front of that Explorer?"

"That's him."

I parked beside the Ford Explorer, taking a good look at the man who I thought was much older because of the way Dee had described him to me. Mr. Willis was very handsome and looked to me to be in his early forties.

"Deavin," he said giving him a fatherly hug. "Glad you two made it."

"This is Shante, Mr. Willis, but she's my Special."

"How you doing?" He gave me a hug. "I've heard so much about you. I'm glad to finally get this opportunity to meet you."

"The feeling is mutual. Dee speaks very highly of you."

He blinked his eyes, shaking his head. "Deavin told me you were beautiful, but he lied. You're gorgeous."

"Thank you," I replied, blushing, staring right into his hazel eyes.

"Let's get inside before Bruce-Bruce get on stage. I don't wanna miss him. I've been wanting to see him live ever since I came home."

Dee put his arm around me and we walked along side Mr. Willis to the club entrance.

"Enjoy the show," the man told us after Mr. Willis handed him the three tickets.

"We certainly will," he replied as we headed inside.

The place was already abuzz by the time we took our seats. Some unknown Eddie Griffin looking comedian was giving one brotha hell. The brotha had the nerve to be wearing a navy blue wool suit with the butterfly collar, in the middle of the summer. On top of that, his hair was done up in thick greasy finger waves. He looked like a character straight out of the movie Super Fly.

When Bruce-Bruce came out to do his thing, the crowd went bananas. Almost every word that rolled off his tongue was funny. He even cracked on Dee.

"Ay, brotha!" Bruce-Bruce said, pointing at our table. Dee held up his hands looking around with the 'who me' gesture. "Yeah, I'm talking to you with that big ass football jersey on! You look like a bench warming, backup tight end on crack!" He joked, causing everybody to roar with laughter.

Dee was the only person I saw not laughing. He was looking like he'd just bitten into a sour lemon. Mr. Willis laughing so hard he had tears in his eyes didn't help make things any better for Dee. I immediately felt sorry for my Boo and decided to speak up in his defense.

"You need to find someone else to pick on, Fatboy! My man ain't the one!" I stood up feeling myself. "You're so big and black the picture on your driver's license looks like a smut print!"

"Alright now, Halle Scary, I mean Halle Berry! I respect a woman who takes up for her man, but if you don't hurry up and sit your pretty ass back down, I'm gonna clown your table all night long."

Since my joke didn't get many laughs from the crowd I quickly sat my ass back down before he changed his mind.

The remaining of the evening went fine and I enjoyed being in the company of two handsome men. Mr. Willis had made the 'since I came home' statement at least four times. I wanted to ask him where he'd been, but since he didn't volunteer the information, I figured I would ask Dee about it when I felt the time was right.

"I had a nice time tonight Mr. Willis, Thanks for showing Dee and I a good time," I said, giving him a hug.

"Anytime, Shante. Anytime," he said. They gave each other a firm handshake. "Take good care of this here woman. I believe she's the one."

"I don't call her my Special for nothing," Dee assured.

"Drive safely," I told him as he got in his Ford Explorer.

"I'm proud of that man, he's come a long way in a short time," Dee said after he and I got into the truck.

I thought that was the perfect opportunity for me to ask him where Mr. Willis had been. However, something deep down inside told me that it was none of my business and to keep my mouth shut.

"Your place or mine?"

"Your place," he responded.

"Alright. We'll stop by my place so I can get my overnight bag. We'll be messing up your clean sheets tonight. We messed up mine last night."

"Oh, you don't want a brotha getting too comfortable at your crib? You must be trying to hide something."

"I don't have nothing to hide. I'm not going to let you run this relationship either. This is a 50\50 thing, not 60\40. Remember that."

"You've read one too many of those Ebony Advisor columns. That kind of shit doesn't work in the real world. You gonna have to come stronger than that when dealing with me." He grinned like it was funny.

"You can take it for what it's worth!" I said with an attitude. "50\50 is what I said. 50\50 is what I meant!"

For the rest of the drive to my apartment we rode in silence. He didn't say a word until he pulled up in front of my apartment.

"You still want me to wait for you?"

"If you're gone by the time I come back out, you might as well stay gone," I said getting out without looking back.

About ten minutes later I stepped out the door carrying my bag and was surprised to see Dee leaning against his truck. He took the bag and opened the Escalade door for me.

"Thanks Boo," I told him after he got in.

"Anytime Special. You know we can't let the small things disrupt the chemistry of our relationship. You and I are both bigger than that." He reached over, taking my hand. "Show a brotha some love."

I leaned over and gave him a kiss that immediately erased all the negative friction between us.

Later that night in his king size bed, he long dicked me, slow dicked me and fast dicked me. I could swear that he'd taken me to heaven. I didn't only stay that one night, I stayed the whole weekend at his place. Things couldn't have gone any smoother.

The only thing that didn't work out for me was that I missed Sabrina's calls. Monica said Sabrina had called twice Saturday and once Sunday afternoon before I'd gotten back home.

DEAVIN

I had just gotten back home from the Run-N-Shoot where me and four other guys ran the court and won six straight games before we lost one. I did everybody who tried to guard me and scored over half of my team's points every game. The last game we won, I had this big kid who was being heavily recruited by Georgia Tech, guarding me. He stood every inch of six-feet-ten and was a beast in the paint, but he didn't have a jump shot. That game became so tense that it seemed like all the players on the other six courts stopped playing to watch us. I even saw a large group of women who had come out of their aerobics class watching us. I had always played my best in front of a crowd of women, so I did just that.

With the three and a half inches and twenty five pound weight difference, the big kid was backing me down to the post and dropping me off like he was Shaq. Since I couldn't do much to stop him down on the block, I had to play 'deny your man the ball' defense on him. Once I had gotten him frustrated, I started dropping deep Stephen

Curry three pointers in his face. Having him trying to defend me out on the perimeter was a mismatch. When he played me too close, I would take him off the dribble and go in for a dunk or whatever else I wanted to do.

My blood was pumping, I was feeling it and there was no stopping me. My team and I ended up winning the game by four points. The seventh game we all basically laid down. We had won enough, plus fatigued had set in. As I was walking off the court, a middle age, bald headed white guy approached me, asking where I played college ball. I told him that I hadn't played organized ball since high school. He was stunned when I told him I'd been out of it for twelve years.

"You're in great shape and have a lot of basketball left in you," he'd said, giving me his business card. "If you contact me, I'm sure I'd be able to get you a tryout on one of the many NBA Development League teams. They are looking for small forwards who can stretch the defense and knock down jumpers consistently. It's also a plus that you have the ability to mix it up in the post too."

That conversation was all I could think about as I headed to my room with my gym bag on my shoulder.

"Ay, Dee!" Mark called from his room, almost startling me.

I peeped into his room. "Yeah, what's up?"

"Ms. Brenda called about an hour ago. She told me to tell you to call her back ASAP."

"Alright man, good looking out."

I went to my room and showered before I decided to call her back. Whatever her reason for calling, I knew it wasn't an emergency because she didn't call my cell phone.

"Boy, what are you doing down there?" She asked in an angry tone.

"I'm making it. How are you and Daddy?"

"This call isn't about me or your father. It's about you. You need to call that sweet girl Tracy. She has something to tell you."

"But mama, we broke up--"

"Hush up lying boy! That's all you do is tell lie after lie, tricking all those women you sleep around with. Keep it up boy and you gonna catch something penicillin can't cure."

"I've changed my life around Mama. I don't be out there messing around like I use to. That was the old me. I'm a one woman man now."

She sighed. "Lord knows I hope you are. Boy you know you left some big problems back here that you need to sort out. You ran off to Georgia thinking you could leave everything behind and start over again. It doesn't work like that son. You can't run away from things, leaving them wide open, everything has to have closure just like life itself. You need to call Tracy and put some closure to y'all's relationship. I don't know what you did to that poor girl, but she loves you dearly. She's having problems right now that's going to involve you in the long run. You need to call her now."

"You and Tammy are both trying to push me off on that woman. It's over between me and Tracy Mama. You two need to understand that and let me move on with my life."

"Your grandmother, father and I raised you to be a man, not a coward. Now, if you don't call that sweet girl like I'm telling you to, don't call back here no more," she said and hung up on me.

My mother had never talked to me like that, much less hung up on me. I felt like shit, still holding the phone to my ear. For the life of me I couldn't figure out what the big fuss about Tracy was about. I knew that in order for me to find out, I would have to call her. Even though I was in love with Hazel Eyes, my feelings for Tracy still ran deep. However, that was one of the reasons why I didn't want to call her, not including all the lies I'd told her.

Almost three and a half months had passed since I'd left North Carolina and I was sure Tracy had finally realized I wasn't going to send back for her. Let me call this woman and let her know what she and I had, is over. I dialed her number.

"This is Tracy William's residence. I am not home right now, but if you leave me your name and number I'll get back to you as soon as possible." Her answering machine said as I was contemplating leaving a message.

"Hello!" She finally answered, sounding as if she was out of breath.

"Tracy, what's up?"

"You."

"My mom told me you needed to talk with me about something. What's up?"

"The only reason you called is because of what your mom said?"

"Yeah. She told--"

She hung up on me in mid-sentence and it really pissed me the fuck off. Who in the hell did she think she was hanging up on me like that? I had to call her back and check her ass. I hit redial.

"What's your damn problem woman?" I barked, the moment she picked up. "You don't hang up on me!"

"First of all I'm not a woman," a deep male voice said. "Furthermore my girl can hang up on whoever the fuck she wants too! If you wanna speak to Tracy I suggest that you change that tone."

"Just put her back on the phone. You ain't got shit to do with this. This is between me and her."

"Hold on..., do you wanna talk to this punk or what?" I heard him ask her in the background.

"Why did you call back here? I'm not looking for your sympathy Deavin!" She snapped. "Don't call me because your mother told you so!"

"Regardless of my reason for calling, you shouldn't have hung up on me. Then you had the nerve to put that wanna be, Ice Cube sounding ass lame on the phone. I don't appreciate that shit."

"His name is Steven and he's not a lame! He's more of a man than you'll ever be. He's the man in my life now and you will respect him every time you call this house."

"Your man! Respect him!" I blew, not believing she was talking to me the way she was.

"That's right. I've never called your house and disrespected you or the person who answered. I expect you to show me and my man the same respect."

"Yeah, whatever. All I wanna know is what is going on with you that got my mom so mad at me?"

"I'm fifteen weeks pregnant with your child."

"Huh?" I murmured, hoping what I'd heard was wrong. "Pregnant?"

"Yes, Deavin. I'm carrying your child."

"How long have you known this?"

"Long enough to know you wasn't sending back for me."

"You could've got my number from my mom or Tammy and called to tell me about it first. You didn't have to tell them. It was none of their business."

"Damn whose business it was! If you had given me your number, I wouldn't have told your family about the pregnancy in the first place. So that's on you, not me. Tammy tried giving me your number several times a couple months ago, but I didn't take it. I'm not gonna chase you or any other man around Deavin. My life goes on with or without you. One monkey don't stop no show," she told me before I heard her say, "Ain't that right baby," she told him.

"You say you're pregnant. What is it you expect out of me?"

"To be a father to your child."

"Why don't you get an abortion? It might not be too late. I'll pay for everything."

"I know you will, you coward ass bastard!" She spat, hanging up on me again.

For the first time in my life, I felt that I was in a situation I couldn't handle. Even though Tracy and I had been having unprotected sex on and off during our relationship, it never crossed my mind that she would ever get pregnant because I knew she was on the pill. I wasn't shocked that she was pregnant, but I definitely was surprised. I was shocked she had a man laying up in her house and she let him disrespect me as if I was nothing. It was my anger from that which led me to tell her to get an abortion. God knows I really didn't mean to say it.

When I finally found the love of my life and stopped chasing after women like a dog in heat, Tracy tells me that she's carrying my child. How in the hell am I supposed to break this news to Hazel Eyes.

As for the relationship between Hazel Eyes and me, it had shot up another level since the evening we'd spent with Mr. Willis at the comedy club, which had been almost a month ago. She and I were spending lots of quality time together and I found myself allowing her to break rules that I had never let other women break before. She left lingerie behind after the first weekend she stayed with me. A few weeks later she cleared out two of my dresser drawers, made room in my closet and filled them with her clothes. Expensive clothes at that. Hazel Eyes had the taste of a Hollywood diva. She had also convinced me to give her a key to my condo. Days later I went out and bought her a $2200.00 platinum bracelet. I was doing things for her that was totally out of character for me.

That's when I first realized that I didn't only love her, I was in love with her. I was falling so deep and so fast for her that it was frightening to me at times because I had never been in that position before. On a nightly basis I would talk to Mr. Willis about her and he would give me strong words of encouragement, letting me know that being in love was a gift from God. I knew all the holes and loops to living the life of a playa, but I didn't know about love. That's why the nightly conversations I had with Mr. Willis helped me out so much.

For a man who had spent so much time in prison, he had a lot of knowledge about almost everything. He's the one who convinced me to buy Hazel Eyes the bracelet after she'd bought me a diamond stud earring. I had never felt comfortable with buying women gifts, especially expensive ones. I didn't want her to get the impression that I was a sucker or trying to buy her love because I didn't roll like that. Hazel Eyes was the only woman, besides my family members, that I had ever spent over $200 on.

"Ay Dee," Mark said, opening my room door. "I almost forgot to tell you. Sabrina came by looking for you earlier. You better watch it man, she might be on some fatal attraction shit."

"I don't know what she's on. What I do know is that she needs to find somebody else to fuck with. I'm already going through enough drama as it is."

"Do Shante know about her yet?"

"I done told her about Sabrina. I just didn't tell her what Sabrina it was."

"You're playing a dangerous game Dee. You need to tell Shante what time it is before the situation gets ugly. Sabrina might fuck around and go postal up in Dolly's one day and your ass will be the one to blame."

"I got this man. I'm gonna straighten it all out in no time."

"You need to. This isn't a fairytale, this shit is real. These women ain't gonna keep letting you run over them like you've done in the past. You need to straighten up and fly right or don't fly at all."

"I been chillin' Mark and you know it. I haven't fucked around on Hazel Eyes. This is the first time in my life I've ever been this committed in a relationship. What else am I supposed to do?"

"Be straight up and tell Shante the truth. That's the only thing I can see you doing that'll be right."

"What he need to tell me about Mark?" I heard Hazel Eyes' voice say. "Fill me in on what's going on? Apparently Dee didn't tell me everything." She entered the room standing beside Mark, cutting her eyes at me.

SHANTE

Prior to me going over to Dee's condo, Sabrina and I had finally gotten a chance to talk. She'd come into work that afternoon looking worse than she did the evening I had given her my phone number. I had been spending so much time at Dee's place that I'd missed all of her calls. Sabrina was looking so hurt that I had no choice but to call her into my office for a quick chat.

"Close my door and have a seat girl. You look like you got a lot in your mind."

"You have got to be the busiest woman I've ever met. It's nearly impossible for me to catch you at home."

"I am so sorry about that Sabrina. I've been spending a lot of time at my Boo's place lately."

"At least one of us appears to be happy." She showed a weak smile. "I've been catching hell lately Miss Blackmon."

"I'm pretty good at solving women problems when it's concerning men. Fill me in on what's going on and I'll help you the best way I can."

She closed her eyes and took a deep breath before speaking. "When I first started working here I met one of the finest men God put on this earth. Uh huh." She shook her head. "Just thinking about him blows my mind."

"He got it going on like that?"

"Yes, Lord. He's tall, dark, handsome and well-endowed. The brotha got it going on all the way around."

"If he's all that, why are you looking like you've just lost your best friend?"

She dropped her head. "I have. He broke up with me last month."

"He must've caught you messing around or something?"

"It was nothing like that, I'm faithful as a woman gets. I don't play the cheating game. Just out of nowhere he up and told me that he didn't want to kick it with me no more. The same day he broke it off with me I saw his SUV parked out in the parking lot, but I didn't see him. He blocked my number. It's just..., I don't understand. I even went by to see him right before I came to work, but he wasn't home."

"Something isn't right about this picture. I'm not lesbo or nothing, but you are a nice looking sista. You have an easy going personality, stacked in the back like most men like it and you keep up your appearance. What more can a man ask for in a woman? Do you think he's one of them down low brothas?"

"He ain't gay," she mumbled, looking as if she was in deep thought. "I don't know. I never really thought about it. He could be though."

"Where does he live?"

"Ansley Park."

"That area is definitely full of gays. He might have a little sugar in his tank girl. "What kind of clubs he go to?"

"I've never known him to do the club scene. See, when I met him he'd just moved down from North Carolina."

Tall, dark, handsome, well-endowed, Ansley Park, SUV, North Carolina, I thought, piecing the puzzle together and fearing the worst.

"What's his name?"

"Deavin. I still can't get over him leaving me."

I felt light headed and almost fainted when that name came out of her mouth. Deavin James. Dee. My bae. I see why he dropped your ass now girlfriend, I came into his life. Thinking back on it, I do remember him telling me that he had been kicking it with a Sabrina, but my employee Sabrina was the furthest from my mind. I am glad to know he left her alone after I told him to cut ties with all his booty calls. I am mad at his ass for not letting me know that he was fucking around with one of my employees.

"Miss Blackmon." She called my name, interrupting my train of thought. "Are you alright?"

"Oh, I'm ok."

"What do you think I should do? I still have feelings for him."

"I really don't know right now. We'll talk again when you come in tomorrow," I said trying to rush her out of my office.

"Tomorrow is Saturday Miss Blackmon. We don't come in."

"You're so right. I don't know where my mind is right now. If you can't reach me at home this weekend we'll talk Monday."

"Alright then. See ya," she said smiling and left my office.

Minutes later I was in my car headed straight to Dee's condo. The faster I drove, the more I thought about him and the time he and I had been spending together lately. He was a man that knew how to make a girl feel like a woman without spoiling her with all the materialistic things. I had used both of my $500 gift certificates that Julian had given me a while back to buy Dee a diamond stud earring. The one he'd been wearing was too small and looked flea market cheap. Two nights after I'd given him the earring he came by my apartment and surprised me with a beautiful platinum bracelet. I looked at it as more than a gift. I felt he thought he was marking me as his property. He thought he was being slick by having his initials engraved in it. I had wanted to say something about it, but he sexed me so good that night, I let it slide.

Besides the gift exchange and the mind blowing sex, our relationship was blossoming into something special. We would cook dinner for each other once a week. Watch movies together and go on long evening walks. He even taught me how to play NBA Live and Madden Football on his XBOX. Never had I enjoyed spending that kind of time with a man. Prior to Dee, a man had to shower me with expensive gifts to keep my interest. However, Dee wasn't the cake daddy type and I didn't expect for him to play that role. I loved him just the way he was.

I made it to Dee's condo in record time. I used the key he had given me and quietly eased into his place. After closing and locking the door behind me, I heard Mark's voice. I wasn't trying to be nosy or anything, but when I heard him tell Dee that women wasn't going to keep letting him run over them like they had in the past, my heart immediately dropped. I stood in the hallway expecting to hear the worst until Dee told Mark that he hadn't cheated on me.

When I heard him say that I exhaled, feeling a sigh of relief because I believed him. What I wanted to know was what Mark wanted Dee to be truthful with me about. Damn this eavesdropping, I want to know what was going on. I entered the room asking Mark a question.

"Special!" Dee said, looking up at me like a deer caught in headlights.

"I'm out of here," Mark replied, making his way towards the door. "Dee got something he wants to tell you."

"What the hell is going on here?" I spat, standing at the foot of his bed with my hands on my hips. "What is Mark talking about?"

"Nothing really. I've told you already."

"This is your last time Dee."

"Why I got to be your Dee again? I thought I was your Boo? Alicia Keys even called Usher her Boo."

"You're full of more shit than a circus and I'm not trying to smell it no more. I'm leaving."

He quickly jumped up off the bed and grabbed me around my waist. 'I knew he would see it my way,' I thought, still putting on a front like I wanted to leave.

"Come on Special, it's not a big deal. Sit down and I'll tell you all about it."

"Get to talking. I can hear standing right here, I don't need to sit on your bed. There's no telling who was laying on it before I got here."

"You can take that elementary psychology shit somewhere else. It won't work on me. We can sit down and talk about it like two mature adults."

He let me go and sat down. I followed suit and sat down beside him.

"What's going on Boo?" I asked, showing my pretty smile.

"Now that's more like it," he said and gave me a peck on the lips. "Remember awhile back when I told you that I stopped kicking it with this girl name Sabrina?"

"Unh-huh."

"What I didn't tell you is that the Sabrina I use to kick it with works at Dolly's." He paused for a few seconds, trying to read my reaction before he continued. "I'm sorry I didn't tell you about it earlier. I guess I was afraid you wouldn't get with me."

He went on and explained everything about their past relationship and told me that she had come by his place while he was away earlier.

"I already knew about you and her."

A frown appeared on his face. "Why didn't you say something to me about it?"

"Just wanted to see if you'd tell a lie. There's a lot of guys who are afraid to tell the truth. I'm glad to know you're not one of them."

He tried to pull me into his arms, but I pushed him away.

"What's the problem now?"

"Sabrina is the problem. That young girl is really hurting right now. She wants you back more than life itself."

"How do you know that?"

"She told me about you before I came over here. She's so confused about why you left her, she thinks you might be gay."

"Get the fuck outta here!" He said, falling back on the bed, laughing uncontrollably.

As bad as I wanted to laugh along with him, it took everything I had in me not to. I waited until he had it all out of his system before I spoke again.

"You think its funny Boo, but this is serious. This girl is crazy about you. She and I had a sista to sista talk and she spilled her guts out to me."

"You told her the reason I left her right?"

"Nope. You're gonna tell her that. You got yourself into this mess, you gonna have to get yourself out of it. You sitting here with that silly grin on your face, but do you realize that you put me in a bad situation too?"

"I can't tell. I'm the one who's got to tell her what's up, not you."

"Do you realize how hard it's going to be for me to face that girl with her knowing I took her man? That's not going to be easy for me to do. Especially with me already knowing how much she still likes you."

"She'll get over it. Fine as she is, she shouldn't have no problems finding another man."

"You know I came over here to kick your butt." I punched him on the arm. "But since you came clean to me, I'm gonna let you slide."

"Don't be hitting on me if you can't finish me off. Cause when I start hitting you," he smiled. "I ain't gonna show no mercy."

"Is that a threat or a promise?" I asked, punching him again.

"It's on now," he said gabbing me. He wrestled me down on my back and pent my arms to the bed.

"You ain't playing fair Boo! You didn't give me a chance to get ready."

"It's too late now." He pulled up my shirt. "You all mine."

"I just got off work Boo. You know I need to bathe first."

"You might be tastier with a little sweat on you. I'm gonna devour you as is."

That's exactly what he did. He took my bra off and began making love to my attentive nipples with his warm mouth before he took the trip down south and ate me alive. He brought me to a screaming orgasm that made me squirt in his mouth. After he'd set off my fireworks, it was time for me to set off his. I instructed him to lay on his back so I could give his dick mouth to mouth. I wasn't fond of sucking dick, but I knew how to please my man. I wrapped my hand around the base of his thick shaft and started tickling the head with my tongue before I took it into my mouth. I massaged his balls with my free hand as my head bobbed up and down on his pole at a steady pace. Once I got into a groove, I envisioned his dick being a sweet chocolate lollipop as it slid up and down my throat. Every so often I would pull it out, jack it and then take it back into my mouth.

"Shiiiiit!" He moaned loudly, thrusting deeper into my throat the harder I sucked it. When he let me know he was about to cum, I came up for air and jacked it until it sprayed my chest.

That had me so aroused that after I wiped up the mess with a damp towel, I straddled him reversed cowgirl style. I eased him into my wetness, grabbed his ankles and began to slowly rock back and forth. I started at a slow pace to tease him. I knew he loved watching my pussy gobble his dick and I enjoyed being on top because I controlled the action. I would speed up, slow down, speed up, slow down. "Uh-huh-uh-huh. Uh-huh! Uh-huh-uh-huuh! Oh ba-beee!" I moaned picking up speed, creaming his long shaft.

"Damn Special," he said, moments after I crawled up beside him." You trying to turn a brotha out."

"If you say so." I smiled, kissing his thick lips. "I call it making love."

No sooner than I made that comment, his telephone started ringing and without hesitating I answered it. Dee looked at me in disbelief, but I didn't trip it. I had begun thinking of his place as my own and felt that I could do almost whatever I wanted to do there.

"Put Deavin on the phone," a female voice said with an attitude.

My first instinct was to curse the caller out for being disrespectful. Instead, I held my tongue and let it go.

"Who's calling?" I asked politely.

"Who's calling?" She mumbled as if she couldn't believe I questioned her. "Tammy, his sister. Put my brother on the damn phone whoever you supposed to be."

"I'm your worst nightmare you disrespectful bitch!" I blew, losing my composure. "It's for you, Boo," I said, dropping the phone on his chest. Before I got up and headed for the bathroom.

****

Finally, I was on my way back to the studio to get the track laid for my song "Gotta Have You." Cool-D had referred me to this brotha named Lamont who had a studio off Campbellton Road. Word on the street was that he was the best beat maker in Southwest Atlanta, the area better known as the SWATS. I'd gotten little to no feedback on the first demo that I had sent out to numerous recording labels. However, I felt the Missy Elliot's, Jermaine Dupris' and the Dallas Austin's would be blowing up my phone after they got the chance to hear "Gotta Have You."

I made it to LMC Recording Studio around 11:30 a.m. Within an hour after I arrived, Lamont had the beat ready and I laid down my vocals. The whole time I was in the sound proof booth I thought about Dee as I sang my heart out.

"Damn Shante," Lamont said when I stepped out of the booth. "Cool-D told me you could sing, but I didn't know you could blow like that."

"Thanks for the compliment," I replied, blushing.

"When I first saw you I thought you was just another dime-piece trying to get in the industry with bad vocals and good looks. You proved me wrong sista. If you stay down with it, you could have a long music career ahead of you, trust me on that. I've heard some of the best. Where's your manager?"

"I'm afraid I don't have one. I never really took my singing seriously until here recently. You really think I need to get a manager?"

"If you are really serious about getting into the industry, you're gonna need one. I can help you if you need me to. I know a bunch of people in the industry."

"Well I do need to meet somebody. Your help would mean a lot to me."

"Enough said, just leave me a copy of your demo and I'll get back with you after I let some people who can pull some strings hear it."

"I don't have a problem with you keeping a copy. If you're a friend of Cool-D, you're a friend of mine."

"You won't regret it Shante. I see big things happening for you in the future."

I left the studio feeling good, even though Dee's sister was mad at us both for me calling her a bitch. Whatever she told him had pissed him off, but it didn't spoil our blockbuster night. We ended up watching "The Real Rucker Park Legends" DVD. Then I spanked him in a game of Madden Football on his XBOX. He'd gotten so mad at me that he didn't say a word to me for a whole hour. I did use Mark's help to win, but it didn't matter much to me because I still won.

Sabrina was another issue and I sort of felt sorry for her. But I had no intentions of letting her have Dee back. I just knew it was going to feel funny at work with her knowing I had taken her man. Dee called her after we'd finished watching the DVD and told her why he'd broke it off with her. I had placed my hands over my ears when he told her I was the reason.

MR. WILLIS

Eight months had quickly passed since my release from the Georgia Prison system after serving nearly 26 years. I had two things on my mind the day I was escorted through the prison gates to my freedom, getting back on my feet and finding my child. I had pretty good success at getting back on my feet, thanks to my young boss Deavin. But I had been running into dead ends when it came to finding my child.

Some months back, I had visited my old neighborhood for the fourth time since my release. On all of my previous visits I didn't seem to have any luck. Fortunately, I bumped into an old friend on my fourth visit. Better yet, she saw me first.

"Is that you Dennis?" A woman asked as I walked past her house.

She was standing on her porch eyeing me with her arms folded at her chest. My whole body became paralyzed at the mention of my name. For years I'd been called Mr.

Willis and hadn't been called by my first name. I stared up at the thick redbone, trying to place her before I answered.

"You talking to me?" I said nervously.

"Oh my God!" She stepped off the porch, coming up to me. "I know them hazel eyes from anywhere. God knows you're still handsome."

For a minute I was speechless. I didn't know what to say or how to respond to this beautiful, voluptuous woman. She stood about average height and was built like a stallion. She had full breasts, thick hips and a big butt.

"Where do you claim to know me from? I haven't lived around here in over a quarter century."

"I know." She rubbed the back of her soft hands across my smooth shaved face. "You just up and disappeared on Carla. We all thought you was dead as the years passed. What happened Dennis?"

I didn't recognize who she was until she mentioned my ex-girlfriend Carla's name.

"Debra Turner!" I couldn't believe it. "Ol' fine ass, Debra Turner."

"That's me." She blushed. "I'm Debra Jenkins these days."

"Married?"

"No honey, widowed."

"I'm sorry to hear that."

"There's no need to be. Henry drunk himself to death about five years ago. He lived for a bottle of Vodka or Christian Brothers after he'd lost his job at the old GMC plant in Doraville."

"You married ol' skinny Henry who use to have the big afro?"

"Yep, Skinny Henry," she replied, looking me up and down. "What brings you back around here?"

"Carla and our child."

She shot me a puzzled look. "You mean, you don't know?"

I shrugged my shoulders. "Know what?"

"Carla married some big shot businessman from up north. He moved her out of the neighborhood well over twenty years ago."

"What happened to the child she was pregnant with?"

"Shanetta-Sharonda, one of them crazy names. That had to be the cutest girl. I always thought she favored you."

"Do you have any idea where I could find them?"

"I believe they moved out of state somewhere. It's been years since I've seen Carla and that little girl. Hell, she should be married by now. The last I heard, she was pregnant. That was about ten years ago. Where you been hiding all these years?"

"It's a long story Debra. I wanna at least tell Carla and our daughter the story first."

"I'm sure my sister knows where they live. She don't do nothing but sit around and gossip with her old church friends anyway."

"If you can find out for me, it would mean a lot to me."

"Come on in so I can give you my number," she said before strutting back up the steps. I couldn't help but watch her plump backside sway from side to side as I followed her. She looked back, making sure her rear had my undivided attention and shot me a flirtatious smile. "My two grandsons live here with me. They're both in school right now."

"How old are they?" I asked, stepping into the house behind her.

"Seven. My daughter LaTanya, had twins. She's in the military and is currently overseas."

"You don't look old enough to be nobody's grandmother."

"Oh, stop it Dennis." She smiled. "You know me and Carla is the same age."

"You don't look a day over thirty five. You've taken very good care of yourself."

"I think I've gained a little too much weight over the past few years."

"Men love thick women." I took a seat on the sofa. "You're the perfect size."

"Would you like anything to eat?"

"I've never turned down a good hot meal."

"I'll take that as a yes. Where you living these days?"

"Over off Wylie Street."

Debra and I sat around and talked for a couple of hours. It felt good to be conversing with someone who actually knew the real me. That first visit inside her home eventually became routine for me over the next few months. Initially, my soul purpose for visiting Debra's house was because I was hoping that she would be able to milk her sister for information concerning Carla and my daughter's whereabouts. Debra's sister might've been a nosy church going gossiper, but she wasn't giving up any information about Carla or my daughter. I'm sure that I was the reason why.

I prayed every day, hoping she would have a change of heart and tell either Debra or myself something. However, during that time, Debra and I started courting. Week after week she would practically beg me to move in with her, but I wouldn't. I wasn't ready to commit myself to her like that. If I wasn't able to locate my daughter, I had planned to start a new family. At forty six, I knew that Debra's biological clock was on its last tick and I didn't want to be its tock. I left room in the relationship for me to exit, if and when I decided to.

Hours after I'd gotten in from work one early morning I was awakened by the ringing of my phone.

"Hello," I answered sluggishly.

"I left a message for you to call me when you got in," Debra said. "Did you get it?"

"Yes Debra, I got it. I didn't want to call you that early. I know how them boys be running you ragged and I didn't want to interrupt you from your sleep."

"They do it all the time," she said, referring to her grandkids. "I'm used to it by now. Anyway, I found out something from old Ms. Wilson last night that I'm sure you'd like to know."

"What is it?" I asked with my fingers crossed.

"She told me that Carla lives in Chicago and is still married to that big shot Ricky Smith. I couldn't remember that man's name to save my life until Ms. Wilson mentioned it last night."

"Did she give you a number or an address?"

"No, I'm still working on it."

"Did she say anything about my daughter?"

"Sorry baby, she didn't. I didn't ask her old evil ass either. I was lucky to get what little information I did."

"Thanks Deb. I appreciate you helping me."

"Always Dennis. I'm hoping to see you in about an hour. The boys will be on their way to school shortly."

"Do you want me to stop by the store for anything on my way over?"

"Let me see..., don't forget to bring the whip cream if you know what I mean," she said seductively.

"I know exactly what you mean. I might as well bring some strawberries too. Remember what we did with them the last time."

"I'll always remember that."

"I'll be there soon as I get ready."

DEAVIN

Some of the strangest things had been happening to me since I told Sabrina I'd left her for Hazel Eyes. At first I thought that Sabrina and Deshundria would try to jump on Hazel Eyes. But to my surprise, things between them didn't end up like I had expected. They continued to get along together. Hazel Eyes had even promoted Sabrina to a higher position.

"Why did you do that baby?" I remembered asking Hazel Eyes while we laid in bed one night.

"You gotta keep your enemies close to you," she replied, showing me an evil smile.

From that night forward I decided not to bring Sabrina's name up in our conversations again. By the following morning, I realized that it was going to be nearly impossible after I discovered someone had flattened all four tires on my Escalade while it was parked outside of Hazel Eye's apartment. Sabrina was the first person that popped in my head as the culprit. My tires weren't slashed, someone had just let the air out of them.

I quickly called for road side assistance and they sent a person out to fix my problem before Hazel Eyes or her roommate had the chance to look out the window to see what was going on. I didn't want her to know what had happened because I didn't want her worrying, especially since it happened in her parking lot.

Days later, while I drove home from work at about 5:00 a.m., I noticed a car behind me damn near riding my bumper. When I sped up, the car behind me sped up too.

"Shit!" I spat, trying to figure out who it was. So I switched lanes expecting the driver behind me to go on about his or her business. That didn't happen and I didn't notice the car was a black Suburban until it pulled up beside me. Even then I couldn't see who the driver was because of the dark tint on the windows. The Suburban continued to ride side by side with me for another mile or two, then it suddenly swerved, trying to force me to slam into the concrete median wall on I-20, near the Hill Street exit.

If it had not been for my quick thinking to immediately slam on the breaks, I would have probably killed myself slamming into the wall at over 65 miles per hour. I was so shaken up by the incident that I didn't even think of getting the Suburban's tag numbers. My heart didn't stop pounding until I made it safely inside my condo early that morning. I thought about calling the police to report what happened, but after giving it some thought, I decided not to. It was probably some young teenage kids playing around in their parent's vehicle.

As serious as that incident could have been, I didn't tell anybody about it until I started receiving threatening phone calls. The first couple of calls nobody said a word, all I heard was heavy breathing. But the last few calls the caller actually spoke.

"I'ma getcha. Watch your back," is what the caller said, muzzling his voice.

After the last call, I left my condo and drove straight to Mr. Willis' place. I had called him in my truck letting him know that I was on my way.

"Hi son," Mr. Willis spoke, greeting me with a firm handshake at his room door. "What brings you out this way with such urgency? And don't tell me its women problems again."

"I don't really know what the hell is going on." I took a seat on his small sofa with my hands covering my face. "All I know is that somebody is out to kill me."

"Damn son," he said, looking concerned. "This is some serious shit. Tell me about it."

Mr. Willis sat down on the edge of his bed and I told him about the flat tires, the Suburban incident and the threatening phone calls.

"Why haven't you reported any of this to the police yet?"

"I don't know." I shrugged my shoulders. "I was hoping all of this shit would just go away. You know what I'm saying?"

"No Deavin." He shook his head looking as serious as I've ever seen him look before. "I don't know what you're saying. This isn't to be taken lightly. Do you have any idea who might wanna hurt you?"

"No, not really. Outside of you, Chuck, Tony, Mark and Hazel Eyes, I don't really deal with nobody else. I don't even know that many people here in Georgia, especially somebody who would want to hurt me."

"What about the girl and her friend who works at the restaurant with Shante?"

"Sabrina and Deshundria. Nah, I don't think it's them. The morning I discovered the flat tires I thought that Sabrina had probably done it, but after the highway incident and the threatening phones calls, I immediately ruled her out."

"After spending over half my life in the big house. I had to learn how to read people in order to survive. And I've read you since the moment you stepped foot through that door. What is it that you're not telling me? Talk to me Deavin. You know that whatever you tell me won't go no further than these four walls. "

"What makes you think I didn't tell you everything?"

"I heard hesitation in your voice and saw it in your eyes."

I smiled. "You're good Mr. Willis. We need to start our own psychic business."

"You best wipe that grin off your face and tell me what's going on before you end up in a pine box."

"I don't think it's that serious. That problem is way up in North Carolina."

"It could've followed you here. You made it down here. What makes you think your problem didn't come behind you? "

"You got a point there. I guess I might as well tell you then," I sighed. "A while back I called one of my ex-girlfriends back home and found out she was pregnant with my child."

"And..., keep going," he instructed.

I went on and explained to him about the conversation Tracy and I had. I even told him about the words I had with her boyfriend, Steven.

"Let's back this up. You telling me you told that woman to get an abortion while her boyfriend was right there with her?"

"Yeah, but...,"

"Are you out of your mind son? You are playing with death by hurting that woman like that in the presence of her man."

"I didn't mean to tell her to get an abortion. I just didn't know what else to say and before I realized it, that abortion shit came out of my mouth."

"Have you called back and apologized to her for what you said?"

"Nope. I have been thinking about it though. "

"What's stopping you?"

"My pride, I guess."

"You need to drop that arrogant ass attitude and put your pride to the side. Call that woman up and straighten your face. Maybe then you'll be able to find out if it's her man who's out to get you."

"I'll do that."

"Have you told Shante about Tracy's pregnancy?"

"Oh, hell no. She'll probably drop me like a bad habit."

"She'll probably end up dropping you anyway if you don't tell her before she finds out on her own. Young men of this generation are full of game," he said with a smirk, shaking his head.

"I'm gonna eventually tell her. I just don't know when."

"You also need to go by the police station and report everything that's been happening to you too. I meant it Deavin. This is serious."

"I know. I'm gonna do everything you said when I leave here, except for telling Hazel Eyes I got a baby on the way."

"Good. That's a start." He stood up stretching. "Now let me get ready. I'm taking Deb and her grand boys out to Grant Park for a barbecue this afternoon."

"Y'all have a good time." I got up and headed for the door. I stopped and looked back at him. "Thanks for being there for me man."

"Always, son. That's the least I can do," he said before giving me a strong handshake.

****

I finally got around to calling the bald, white guy who had given me his business card at the Run-N-Shoot. He arranged for me to work out in front of a group of coaches at Life College. When I got there and entered the locker room there were seven other guys already in there dressing out.

"Y'all fellas are here for the tryouts too?" I asked, sitting in front of a locker unzipping my gym bag.

"Yeah," a tall light skinned brotha about my height answered with a smile, showing off his gold teeth. "I've been waiting for this moment ever since I went undrafted out of college a few years ago."

"Tell me about it," another brotha said, closing his locker. "This is a chance of a lifetime for me. I gotta make the best of this opportunity. You know we'll probably never get another chance like this again fellas, good luck y'all." He walked out of the locker room heading towards the ball court.

"I don't know about you guys, but I'm trying to use this as a stepping stone to get to the NBA," one of the guys said, standing up. "They always need big bodies in the league."

"You right, big man," the brotha with the gold teeth added. "The NBA do need big bodies, but they need guys with big bodies who know the game and can play."

"Shit, I can play!" The big guy spat in his defense. "Plus I'm almost seven-feet tall."

"Yeah," the brotha with the gold teeth shot back. "A seven-footer with two left feet. The NBA already got enough Kwame Browns and Hashem Thabeets taking up bench space. I saw you play at Center Court a couple times too, I know you ain't working with nothing."

"I'ma let my game speak for itself," the big guy said, storming out of the locker room.

"What game?" Another one of the guys hollered, causing us all to burst out laughing.

"Let's get a move on guys," a tall black guy said, coming into the locker room with a clipboard in his hands and a whistle around his neck. "We don't have all morning. I need you guys out there on the floor in five minutes."

I quickly put on my ball gear and jogged out onto the court. The coaches worked us out in pairs for about twenty minutes before they put together two, four on four teams and let us scrimmage each other. They wanted to see how good our game was against stiff competition. I was nervous at first because I was the only guy out of the eight that didn't have any college experience. I started off kind of slow, but once I shook the butterflies and my body heated up, it was on. I wasn't able to dominate them guys the way I knew I could have, however, I felt that I was arguably the best player there.

At the end of the intense workout, Coach Terry called me and this brotha Sammy, who had the gold teeth, to the side.

"After you two get dressed, meet me back here. I believe you two have what it takes to make it to the next level," he said, scribbling something down on his clipboard.

"Okay Coach," I replied, feeling like I had just hit the lottery. Twenty-five minutes later, I was in Coach Terry's office, and he was winding down our short meeting.

"You've earned yourself a guaranteed roster spot for the Fayetteville Flyers of the National Basketball Association Development League. All you need to do is show up for the training camp next month, ready to play." He handed me a large manila envelope. "Everything you'll need to know about contracts, the league, etc., is in this envelope. Read over all the contents well and give me a call in about two weeks."

"I will definitely be calling you coach," I said, shaking his hand before I exited his office.

I drove home from Life College listening to Sarah Vaugh, on a natural high, feeling like I was on top of the world. At the moment, I really was on top of the world, I was running my own successful business, had a beautiful girlfriend that I was happy and in love with and I was on my way to playing professional basketball. What more could a brotha ask for?

Soon as I entered my condo the phone began ringing.

"Hello," I answered.

". . . I followed you this morning," the muzzling voice said and hung up.

It had been almost a week since the last threatening phone call and I was beginning to think things were back to normal. I didn't report the incidents to the police like Mr. Willis had told me to do, nor had I called Tracy back.

Let me call this woman and see if it's her crazy ass boyfriend threatening me.

"How you doing Tracy?" I spoke, after she answered.

"I'm good and you?"

"Not too good right now and I'm sure you know why."

"I wish. I'm trying to figure out who put a gun to your head and forced you to call me. I'm sure you didn't do it on your own."

"Why would you think somebody had to force me to call? You must've sent a hitman after me."

"What if I did? You deserve all the bad luck a person can have. I wish your black ass was dead."

"Damn Tracy that was a low blow."

"That can't be no lower than you telling me to kill our baby. I cried in Steven's arms for hours after you told me to get an abortion. It's still hard for me to believe you even told me to do some shit like that Deavin. You've changed into another person since you left."

"About the abortion," I said taking a deep breath. "I'm really sorry for letting those words come out of my mouth. I wasn't thinking before I spoke Tracy. God knows I wasn't."

"You meant it Deavin. I heard it in your voice."

"I only said it because I was mad at you at the time."

"Mad with me! You need to switch that around. You're the one who lied to me Deavin. I've never did anything to hurt you. All I ever gave you was my love and you abandoned it. So don't try to use that bullshit reverse psychology shit on me. If you was mad about anything it was because me and Steven was laying up when you called."

"You're wrong."

"You're something else Deavin," she chuckled. "You think I'm really stupid, don't you? You're jealous of Steven. You're jealous because I have a man that loves me and treats me with respect. That's it, isn't it?"

"I ain't jealous of nobody."

"You got some helluva nerve. You don't want me no more, but you don't wanna see me happy in a relationship with another man. Am I right Deavin?"

"Only if you say so," I answered, thinking about the conversation that Mr. Willis and I had. "I would like to apologize about the abortion thing and for making false promises to you before I left North Carolina."

"Your apology is accepted. There's one thing I'd like to know Deavin?"

"What's up?"

"Did you ever love me?"

"Yeah Tracy. You are the first woman I ever loved."

"If I'm the first, there has to be a second. Do I know her?"

"No. I met her after I moved down here."

"I see." She sucked her teeth. "You know we need to talk about our child. I'm going on my twenty-second week."

"I know, I'm counting. Thanks for not getting an abortion. That was the dumbest statement I've ever made in my life."

"You're forgiven. At least half forgiven anyway."

"Thanks. That really makes me feel a lot better. Where's Steven? Tell him I'm really sorry about what happened the last time I called."

"He's down there in College Park, Georgia somewhere. You just might bump into him. I'll tell him what you said when he calls tonight."

"You do that. I'll talk to you later and if you need anything, call me."

I hung up with my mind focusing on Steven. I think he's my man.

SHANTE

I left work early so I could make it to Diamond Facez in Buckhead on time for my appointment. My cosmetologist, Sha Sha, had the best skin care bar in Atlanta and she didn't have you sitting in her shop half the day. It had been a few months since I had gotten my last facial, The Glow Experience and I couldn't wait to make it to the shop.

The day before, while Monica was telling me about the problems she and Trey were having, I got a call from Lamont. He told me that somebody big time wanted to meet me and for me to be at his studio by 6:30 the following evening.

"I believe you're on your way girl," he'd said to me before hanging up.

I was so excited when I got off the phone that I talked Monica's ears off about my future music career. I barely slept a wink that night. I tossed and turned until it was time for me to get up for work. When I got out the bed, my first instinct was to call Dee because I knew he would just be getting back in from work.

Soon as I pulled out of Dolly's parking lot in route to the beauty salon, I called Dee.

"Hey Boo," I said when he answered. "Did I wake you up?"

"Yep, but you can wake me up anytime. What's going on? You don't normally call this time of day."

"I'm supposed to be meeting someone at Lamont's studio this evening. So I took off work early to get my facial and my nails done."

"That's what's up. Do you have any idea who you'll be meeting with?"

"Not even the slightest clue. Lamont only told me that it's going to be someone big time. I'm hoping that person is Tony Vick or Vince. You see how quick Vince helped Tamar blow up."

"You're right about that. She's doing her thing now. I'm hoping my Special will be next."

I smiled. "I hope so too. This time next year I might have a video on BET, while you're playing in the NBA."

"You got half of it right."

"Huh," I murmured, not understanding what he was getting at.

"You might have your music video on BET next year, but I doubt if I'll be in the NBA."

"That's all you've talked about since you earned that roster spot last weekend. What's the matter Boo?"

"Nothing really. I was just watching sports center when I got in this morning and they were showing all the young stars like Russell Westbrook and Stephen Curry--"

"And…, what's that supposed to mean?"

"I'm pushing thirty-one Special. Them young boys will run circles around me. Of course, I'm gonna give it my all, but I'm not gonna keep hyping myself up, thinking I'm gonna be in the NBA anytime soon."

"Don't let that get you down Boo. Just stay focused and everything will work out."

"You can count on me to give it my all. Oh yeah, I almost forgot to tell you. Mark gave us four tickets to this Old School Costume Party that's happening next Friday. You wanna go?"

"You know I'm not into the club scene, but there's no way in hell I'd miss that party. That's all the girls at work have been talking about all week."

"I don't have no use for the other two tickets. Maybe you can sell them to the girls at your job. They cost like $30 a piece."

"I won't sell them. Would you mind if I gave them to Monica and Trey? They would probably love to go."

"You know I don't care Special. Now let me get my butt out of this bed so I can go trade my truck in."

"I thought you was gonna do that next week?"

"I thought I was too, but since I have nothing else to do today I might as well handle my business and get it over with."

"I'm pulling into Diamond Facez right now, call me back later. You know Sha Sha don't play that showing up late for appointments mess. I gotta get in there."

"Do your thing baby and good luck at your meeting too."

"Love you Boo."

"Love you more."

I turned off the phone and smiled. My parents would never believe that their spoiled daughter had finally found love in her life. Sometimes I couldn't believe it myself.

"Hey girls," I spoke when I entered.

"I'll be with you in about five minutes. I'm running a little behind today." Sha Sha told me as I sat down.

I nodded my head, letting her know I was okay with it and picked up the latest issue of SISTER 2 SISTER, to see what Jaime Foster Brown was talking about.

For the next hour and a half I sat up in Diamond Facez listening to all kinds of gossip. For the life of me, I never understood how women can air their dirty laundry out in public to people they don't even know. While Sha Sha was doing my facial, this one sista started telling us all a story that I thought was a little too personal to be airing out to total strangers.

"I work third shift, you know," the sista appeared to be in her early thirties said, telling her story. "See Monday night I only worked an hour before I left early, telling my supervisor I was sick. As I drove home all I could think about was how I was going to surprise my man with some good midnight loving. Soon as I stepped foot through the front door I heard loud panting and moaning. By the time I got down the hall I noticed it was my daughter's room. I knew my daughter KeKe was hot in the ass because I had caught her and some young boy getting it on a couple months back. Before I opened her room door I peeped in my room to see if my man Ronnie was in there sleep. When I didn't see him, I had assumed he was out with the fellas. Y'all know how men do," she said, causing the crowd to nod their heads and mumble in unison. She continued, "When I tried opening her door, I realized that she'd locked it. I didn't wanna knock on it cause I knew that whoever it was in the room with her would have time to snatch up his clothes and jump out the window. I also knew that KeKe would make up some kinda lie, claiming that she was making the noise because she was sick or something. Not tonight, I mumbled as I rammed my shoulder into the door, causing it to swing wide open." She sighed. "What I saw made my body go numb. My sixteen year old baby was butt naked, fucking my man. No..., let me rephrase that, my ex-man. His eyes almost popped out of his head when he looked up and saw me standing in the middle of the floor. KeKe jumped up and ran past me, locking herself in the bathroom. He stood up eyeing me like he was a sick puppy with his dick hanging damn near to his knees. And guess what he had the nerves to say before I put the broomstick on his sorry ass?"

"What?" Everybody sked at once.

"It ain't what you think baby, I can explain. I grabbed the broom from behind the door and beat his skinny ass out my front door butt ass naked. And then threatened to put the police on him if he ever came near me or my child again."

"That's one trifling ass nigga," Sha Sha added. "I hoped you burned all his shit."

"I tried to. See, after I had all his shit stuffed in plastic bags, my daughter went behind my back and took it all back to him the next day. I haven't seen her since, but she did call yesterday telling me she was okay and that she was sorry for hurting me."

"I know she's not living with his trifling ass?" One of the sistas asked.

"Yep," she answered with a look of defeat in her eyes. "My baby girl think she's a woman now."

"Damn, that's fucked up, Sha Sha," I told her getting out of the chair. "I've heard enough today to write a book."

"I've heard much worse than that girl. Believe it."

I paid and tipped Sha Sha, then hurried next door to get my nails done. The buzz in the nail shop was about a female author name Honey B. Morrison.

"I am telling y'all, Honey B is the best out there right now," this tall dark skinned sista said, pulling out her Coach bag.

"What kind of books does she write?"

Immediately after I asked that question, all the women in the shop stared at me like I had a red light blinking on my forehead.

"Was that a trick question or are you serious?" The tall dark skinned sista asked me.

"As a heart attack."

"Take this one," she handed me the book she had taken out of her bag moments earlier. "I've already read it four times."

"Are you sure?" I asked placing the book in my lap.

"Yes girl. I've had it long enough. The name of that one is SEXCAPADE and girl, it's going down."

"Thanks. Do I owe you anything, Miss--?"

"It's Nita. And no girl, you don't owe me anything."

"I'm Shante. Thanks for the donation."

Since I wanted to read the Honey B. Morrison novel later, I picked up an After 5 Atlanta magazine off the table and flipped through it while I waited.

When I returned home I spent over an hour picking through and trying on outfits before settling for a simple pair of Deron jeans and a blouse. There was no sense in me trying to dress up all elegant, the meeting was for my vocals, not my body. Even though I didn't dress up, I still looked stunning in what I had on. Not meaning to brag, but I knew I would look good if I was forced to wear one of Celie's outfits from The Color Purple.

I was a few minutes late arriving at the studio, but what the hell, I made it. I parked beside Lamont's burnt orange Lincoln Navigator, which was sitting on 28" rims. Parked on the other side of the Navigator was a black Denali.

"What's up Shante?" Lamont's assistant, Buggy Hugh, said after letting me inside.

"I'm good. What about yourself?" I replied feeling a bit nervous.

"I'm hanging in there. Lamont and the black Clive Davis himself are in the office waiting on you. Let me tell them you're here. It'll only take a minute."

I wanted so badly to ask Buggy who the black Clive Davis was before he walked away, but I didn't. It wasn't a hot thirty seconds later that I was entering the office, staring at Tee Wiley, the super producer.

"Glad you made it Shante," Lamont said, greeting me with a hug. "Have a seat so we can get this show on the road."

I sat down with my eyes still fixed on Tee Wiley, not believing it. Initially, I had expected to see London or 808 Mafia. Never did I expect to see Tee Wiley. Not only was he a great producer, I'd heard people refer to him as the Quincy Jones of his era and I felt damn good knowing he was there to see me.

"I'm sure you already know who this is," Lamont said, pointing at him. "Shante, this is Tee. Tee, this is the woman with the beautiful vocals behind 'Gotta Have You,' Shante Blackmon."

"Hi Shante," Tee said, extending his arm over the table to shake my hand. "It's a pleasure to meet you."

"It's a pleasure to meet you too Mr. Wiley," I said cheesing.

"I had Lamont arrange this meeting so we could discuss business, the industry and to get a chance to know you, cause I'm hoping we'll be working together soon. I also want to hear you sing.

I felt like a real R & B Diva for the next couple of hours while I was in Tee Wiley's presence. He treated me with a lot of respect, but at the same time he didn't hesitate to let me know when I was singing off key or when I needed to raise or lower the pitch of my voice. At first, I thought he would try to act all stuck up and arrogant because of his status in the music industry, but he didn't. He was down to earth.

"So far so good," I said to Lamont when he walked me to my car, minutes after Tee Wiley had left.

"What are we getting into tonight?" He asked, palming my butt as I opened the car door.

Lamont was a good looking brotha, but I wasn't attracted to him. Inside the studio he was very professional and strictly business. Outside the studio I quickly realized he was the total opposite.

"Don't get it twisted Lamont," I turned around facing him. We are not getting into anything tonight. I got a man and he won't appreciate you grabbing my ass..., I mean his ass, like that."

"My bad." He held up his hands and took a step back.

"There's a first time for everything. Don't let it happen again. And for the record, I don't mix business with pleasure. You got that?"

"I feel you, but I had to at least try."

"Now you know." I sat in my car. "Call me when Tee is ready for me to sign."

"Okay."

I closed my door and pulled off, thinking about Dee. I had been missing him so bad that I drove straight to his condo.

Neither Dee nor Mark was home when I got there. However, that didn't stop me from making myself at home. I went into Dee's room and stripped down to my cream colored, signature, Christian Dior bikini, slipped on my silk teddy, took the Honey B. Morrison book out of my bag, sat up in the bed and started reading. Nita was right about the book. I couldn't put it down after reading the first two chapters, I was hooked.

Three to four chapters later, my nipples were hard and my panties were damp. Just when I was about to use a finger to do a little exploring, I heard Dee coming through the door, singing Major Harris, classic hit "Love Won't Let Me Wait." Dee couldn't sing a lick, but at the time, I was so sexually aroused that the song sounded good coming out of his mouth. I hurried up and slid the book under his mattress because I didn't want him to know that I'd been reading an erotic novel.

"How was the meeting baby?" He asked, giving me a hug and kiss.

"Everything went fine Boo. I met Tee Wiley."

"Tee Wiley!" He blurted excitedly.

"Yes Boo, Tee Wiley," I said, pulling him on top of me. "We'll talk about how the meeting went later. Right now I want you to make love to me."

"I love a woman who's not afraid to ask for what she wants."

"You know me Boo," I told him between kisses. "I'm very straight forward."

Honey B. Morrison's SEXCAPADE had set my whole body on fire and I couldn't wait to feel my Boo deep inside me.

For close to an hour he and I went at it almost nonstop. The only time there was a break in the action was when we changed positions, which we did four to five times. After our hot steamy sexscapde was over, I figured it was the perfect time for us to talk about how our day went.

"What kind of car did you get?" I asked, sitting up in bed.

He followed my lead and sat up too. "I traded my Escalade in and bought a pearl black LS 430 Lexus."

"I'm glad you got something that I'll like driving," I responded, unable to conceal my smile.

"I also leased a Yukon Denali."

"No, Boo. Tell me you didn't."

"Yes, baby. You know I got a business to run."

"In a new Denali? That's just wasting money Boo."

"When did you become so interested in how I spend money?"

"The day I fell in love with your black ass. I don't wanna see you struggling trying to live from check to check, I want you to succeed. Now, if I was a gold digger, I would have already dug a mine in your pockets. Bank accounts too. Believe that," I said, rolling my neck and snapping my fingers.

"I have yet to meet a woman who could accomplish that with me. I've never played the role of a fool. As for the Yukon, I leased it through my business so I basically get to drive it free for two years."

"Good thinking," I kissed the corner of his lips. "Do you wanna go another round? I'm still wet."

"You know I do."

"You gotta catch me first."

I jumped out of bed and ran into the bathroom. Seconds later, he was behind me.

"Goddamn Special," he said, staring down at my naked butt, stroking his erection. "When you gonna let me slide up that back door?"

"Never," I spat seriously. "Your dick is too big to be going up my ass."

"Come on baby, I'm gonna take it easy on you."

"No. No. No. A tongue is all you get in that hole." I turned the shower on. "No dicks."

He picked me up. I wrapped my arms around his neck and wrapped my long legs around his waist before he pinned me against the wall. He eased his shaft inside me and gave it to me like he never had before. At times I didn't know if I was supposed to scream out in ecstasy, or cry. He put the dick on me so good that I rewarded him with some mouth to mouth action when we got in the shower. I even let him stay in long enough to spray the back of my throat. He was surprised by that. I was too.

"Oh yeah, baby," he said while we dried each other off. "What happened with Tee Wiley?"

"He wanna sign me to his label."

TRACY

I woke up feeling energetic, which was a good thing for me because I was in my fifth month of pregnancy. It was also the first morning in weeks that I had woke up without feeling any morning sickness. Even though I'd been sleeping in my bed by myself on and off for the past month, I still didn't feel alone because my unborn baby was giving me all the comfort I needed. I'd had an ultrasound earlier in the week and it revealed that I was carrying a girl. I had been hoping it was a boy, but I was satisfied with what the good Lord was blessing me with.

Every Wednesday I would attend Lamaze classes at Cape Fear Valley, off Owen Drive. I use to enjoy the classes when Steven attended them with me. He'd missed two straight classes because he was out of town and I couldn't wait until he got back. Ever since that day Steven and Deavin got into it over the phone, he'd been pissed off. It really wasn't the little argument they'd had, Steven was mad at Deavin because of the way he handled our relationship. But when Deavin told me to get an abortion, that did it and Steven lost it.

"You shouldn't have never talked to his selfish ass!" He had shouted. "I shouldn't have gave you the phone back. I was supposed to curse his bitch ass out and hang up on him."

"It's gonna be alright," I told him, rubbing his back. "I know how to deal with Deavin. He thinks he's God's gift to the world. He'll have to face reality one of these days."

"Stop fooling yourself Tracy. You're not all right. You haven't been all right since you realized he wasn't coming back for you. I'm not going to continue to lay up in here watching you suffer like this. I got too much love for you." He sighed." I'll do his ass if he keeps hurting you."

"Don't do nothing to him Steven. It's not even worth it."

"Yes it is. Remember how me and my boys fucked up that dude Jason when we were in college?" He asked with malice in his eyes. "Deavin's ass just might be next."

"Don't go there with it. It's not that serious," I said praying he wouldn't.

Back when we were in college, this guy Jason, who I had a short fling with, started stalking me after I broke it off with him. He wouldn't only not take no for an answer, he'd broken into my dormitory room while my roommate Iris was out and tried to force himself on me. I was sleeping when all of a sudden I was awakened feeling somebody's hand rubbing between my thighs. I'm gonna whip that dyke bitch ass, I thought, expecting to see Iris when I opened my eyes.

It wasn't Iris, it was Jason sitting on my bed. My first instinct was to scream, hoping the dorm monitor or somebody would hear me. However, I figured that could turn fatal on my part by me not knowing what kind of weapon he had or how he would react. I closed my eyes and said a little prayer and tried to remain calm until I felt that I was in a good position to make my getaway. I opened my legs wider, allowing his roaming hand easy access to what he wanted. I even began rolling my hips with the movement of the fingers he had inside me. I opened my eyes and watched him for a good minute before he and I caught eye contact. By then, he was too far gone and his comfort zone had set in.

"You should've called me and let me know you was coming over," I said calmly, but I was nervous and scared to death.

"But-huh-you," he stuttered. "You stopped taking my calls. You-you haven't said two words to me since the day you kicked me out of here last month."

That statement had really frightened me more because a frown appeared on his face and I couldn't see what he held in his free hand.

"Don't worry about that now. All that matters is you're here now."

"You mean-you serious?" He asked, looking unsure if he wanted to believe me.

"Yes Jason, I'm serious. Hand me my pocketbook off the nightstand so I can get a condom out for you,"

Without hesitation he got the pocketbook and gave it to me.

"Why don't you take off your clothes? You see I'm almost naked."

Like a dummy, he looked down to unbutton his jeans. In that split second I took my pepper spray out of my pocketbook and hid it under my pillow. When his eyes darted back on me, I was holding two condoms in my hand. He took the condoms and put the pocketbook back on the nightstand. With my night light on, I was easily able to see that Jason didn't have a weapon on him after he'd took off his jeans. I pulled up my night gown, exposing my nakedness, hoping he would feel more comfortable.

"No Tracy," he spat, giving me the evil eye. "I don't wanna do it like that. I want you to ride me."

"That's okay with me."

He got on the bed and I straddled him. His dick hadn't entered me and I had no intentions of letting it get that far. I leaned forward, allowing him to take my big juicy breast into his mouth. While he feasting on my nipples, I reached under the pillow and got my pepper spray. When I looked down at his eyes they were still open. So I started rubbing his dick between my warm thighs until his eyes finally shut. BINGO! I raised the can of pepper spray and sprayed the shit out of him. I made sure it went in his eyes, mouth and up his nose. He started coughing gagging and kicking his legs, trying to get me and my can of mace off his ass.

By the time he was able to push me up off of him, he tried to get up and run, but he tripped and fell down almost immediately. I jumped back on top of him, clawed his face with one hand and continued to mace him with the other.

"Plee--eeze!" He cried out between his coughing and gagging. "Let me make it outta here alive, you...you tricked me!"

I finally stopped my assault after the pepper spray started burning my eyes.

"Get your sick ass out of my room before I call campus security!" I spat stepping back, allowing him to scramble for his pants.

"I can't see! My eyes are burning! I need water!"

"Get it somewhere else fucker!" I barked, using my feet to literally kick him out the door half naked.

I didn't report the incident because he didn't hurt me and the fact that I didn't want to be known as the girl on campus who had almost gotten raped by her ex-lover. I did call Steven early the next morning and told him about it.

"Are you sure you're okay girl?"

"Uhm-hmm," I mumbled. "I'm kind of scared that he might try to harm me later."

"Don't worry about his bitch ass. Me and my boys will take care of him."

That's exactly what Steven and his homeboys did. They caught up with Jason later on that day and beat him damn near into a coma. I never saw Jason again after that night. The word on campus was that he transferred to Johnson C. Smith University in Charlotte.

With no morning sickness symptoms slowing me down, me and my fat belly was up and out of the house in no time. I was on my way to the Westwood shopping center, to meet Tammy. As I drove my late model Accord down Reaford Road, I couldn't help thinking about the possible threat Steven had made about hurting Deavin because I knew he was more than capable of carrying it out.

Steven had moved in with me the same week I found out I was pregnant and had only missed two or three nights out of the comfort of my bed. That is until he left for Georgia some weeks back. I had an uneasy feeling in the pit of my stomach about Steven seriously hurting Deavin. But each time I questioned him about it, he'd tell me that he was spending a lot of time in Georgia on business. I constantly prayed, hoping his business had nothing to do with harming Deavin.

Even after all the deceiving and heartaches Deavin had caused me, I still loved him and wanted him to be my Boo again. Just the night before he had called about five minutes after I had hung up with Steven. I was angry with Steven because he'd told me he would be in Georgia a few days longer than he'd promised me. However, when Deavin called my anger for Steven immediately stopped.

Since the day Deavin had told me to abort our child, he'd been sort of calling on a regular, but there was something suspicious about his conversation that I just couldn't put my finger on. For one thing, he was just too apologetic about small things and he wanted to know where Steven was. Regardless of all the suspicions I had about him, I was just glad to have the opportunity to try to rebuild our old relationship. When it dawned on me that he was jealous of my relationship with Steven, I would find ways to ease Steven's name into our conversation to give him the impression that another man had come along and swept me off my feet. I waited until he was about to hang up before I told him the results of my ultrasound.

"A girl. You're having a girl?"

"No!" I spat. "We are having a girl. You and I. Me and you. Us. Do you understand? I didn't get pregnant by myself Deavin. You played a role in it too and our daughter was conceived out of pure love. Wouldn't you agree?"

"Without a doubt Tracy, I agree with you a hundred percent, but you didn't have to come off on me like you did. I know we made our daughter together and I'm gonna handle my role as a father."

"That's good to know. I also hope you know that it's gonna take more than you sending me money to raise our daughter properly. You're gonna have to play more of a hands on role as well."

"Enough already Tracy. I understand and I'm gonna be there for our daughter the best way I can."

"Good. Just don't renege on your words. Now I need you to make me a promise."

"What kind of promise?"

"To be at the hospital when I give birth."

"All I can say is that I'll try. Atlanta is a good six hour drive from Fayetteville and it's gonna be nearly impossible for me to get way up there in time."

"I'm sure you have enough money to afford a plane ticket."

"I'm going to do my best to get there as quick as possible, when that time comes."

"Ok...," I said, scheming up something to say to make him jealous. "Let me get off this phone so I can hurry up and get ready to meet Steven at Applebee's. Bye." I hung up, not giving him a chance to respond. He wasn't the only one who could play games, I could play them too.

I spotted Tammy's white Nissan parked near the front of the shopping center when I got there. She and I had planned to meet up to do a little shopping, mainly for my baby. Even though Deavin and I were no longer together, his sister and I stayed close friends. You couldn't have pried our friendship apart with Denzel and Taye Diggs put together.

SABRINA

Deshundria thought I was tripping, but I wasn't, I was only trying to straighten my face. There was no way that I was going to allow Deavin or Shante to get away with making me look like a fool. It didn't seem like it, but three months had passed since Deavin had broken it off with me and I felt like he and Shante had sort of put me on the back burner. That was all fine and well for me because I was out for blood for both of them.

I had already flattened Deavin's tires, which was easy to do. Little did he know, but that was only the beginning. As for his saditty ass bitch, she was getting on my nerves. Every day at work she would brag and boast about something she and Deavin had done together, or about something they had accomplished. One week she bragged about how much fun they had at the bowling alley. That following week, all she talked about was how Deavin had made some professional basketball team and how he should be playing in the NBA by the next NBA season. Then the week after that she boasted about how she had met and sung for Tee Wiley. I knew she had to be lying about that, I couldn't see Tee Wiley coming all the way to Atlanta from New York just to hear her tired ass sing. She also had the nerves to top that lie by telling everybody Tee Wiley was in the process of signing her to TW Records.

At times I wanted to just grab her around the neck and choke her prissy wannabe diva ass out. She'd driven a brand sparkling new, black $60,000 Lexus to work days ago. Seeing her in that car had really made me hate her even more. What surprised me the most was that I didn't hear her say anything about the car. I assumed that Deavin's good pussy eating ass had bought it for her. It crossed my mind to take my keys and rake it through the pretty pearl black paint, just to see her expression after she discovered it. The only thing that stopped me from doing it was the fact that I would have been the prime suspect.

Shante had even thought she was being slick by promoting me to the assistant supervisor position. Deep down inside I knew she wanted to fire me after finding out I was Deavin's first Georgia Peach, but she didn't have a legitimate reason to. I also felt she had given me the promotion out of fear of me whipping up on her ass for stealing my man. I had never got into a physical confrontation with anyone at work, but thanks to Deshundria's big mouth, the majority of the employees at Dolly's knew all about the fight I'd had with my ex-roommate for sleeping with my man.

Back to Shante, she had the nerves to come at me with that sista-sista talk bullshit.

"Hi Sabrina," Shante spoke, stepping out of her office when I passed it. "What have you been up to girl?"

Plotting to fuck up you and your boyfriend. "Besides working hard, I'm trying to concentrate on school."

"Yeah," she said, showing her phony ass smile. "You're a senior this year, I almost forgot.

You haven't forgot a damn thing about me bitch. You probably know when I wipe my ass, you be sweating me so hard on the sly. What's the point of you trying to socialize with me anyway bitch? I know your wannabe diva ass don't like me. "Yep," I replied as if I wasn't interested in the conversation. "I'll be graduating next spring."

"What are you getting into tomorrow night?"

"Nothing, why?"

"I thought maybe you and Deshundria would be interested in going to the Old School Costume Party. You know it's going to be turnt. I have a couple extra tickets. You're welcome to have them if you'd like."

"I'll pass on the tickets. Thanks for the offer though."

"Ok, I was just checking," she said before stepping back into the office.

Bad as I wanted to accept the tickets from her, I just couldn't do it. I felt like she was trying to handle me like I was some kind of charity case. She might've stolen my man, but I wasn't about to let her think she could buy my friendship, which wasn't for sale, it had to be earned.

Little did she know I already had two tickets for the party and Deshundria wasn't the person going with me, I had a date, a date she knew very well. "We'll see you at the party bitch," I mumbled under my breath after she'd closed her office door.

"It was about a month ago when I ran into one of Shante's ex-boyfriends. Come to think of it, it might've been a little longer than that. Anyway, around closing time that night, this thuggish, rough neck looking brotha had come into the restaurant. He stood about five-foot-ten with a stocky build, bald head and wore baggy blue jeans with a Straight Outta Kirkwood T-shirt. With all the bling he had around his neck and wrist, it immediately gave me the impression that he was either a professional athlete or dealt drugs. After observing the thuggish, but handsome looking brotha for a minute, I stepped to him to see if I could help assist him with anything.

"Excuse me sir. Can I help you?"

He examined me from head to toe before he answered. "I'm looking for an old friend of mine. A few of my homies told me she worked here."

"Who might that friend be?"

"Precious. Y'all might call her Shante though." He smiled, showing his pearly whites.

"Shante, huh. I might know her, but I don't give out information to strangers."

"I'm Jay." He extended his hand to me. "Me and Precious..., I mean Shante, we go way back. Is she here?"

GO WAY BACK.

"No, she's not here," I said, extending my hand to his. "I'm Sabrina, the shift supervisor." I can be one helluv'a consultation prize.

"Nice to meet you Sabrina. I don't mean to be annoying or anything, but is there any kind of way you can get in contact with her for me?"

"Sure," I shot him a flirtatious smile. "What would I get out of the deal?"

"Anything you want," he replied, eyeing me from head to toe again.

"Mmmm," I licked my lips. "Anything?" I touched his chest. "It'll be another twenty to thirty minutes before I close up. You can leave and come back later or you and I can sit at one of the tables and get acquainted while my staff clean up."

"I ain't in no rush to go nowhere."

Four hours later I was laying up in Jay's bed, getting my back beat out. I didn't normally give up the booty on the first night. Thanks to Deavin and Shante, Jay was the first one to hit that quick. I didn't even feel bad about sleeping with him so soon. I looked at it as revenge sex. As you already know, Jay held up to his end of the deal, but I didn't hold up to mine. By the time he'd finished sucking and beating my nookie he didn't mention another word about me contacting Shante for him the rest of that night.

Before he and I got in bed together he told me a lot about himself and his past relationship with Shante. That information alone made me want to get closer to him. Most of the employees at Dolly's knew about Julian, Deavin and the lawyer guy who drove the Porsche that Shante had dated. Nobody had ever heard of Jay. *The Mystery Man*, is what I thought of him the night I followed him to his loft at

Atlantic Station. I wanted to find out all the dirt I could on Shante, if any. Boy, was I in for a surprise. Better yet, I was shocked by what he'd told me. Shante Blackmon had enough skeletons in her closet to make her own horror movie.

"I bagged Precious back when she was in high school," Jay said, referring to Shante. "Her parents were real strict on her. They barely allowed her to talk to boys on the phone back then and going to her house while her parents were home was out of the question. So for nineteen months we kicked it behind their backs. All that shit came to an end during her senior year when I took her to the prom.

Neither one of her parents wanted me to take her, but I wasn't hearing that shit. Precious wasn't either. She stood up to them for the first time. After nearly thirty minutes of us all arguing back and forth, me and Precious was in my Benz on our way to the prom. That prom night changed both our lives forever," he said looking as if he'd lost his best friend.

"What happened?" I asked, thinking they'd had a terrible car accident.

"I took her virginity. A month later I took her to the clinic for a checkup and found out she was pregnant."

"Preg-nant!" I repeated, not believing my ears. Miss wannabe diva ain't so perfect after all.

"She told her mom about it the next day because she was scared and didn't know what to do." He took a deep breath. "That's when all hell really broke loose. Her parents popped up on my doorstep around eight o'clock that same evening like they were the feds coming to arrest me. They made Precious stay in the car while they stood outside my door threatening to have me put in jail if I didn't stay away from their daughter. I didn't worry about the bullshit threats because Precious was eighteen. When I got tired of hearing their bullshit I told them I would have them arrested for trespassing if they didn't get off my property. Moments after I told them that, they left. Believe it or not Sabrina," he said, softly. "I haven't seen her since that day. We talked on the phone the next few days and I tried my best to convince her to move in with me, since she only had a couple weeks before her high school graduation. I literally begged and begged that girl, but she was too scared to leave her parent's house." He grinned. "I loved Precious. She was the most beautiful girl I'd ever seen in my life and had that sassy attitude to go with it."

"Still got it too. So what about the baby?"

"She never had it. She wrote me while I was in jail, telling me her parents made her have an abortion. *'I didn't want to do it, Jay. Please believe me'*, she'd told me in that letter. From then on, I never heard from Precious again."

"Jail... Abortion! You mean that stuck up bitch killed the baby? That's some bullshit. She didn't have to have an abortion at eighteen. She was legally grown."

"I know. That's what I don't understand about the whole situation."

"I knew that bitch was up to no good. She walks around that restaurant like her shit don't stink. I got something on her ass now. Oh yeah, what you go to jail for?"

"Bout a week after Precious' parents had come to my house, the police ran up in my shit and found two guns, a brick of powder and sixty stacks. I was in the bed asleep when the Black Cats busted in. I got arrested and ended up serving seven and a half years in prison on those charges. I felt that I got off easy because the state prosecuted the case. They could've easily turned it over to the feds. I'm glad they didn't."

"Do you think Shante had something to do with you getting busted?"

"At first I didn't because I didn't wanna believe she would hurt me like that. Even right now I'm still not sure what role she played in it. I'm sure her parents had something to do with it though."

"Was she holding any of your money before you got arrested?"

"No, I didn't play that. I did spend a lot on her though. Precious was already high maintenance when I met her. Everything was Prada, Donna Karen and Gucci. She wouldn't get caught dead wearing none of that bootleg knockoff shit. How she became that way so young, I don't know. I was her first boyfriend."

"Well, if you're wondering, she hasn't changed a bit. She's still a gold digger."

He and I had sat in his living room trading stories for hours before we had sex. I felt like I'd been knowing him for years after that night. Since then, he and I had been sort of an item.

Jay hadn't long ago got off parole, so convincing him to help me fuck Deavin up was next to impossible.

"He's your problem Brina. I can't put myself in no position to end up back in prison for fucking up some nigga I don't even know. I don't play the game like that," he'd told me a few weeks after we'd been together. "As for Precious, she's a different story. She's my problem and I'm gonna deal with her when the opportunity presents itself. Now if her nigga try to play hero, I'm gonna light his ass up."

I accepted that from him then because I had a couple more weeks to change his mind about Deavin. I wanted his ass fucked up regardless.

From that day forward, I put the sex down on Jay like I was a real nymphomaniac. I was willing to do almost anything to get back at Deavin and Shante. I had convinced Jay to stay away from Dolly's and not try to confront Shante until we had our plan set.

'I'll be seeing your Miss wannabe ass at the old school costume party tomorrow night and it won't be pretty,' I thought as I watched her get off work.

DEAVIN

I had finally gotten around to calling Coach Terry and agreed to sign on to play with the Flyers. Prior to me calling Coach Terry, Hazel Eyes and I had a long talk about me leaving town to pursue my basketball career.

"What do you think about me going to play for the Flyers?" I asked her earlier that week while she and I strolled through Piedmont Park.

"You know I'm your biggest fan Boo, I'm behind you all the way. The best thing about it all is that you won't even have to leave Atlanta. Fayetteville is in Fayette County, which is only about a thirty-five minute drive."

"No Special," I stopped walking, looking into her eyes. "The Flyer isn't a Georgia team. It's a team in my hometown of Fayetteville, North Carolina."

Her facial expression went from a smile to a frown in a split second. "I can't walk no more. We need to sit down and talk about this."

I led her to the nearest park bench and we sat down.

"Why are you telling me this at the last minute?"

"I just found out myself last night when I was reading over some of those papers. This will be the Flyers inaugural season in North Carolina, the team wasn't there before I moved. That's why I thought the Flyers were in Fayette County too. Do you still want me to pursue my basketball career now?"

"Yeah I do, but I don't want you to have to leave town to do it."

"I really don't care to move back home temporarily either, but I got a chance to make it to the next level."

She sighed. "What are you considering temporarily?"

"Five to six months and that's only if one of the thirty NBA teams don't call me up first."

"What about the business, are you just giving up on it?"

"I'm planning on running it by phone and leaving Mark as the boss while I'm away. The salary that I'm gonna be making from playing basketball should help me to expand the business and possibly buy a house a lot sooner than I had ever expected to."

"Just when I thought everything was going good," she said as she rubbed her soft hand across my head, eyeing me with a sad face. "You're being taken away from me."

"I'm not being taken away from you baby." I gave her a peck on the lips. "I'll drive down to spend as much time with you as I can."

"I hope so," she replied, flatly.

"You do want me to make it in the NBA, don't you?"

"You know I do, but..."

"If an NBA team does eventually sign me that means I'll be playing in another city besides Atlanta, if I don't get picked up by the Hawks, which I doubt. What if the New York Knicks sign me? I'll be over a thousand miles away from you then."

"Oh no you won't," she said with sass. "I'll kiss Atlanta goodbye and go with you."

"What about your job?"

"What about it? If you make it to the NBA I'm gonna be sitting court side at every game, supporting you a hundred percent."

"You got it all mapped out, don't you?"

"Just as sure as my name is Shante Tara Blackmon. It's a two way street with me Boo. If by chance I make it big and you don't, I already have plans of taking you on tour with me."

"I'm glad to know that. What I wanna know is, will you support me a hundred and ten percent if I go back home and play for the Flyers?"

"My support is always gonna be there for you. I just don't want you thinking that you can reactivate your life as a playa because you're away from me."

"Never that baby." I pulled her into my arms. "I retired that life the same day I told Sabrina it was over. You're all the woman I need."

"And you're all the man I need Boo."

She and I sealed the end of that conversation with a long loving hug.

It wasn't long after I hung up with Coach Terry that Tracy and her being pregnant began to dominate my thoughts. Knowing that I was going back to North Carolina for a while, I realized that I was going to be there with Tracy when she gave birth to our daughter.

Me, Deavin James, in love with one woman while another woman is about to have my baby. Becoming a father was something I never gave much thought to until Tracy told me about her pregnancy. Apparently, the birth control pills stopped working the last time Tracy and I had sex, unless she stopped taking them and planned her pregnancy. I wasn't sure if that was the case or not. Planned pregnancy or unplanned pregnancy, the bottom line was that I was about to become a father from a woman that I still loved.

I know it's hard to believe that a man could abandon a relationship with a woman he still loved. However, in my case, had I stayed in Fayetteville around Tracy for a couple more months, I knew that I would have definitely fallen in love with her. Being in love was something I wasn't ready for at that time.

That is until Hazel Eyes came into my life. As for Tracy, I knew it was going to be hard for me to distance myself from her once I got back to Fayetteville because of my feelings and physical attraction to her. I was glad that she would be at least six months into her pregnancy by the time the Flyers training camp started. I was hoping she looked fat and unattractive by the time I saw her, I couldn't imagine having sex with a big belly, fat faced, swollen footed woman.

With that alone, I felt I wouldn't have any problems controlling my hormones around her. I was also sort of glad that Tracy and I were on friendly speaking terms again. Since the last time I talked with her on the phone, nothing strange had happened to me. Even the threatening phone calls ceased. I didn't know what business Tracy's boyfriend Steven had in College Park, but I hope it had nothing to do with getting back at me. I did consider myself a fairly tough guy and I wouldn't hesitate to kick some ass if I had to. Fighting was never my thing. I left all that bad boy stuff to the wannabe thugs and gangstas.

I wanted to know how Tracy had ended up with Steven as her live in boyfriend so fast. Yeah, I know that Hazel Eyes and I were together and all, but my point is, I knew Tracy wasn't the type of woman who would let a man move in with her after only kicking it with him a few months. That just wasn't Tracy's style. Did I hurt her bad enough to change her ways? It's possible, but doubt it. If she let this Steven dude move in with her so fast, then she had to have him on the side when we were still together. She had to be playing me the whole time.

Instead of me racking my brain about the situation, I called my sister trying to find out who Steven was and if I knew him.

"You need to be ashamed of yourself boy," she said to me. "You lied to that girl about letting her move to Atlanta with you. Now you're trying to find out who she's laying up with. You got some helluva nerve. I know what your problem is..."

"What?"

"You're jealous of Tracy being with Steven. Admit it."

"I've never been jealous of another man and I ain't about to start now."

"Save that lie for one of your dingbat girlfriends. You know I ain't the one. I'm your sister, remember. I know everything about you."

"Some kind of sister you are. You're supposed to be on my side, not against me."

"I am on your side big brother," she giggled. "And that's why I'm gonna call Tracy and tell her that you was asking me about her and Steven."

"Don't do that Tammy!" I pleaded.

"Don't start copping deuces now playa. I'm telling her."

"You ain't nothing but a hater."

"A snitching hater at that. Bye!" She hung up on me laughing.

With my sister telling Tracy about our phone conversation. I knew for a fact Tracy would start thinking I was jealous of her and Steven's relationship. As bad as I didn't want her thinking that I was actually jealous of her, it was the least of my worries. My biggest worry was Hazel Eyes and the bomb I was going to drop on her about Tracy carrying my daughter. I had no idea how she was going to take it, but I had to tell her. I guessed I would do it now.

"How was your day baby?" I asked after she answered the phone.

"It was okay, I'm a little tired right now. What have you been doing?"

"Nothing yet, I just woke up. You need to start taking a midafternoon nap."

"As bad as I would like to, I can't right now."

"Why, what's up?"

"I gotta go shopping for an outfit for the party tomorrow."

"What time are you going?"

"I was in the process of leaving before you called. Want me to get you anything?"

"Nah, I'm straight. Me and Mr. Willis are supposed to be dropping by a thrift store to get our outfits later. By the way Special," I said as my heart began to beat faster. "I need to have a serious talk with you."

"Is it an emergency?"

"Of course not."

"We'll talk about it when I get back from shopping. Is that okay with you?"

"Yeah, that's okay with me."

"I'll talk to you later Boo." She blew me a kiss and hung up.

I was sort of glad she had something to do because deep down inside I wasn't ready to drop the bomb on her.

SHANTE

I was totally beat after I got back in from shopping. I had gone from store to store until I had my Chaka Khan outfit in tack, big wig included. Chaka was my favorite old school R and B singer. That's why I had chosen to go to the party dressed as her.

Before I got back home with my outfit I stopped by the Shrine of the Black Madonna bookstore. What I initially thought would be a five to ten minute pit stop, turned into thirty minutes. I was like a kid in the candy store as I browsed up and down the aisles, checking out the books. I had to admit that prior to me reading Honey B. Morrison's novel "Sexcapade", I had never been interested in reading books. Hairstyling and fashion magazines was the norm for me. I read them faithfully. Now thanks to Honey B, I became a novel reader too.

I left the bookstore with five novels. Of course I had "Married On Monday" and "Unconditionally Single" by Honey B Morrison. I also had "A Hustler and the Married Woman" and "The Come Up 1 & 2" by Da'Author Raymone.

A woman I had met inside the bookstore had suggested the three Da'Author Raymone novels to me. She told me her husband had read all his books and that I would probably enjoy reading them too. Even though I was tired when I made it home, I did want to start reading "Married On Monday" but Monica wanted to talk about the problems she and Trey were having.

She said that things between them were getting better and asked me if I still had the two extra tickets.

"You better be glad Sabrina didn't want these," I said, handing her the tickets. "Consider yourself lucky."

"Thanks girl. I wouldn't know what to do without you." She grinned. "Trey is gonna be happy I got these. He told me he tried to buy some yesterday, but it was already sold out."

"Who are you planning to dress up as?"

"Hell, I don't know. Probably Diana Ross or my girl Patti. That's all my mom played when I was coming up."

"If you're going as either one of them, you're gonna need a wig. You better be glad I bought two of them today. You can wear one."

"You're a lifesaver. What else did you buy that I might be interested in?"

"You already know my clothes are off limits unless I've worn them before. I bought five books that you are welcomed to read anytime."

"I haven't even started reading "Sexcapade" yet. I'm still reading "King of the Streetz"."

"Sounds like a gangsta novel. Who wrote it?"

"Charles Broadie, he's written a whole series. Trey gave me the book last week."

"You need to hurry up and finish it so you can get started on "Sexcapade". That book hooked me after the first chapter. Once you start reading, it's gonna be nearly impossible for you to put it down."

"If it's all that, I'm gonna finish up the last couple chapters of "King of the Streetz" so I can jump to it," she said heading to her room.

I was so sleepy that I almost forgot to call Dee back. Since he'd told me earlier that he needed to have a serious talk with me, I called him. Mr. Willis answered Dee's phone, telling me Dee was in the dressing room trying on clothes. Waiting for him was out of the question. I told him to tell Dee that I would call him back if I didn't fall asleep first. I took a hot bath and climbed in bed. Minutes later I dozed off.

Time went by slow at work the next day. I thought 2:00 p.m. would never roll around. Sabrina had come in about an hour before I left, acting sort of weird. I was almost sure she hadn't gotten over me taking Dee from her, but this specific day she didn't act like it. For the first time in months she looked happy. I was glad for her because it was easy to see that she had a new man in her life. She even had on an expensive looking gold friendship ring. What took me by surprise was when she stuck her head into my office to speak to me.

"How are you doing Miss Blackmon?" She asked with a big smile that made me do a double take.

"Good and you?"

"I'm good, I'll be doing much better tonight. See you then." She closed the door and stepped off.

I didn't understand her "see you then" comment. It hadn't quite been twenty four hours since she had passed up the free tickets I'd offered her. I guess she changed her mind and found tickets elsewhere.

When I got in from work that afternoon I decided to call my mother back. She had left a message with Monica for me to call her while I was asleep the night before.

"How you been doing Mama?" I asked when she answered.

"Great, I feel twenty years younger."

"Daddy must be taking them Viagra pills again."

"Viagra," she repeated, laughing. "Child no. That stubborn man don't even like to take his prescribed medication no more. He doing good since he had that prostate surgery."

"I wanna talk to him before we hang up."

"He's not here. He's out golfing with one of his buddies."

"Why you feel my age all of a sudden if daddy ain't using Viagra?"

"Y'all young generation think that good sex is the key to feeling good, but y'all got it all wrong. Good healthy eating and running three miles, five days a week is what has me feeling so young. Just the other day when Ricky and I were out shopping, the store clerk mistook me for being his daughter instead of his wife."

"Cut it out mama. You can't be looking that young."

"Compared to Ricky, yes. You know he's thirteen years older than me. Besides our age gap, I can still pass for my late thirties any day."

"It's about time I take a trip up there to visit."

"You need to bring that handsome man of yours up here when you come. Monica told me all about him last night."

Nosy Monica and her big ass mouth. "That figures."

"Don't try to keep everything from your mother. Fill me in. Are you in love?"

"I honestly think I've finally found my soulmate."

"But are you in love?"

"For the first time in my life I can honestly say that I am in love."

"I don't know about it being your first time Shante."

"What do you mean?"

"You were in love with that young man Jason when you were in high school."

"No Mama, I was never in love with Jason. I cared four him and loved the way he use to spend all that money on me."

"You could've fooled me and your daddy then."

"I guess you two was fooled then," I said, thinking about a past that I wanted to forget. "I don't wanna talk about Jason so would you please change the subject?"

"Have you told your boyfriend about what happened yet?"

"Mama!" I spat, getting irritated.

"Don't Mama me girl. I'm trying to tell you something for your own good. If you're in love like you say and it's as serious as Monica told me last night, you need to sit that man down and tell him about your past. Especially if you're intending on marrying him one day."

"I don't think so. Since it's not broke, I'm not trying to fix it. Where did you get the idea of marriage from anyway? You need to pump your brakes and slow it down. You got it all twisted."

"You need to watch your mouth child. Just because you're grown and a thousand miles away doesn't mean you can talk to me like I'm one of your friends. You understand me Shante?"

"Yes Mama, but..."

"Ain't no but, Shante."

"I'm sorry Mama," I said, trying to ease the mood. She was the last person on earth I wanted to argue with.

"Your apology is accepted. Let me tell you what I wanted to tell you when I called last night. Your father..., I mean Howard, is seeing an old friend of mine."

"How do you know?"

"I still keep in touch with a few friends from the old neighborhood."

"I haven't really thought much about him since the time you told me he was looking for us. Have you found out where he's been living all these years?"

"No sweetheart," she answered softly. "I would like to find out though."

"Are you?"

"I'm still undecided about it. What do you think?"

"I really don't know. I never met him. I'm gonna leave that up to you."

She took a deep breath. "I'm not gonna lie to you Shante, I wanna see him. I wanna sit down and talk to him face to face about why he just up and left us. He's the only man I ever truly loved."

"What about Daddy?"

"I grew to love Ricky over the years. I married him to make a better life for us both." She sighed. "You grew up in a nice home, got everything you wanted and went to college. I guess it all worked out fine."

I couldn't believe what my mother was telling me. She had married for security.

"Are you happy Mama?"

"Don't worry about me child. I've made it all these years and I'm gonna continue to make it."

"Does Daddy know what's going on?"

"About what?"

"My real Daddy resurfacing after all these years."

"I haven't told him a word. If I do decide to look up Howard, Ricky will be the first to know."

"Let me know whenever you do decide to set up a meeting with him. I might wanna see and question him myself."

"Why the change of heart?"

"We only live one time, so I guess I'd like to meet him to at least see what he looks like. See if I favor him.

Meet the man who stole your happiness so many years ago. I don't know mama. Am I making any sense?"

"You're making all the sense in the world sweetheart. I believe every child needs to see what his or her parents look like, if only out of curiosity. I still have the pictures of him that you never wanted to see when you were growing up. Would you like for me to send them to you?"

"Yes Mama. It's about time I see what he looks like."

"I'm gonna dig them up and send them off to you in the morning."

"That'll be fine."

My mother and I talked a while longer. I told her about my up and coming singing career and filled her in on my relationship with Dee, which really wasn't much because Monica had told her almost everything.

After hanging up with her I should have been feeling good, but I wasn't. Her bringing Jason's name into our conversation had really thrown me for a loop. I hadn't thought about him in years. Why my mother brought up his name, I didn't know. I assumed that since she was forty-six she was ready to be a grandmother. That wasn't my fault though. She and Daddy were the ones to blame for that.

Dee and I were in our new car on our way to the Old School Costume Party. I called the Lexus our new car because I drove it more than he did. Transforming myself into Chaka Khan had been a lot harder than I had first expected.

Chaka was short and thick with large boobies and wore lots of makeup. I wasn't short and my boobies were nowhere near her size, but I did have a lot of junk in the trunk that turned guy's heads when I passed them by. However, after I put on a padded pushup bra, makeup, big curly wig, tight leather black jeans, maroon blouse and patent leather pumps, I was a Chaka clone, with the exception of my height.

As for Dee, he was working his Teddy Pendergrass outfit. He wore a black wife beater tucked into a pair of jeans with a tan blazer, black boots, a cowboy hat with rhinestones and a scarf, tied loosely around his neck.

"Where's your jewelry Boo? You know TP always worse several gold necklaces," I asked him when he picked me up.

"This is a platinum era Special. I don't own any gold necklaces."

"Well I do. Hold on a minute," I said before going to my jewelry box and taking out four gold necklaces that I'd had since high school. "Let me put these on you Boo. Then you'll be Mr. TP himself."

The club was getting crowded by the time Dee and I got there. Evelyn Champagne King's "Shame" was playing as we found our table in VIP.

Mark and his girlfriend Christine were already seated with two bottles of Armand de Brignac's champagne. Mark was working his Rick James outfit, long braids included. Not to be outdone, Christine had her Teena

Marie look going. She wore a pink hat, broke down on her long reddish looking hair like Teena use to wear.

No sooner than we settled in, the deejay put on Freddie Jackson's "Tasty Love."

"You don't know nothing 'bout that Special. You wasn't even born when that came out."

"Let me show you what I know," I replied, grabbing Dee's hand and leading him to the VIP dance floor.

MR. WILLIS

For the first time since I came home, I decided to go out to a club to unwind. Mark had given me two tickets for the Old School Costume Party. *"Hell..., why not?"* I thought when he offered me the tickets. I didn't care much about that hip hop mess, but I was crazy about me some old school R & B. So going to the party was a must for me.

I chose Debra as my date of course and I dressed as my boy Howard Hewett. People use to say he and I favored each other back in the day. My ex-girlfriend Carla had even given me the nickname Howard. Debra dressed as the Disco Queen, Donna Summers.

When Debra and I entered the club it was jammed packed. Stevie Wonder's "Reggae Woman" was playing.

"Let dance," Debra said, pulling me towards the large dance floor. "You know I love me some Stevie."

"Not now, Deb. We need to find our table first. I know everybody else is waiting on us."

"With all these folks and tables in here it's gonna be nearly impossible for us to find that table."

"Not when it's reserved in VIP."

While making our way to VIP I spotted a guy dressed up looking like Isaac Hays and he had his arm around a young lady who favored Sade. It wasn't until Debra reached the VIP section that I remembered who the guy was, his name was Jason Chambers. I'd met him when I was in prison. I didn't befriend many guys during my incarceration, but Jason was one of the guys I befriended. He use to always talk to me about his personal problems when things got tough. If he wasn't telling me about how his brother was messing up the money he'd left behind, he was telling me about his ex-girlfriend Precious who had aborted his child while he was in county jail. Every time he talked to me about Precious, I could see the hurt in his eyes.

"I don't know why she refuses to answer my letters Mr. Willis," he'd told me. "I've written her at least once a week ever since I got locked up fourteen months ago. What do you think I should do?"

"Ain't much you can do in this position son, just stay strong and try looking her up when you get out. Then you ask her why she did what she did. You know we're both riding in the same boat Jason, I got an ex-girlfriend to look up myself. Hell, I left her out there pregnant too."

That old conversation was replaying in my mind when I spotted Deavin and Mark at the table. I introduced Debra to everyone at the table that I knew. Then Deavin spoke up and introduced Debra and I to Monica and Trey. She was dressed as Patti Labelle and he as Marvin Gaye. Once we had all gotten acquainted and talked about the

$1000 prize for the best dressed Old School Couple Contest, we all hit the floor.

"Dennis," Debra whispered in my ear while we were slow dancing to Heatwave's 'Always and Forever'. "That girl dressed as Chaka Khan looks familiar to me."

"You probably know her from that soul food restaurant downtown. She works at Dolly's."

"That's not it sugar. I know her from somewhere else."

Debra kept me on the dance floor nonstop for over thirty minutes while the deejay played all the oldies but goodies. I didn't spot Jason again until Teena Marie's "Square Biz" started playing. By then I was ready to sit back down. Since I had yet to tell Debra about the long prison sentence I'd served, I sent her back to our table before making my way over to chat with my buddy Jason.

"All the old school dressed couples who are participating in the best dressed competition please report to the side of the stage to get your contestant number! The competition begins at twelve thirty!" The hostess, Missy E, the Party Doll, announced moments before I tapped Jason on the shoulder.

He turned around and stared at me for what seemed like an eternity before he recognized me. "Mr. Willis!"

"How's it going Jason?" I spoke, giving him a father-son embrace.

"Things couldn't be going any better. When you come home?"

"Bout a year ago. Is that your girlfriend Precious?" I asked, referring to the beautiful woman who was dressed as Sade, standing behind him. When her cute smile turned into a frown I immediately realized I shouldn't have asked that question in her presence.

"Nooo Mr. Willis." He pulled her to him and kissed her on the lips. "This is my girl, Sabrina. Sabrina, this is my ol' buddy Mr. Willis."

"Nice to meet you Sabrina." I extended my hand to her. "Sorry for the misunderstanding."

She shook my hand. "Don't worry about it sir, I understand."

"We got a table over in the corner. Would you like to join us?" Jason asked.

"I can't stay too long. I don't wanna keep my ol' lady and friends waiting."

"Your ol' lady..., the one that was pregnant?"

"I wish," I answered as we headed to their table. "Haven't found them yet, but I'm still searching. What about you? Have you had any luck?"

"Oh yeah, thanks to Sabrina. I haven't had the opportunity to confront her yet."

"He will tonight," Sabrina interjected.

"She's in here somewhere. I'll see her after the club closes."

"We might see her before then, 'cause she loves attention," Sabrina said.

I sat down with them and chatted for about fifteen minutes before I made my way back to VIP.

Debra was sipping on champagne and talking to Monica and Trey when I got back. They told me that Dee, Shante, Mark and Christine were entering the contest.

JASON

After eight long years I was about to get the opportunity to confront my ex-girlfriend. During all my years of living I'd never seen or met a woman as fine as her. I had met Precious at South DeKalb Mall when she was sixteen years old. At that age she was matured way beyond her years. Even though I was a twenty two year old playa back then, I knew I had to have her.

When I first stepped up to her inside the mall that memorable day, she put on a front, acting like she didn't want to be bothered. So being the playa I was, I went back outside to my car and waited until she stepped out of the mall, then I pulled up on her in my big boy Benz.

"Wassup Shawty," I spoke as she stood on the sidewalk holding a Rich's shopping bag like she was waiting for someone to pick her up.

"I ain't no Shawty for your information," she said, rolling her neck.

"What are you then?"

"Nothing!" She blurted mistakenly, embarrassing herself, trying to be a smart mouth. She laughed it off.

"Ok nothing," I told her as I wrote my name and number on a hundred dollar bill. "Give a nigga a call when you come down off that high." I handed her the money. "You ain't all that Shawty." I pulled off before she was able to respond.

While eyeing her in my rearview mirror, I watched her hold the hundred dollar bill up in the air, checking to see if it was real. Then she watched my car until it disappeared out of sight. She called me a month later and I picked her up from school that same day. What surprised the fuck out of me was that she still had the same one hundred dollar bill I had given her at the mall.

"Thanks, but no thanks Jason." She gave me the money back after she'd gotten in the car. "I ain't that cheap."

From that day forward I knew I wasn't dealing with the average teenager. Again, with me being six years older than she, I automatically thought that I would get the pussy in a few days. However, I had never been more wrong about anything else in my life. It had taken me nearly nineteen months to hit it. By then, I was already in love.

The night she gave me her virginity I intentionally came inside her, hoping to get her pregnant and it worked. It was most guys dreams to have a baby mama as fine and as beautiful as Shante "Precious" Blackmon. I didn't just want her to be my baby mama, I wanted her to be my wife.

I knew that getting her to marry me was going to be a hard task because of her parents. They were super strict on her and thought that no man was good enough for their daughter. So by me getting her pregnant, I thought her parents would give in and see things my way.

"You got her pregnant? You gotta marry her!" Is what I had expected them to say, but I was totally wrong. Instead, they flipped out on me like I was the devil himself and days later I was sitting in the DeKalb County jail without bond.

Besides me losing Precious and the unborn child, I lost my $190,000 home, Benz, $23,000 worth of jewelry and $60,000 in cash. I lost a lot, but I felt that losing Precious and our baby was the biggest loss of all. I still wasn't sure if her parents were to blame. There were a lot of questions that I wanted answered and I was sure Precious knew all the answers.

"Jay!" Sabrina called my name, shaking me from my thoughts. "There she go."

I looked up on the stage and there stood my Precious. Even though she had on a wig and makeup I easily recognized her.

Damn! She's still beautiful and fine as ever. "That's her alright," I mumbled in disbelief.

"I told you we were gonna see her ass before the club closed. She craves attention too fucking much!"

Attention is what she got as she sashayed across the stage in the tight leather pants she wore. The guys were hollering and whistling so loud that you could barely hear what Missy E, the Party Doll was saying. Precious was practically stealing the contest. She and her Teddy Pendergrass dressed looking boyfriend weren't the best dressed old school couple. That belonged to the Rick James and Teena Marie couple. I had to give them credit, Rick and Teena had their shit together. But in the end, the crowd roared the loudest for Precious and her man.

"Sista girl! Yeah, you Chaka. You wearing the hell out of that outfit, but can you sing?" Missy E, the Party Doll asked before she was able to step off the stage holding her boyfriend's hand.

She turned around and walked up to Missy E, the Party Doll and got the microphone.

"Give me the closest thing you can get to Chaka's 'Sweet Thing' instrumental," Precious requested from the deejay.

Within thirty seconds the instrumental came on. Precious tore off into the song as if she was Chaka herself. She could really sing as she held her boyfriend's hand and stared up into his eyes.

The crowd erupted into cheers when she finished. She handed the microphone back to Missy E the Party Doll, before exiting the stage.

"Now that sista needs a record deal!" Missy E the Party Doll announced.

"That bitch's head is up past the sky right now!" Sabrina spat, eyeing Precious with an evil look. "I can't wait 'til you bust that bitches bubble."

"Let me have this dance." I grabbed her hand and led her to the dance floor. Atlantic Starr's 'Send for Me' had just come on. I pulled her into my arms and held her tight. "This dance is all about you Brina. Forget about all the negatives and relax."

The next couple of songs I thought about Sabrina and only Sabrina while we slow danced.

When I first met her I thought she was a hood rat because she let me beat the pussy up on the first night. I thought it was my playa skills that led her into my bedroom, but I later found out differently. Two weeks after the night we met, she told me her reason for wanting to get close to me and apologized about it. I didn't get mad at her about it because I had my reasons too. Even though she and I were both trying to find closure in a past relationship, we still decided to give each other a chance.

When I finally got to know her for who she really was and not for the person she became after Precious had stolen her man, I started feeling her. I was hoping that once she was able to get Precious and Deavin out of her system we would be able to put it all behind us and move forward with our lives. Sabrina wasn't as fine as Precious, but she was still a dime piece and was in the process of getting her bachelor degree in Journalism.

"Let's make it happen Brina," I told her as people started to exit the club.

Soon as Sabrina and I made it outside I went straight to my truck and got my gun, just in case Precious's tall ass boyfriend decided he wanted to play hero. My knuckle name was tight, but I wasn't about to swell them up in no street fight. I figured I would just bust a cap in his ass and get it over with real quick.

Parked only three cars down from my Tahoe was a black Lexus that Sabrina said belonged to Precious.

"We'll wait right here for them. They should be coming up outta there any minute now," I told Sabrina as I leaned back against the Lexus with my arms folded.

DEAVIN

"I'm in love with this woman," I told everybody at our table when Hazel Eyes and I got up to leave.

"Hell," Mr. Willis said. "We're right behind y'all. Come on Deb."

With the club crowd thinning out, it didn't take Hazel Eyes and I long to get out of there.

"Your place or mine?" I asked as she and I strolled hand in hand to the parking lot.

"It doesn't matter to me Boo," she said as she shot me a seductive look. "I'm gonna put it on you regardless what bed we get in."

"I'm with whatever." I passed her the car keys. "We can take it to the Hilton if you want too. Wherever we go I gotta have a serious talk with you first."

"Ok Boo."

No sooner than those words left her mouth, I swore I saw the same black Suburban with the tinted windows that had tried to run me into the median wall, cruise by. As Hazel

Eyes and I continued walking, I kept looking back over my shoulder to see if the Suburban was going to turn around.

"What's the matter Boo? Are you ok?"

"Yeah babe, I'm straight," I answered, looking back before we bent the corner. What the fuck is up with that Suburban?

"Hey Precious..., long time no see." A bald headed, stocky looking guy said, standing beside my car.

"I told you at work earlier today that I would be seeing you tonight," Sabrina added, standing next to the bald guy with her arms folded.

"What's up?" I asked the two.

"Ask your girl Precious," the guy said. "Her folks set me up and she aborted our child."

"I don't know you or this Precious chick you're talking about. So would you please excuse us?"

He eased his hand inside his jacket. "Not until your girl Shante, who I know as my ex girl Precious, answers my damn questions!"

"Do you know what the fuck this dude talking about?" I asked Hazel Eyes.

She stared up at me with a blank expression and nodded her head. "Yes," she sighed. "But I don't know nothing about him being set up."

I was confused at that point and didn't fully understand what the hell was going on.

"You left me for that stuck up saditty child murdering bitch!" Sabrina shouted at me.

"Child murdering," I repeated, staring at Hazel Eyes. "You ain't never had any kids..., have you?"

She peered at the ground without answering.

"Tell'em Precious. Tell'em why you aborted our child. I been waiting for over eight years now to hear your side of the story," he said with his hand still inside the jacket. "You gonna tell me something right here tonight!" He demanded.

"Is that true babe?" I asked getting agitated. She continued peering at the ground, disregarding me. "So it's like that now? You can't answer me? I'm outta here."

I walked out of the parking lot and headed down the street looking for a cab. After I'd walked about forty yards past the club entrance, I spotted the black Suburban again. I watched as the passenger side window came down. Before I was able to react and dive for cover, I heard multiple gunshots.

"Shiiiit!" I screamed when I realized I'd been hit. I immediately fell to the ground. As I laid there gasping for air on the cold pavement, I felt a burning sensation in my chest and my side as I was beginning to bleed badly.

"I need a drink of water. My eyes are getting weak. Somebody please help me... I'm... losing... consciousness."

SHANTE

I can't believe Dee left me out here by myself with the ghost of my past and the bitch who loves to hate me. Stay strong, keep your composure and don't let them see you sweat.

"I see your man bailed out on you Precious. I guess you never told him about us," Jason said, standing beside my car.

"No, I didn't. You shouldn't have either." I stepped forward. "Would you two please excuse me?"

"Not until you talk to me..., I mean right fucking now!"

All of a sudden somebody down the street started shooting. There were only about three to four shots fired, but were warning enough to let me know it was time for me to go.

"I'm out of here," I said, trying to squeeze between the two to open my car door.

Sabrina shoved me so hard that I almost lost my balance and fell. "If you brush up against me again you child murdering bitch!" She spat, balling up her fist. "I'm gonna beat your ass!"

"Somebody got shot! Somebody got shot!" A crowd of people shouted simultaneously, scrambling to get to their cars. The parking lot scene had turned straight pandemonium in a matter of seconds.

"I'll talk to you Jason, but not out here," I said, taking off my pumps. "And you," I pointed at Sabrina. "If you lay another fucking finger on me, you best kill me bitch! Cause that's exactly what I plan to do to you! Now step outta my way bitch!"

Jason grabbed her and pulled her to the side before whispering something in her ear. Moments later, he handed her some keys and she walked off towards a grey Tahoe.

"I'm riding with you while she follows us. It's getting too hot out here and you already know that me and the police don't get along."

I can't be driving him around in my man's car. What the hell am I thinking, Dee left me. I'm on my own again and I gotta do what I gotta do.

"Let's go Jason. You better not try nothing crazy either."

"Have I ever?" He replied, opening the passenger door. "Don't keep calling me Jason either. You know I like to be called Jay."

"Alright Jay. There's a first time for everything."

"I know there's a first time for everything. I found that out eight years ago."

I didn't respond to the comment and pulled out of the parking lot, making a left on Peachtree Street. As I turned, I saw police cars stopping at the scene of the apparent shooting. That's why I don't like going to clubs, our kind just don't know how to act civilized in public.

After driving a mile or two in silence I was undecided as to where I was headed to. I definitely wasn't going to take him back to my apartment and going to his place was out of the question. So when I felt the hunger pains in my stomach I decided to stop by Gladys Knight Chicken and Waffles.

"We'll talk about it over an early breakfast," I told him as I turned into the parking lot. "My treat. Just me and you." I looked in the rearview mirror watching Sabrina pull in behind us. "I don't want her all up in my business."

"Ok Precious, I'll handle that."

"Thanks Jay. I appreciate it."

He got out and went straight to the truck to talk to Sabrina while I went inside the restaurant. It didn't dawn on me that I was still wearing my old school costume until this guy in the restaurant thanked me for my Chaka performance. After running into Jason and Sabrina and Dee abandoning me, my mind was a million miles away.

"Why Precious?" Jay asked while he and I sat waiting to order.

Looking into his eyes brought back many old memories. Some bad, but mostly good. "My parents, Jay. They're the ones to blame."

"Your parents! You were eighteen then. You didn't have to listen to them."

"I might've been eighteen. What you don't understand is that I was an eighteen year old high schooler, still living under my parent's roof. You were locked up Jay, what was I supposed to do? Who was I supposed to turn to? I didn't want to have an abortion. I wanted to keep our baby. I cried on and off for weeks after leaving that clinic," I said, trying to hold back the tears as I waved the waitress away. "You know my plans were to move in with you after I graduated, but things didn't turn out like that. My parents knew you were the only person I could turn to for comfort. So after you got arrested they flipped the script on me. They threatened to take the car back they'd bought me for Christmas. They even threatened to put me out on the streets with nothing. 'You won't be having no bastard child in this house. I won't be raising two of them', my father had told me days after you got locked up. Those words coming out of his mouth had really hurt me to the core. I couldn't believe he'd said that to me. At the time I had nobody else to point the finger at but you. You left me pregnant out here in this big world alone and I started hating you for it." I sighed. "Up until a year after my parents basically forced me to abort our child, the 'what if' questions dominated my thoughts. In order for me to get over it all and move on with my life, I had to forget about you and everything else that happened. When my parents moved to Chicago they tried to make me go with them, but I wasn't hearing it. At nineteen I finally stood my ground against them and made my own decisions. I ended up staying here and finished college. Even though my parents were against me living alone, they continued to pay my car notes and the rent to the apartment I'd moved in."

"I wrote you letters every week for almost a year and a half Precious. Why didn't you ever write back?"

"What are you talking about Jay? I responded back to every single letter I received from you. I thought you had got mad with me about the abortion and stopped writing me. I never received another letter from you after I wrote telling you about it."

"You gotta be bullshitting me, Precious."

"I'll never lie to you, Jay." I reached over the table taking his hand in mine. "I've always been straight up with you. As for the letters you said you wrote me, I believe you. I have no other reason not to. My parents had to intercept the letters so I wouldn't get them. It wouldn't have been hard for them to do because I had moved out when I went to college. I promise you that I'll be finding out what happened to those letters when I call my mother tomorrow."

"Do you think your parents had anything to do with me getting locked up?"

"I wouldn't put anything past them, Jay. If they hid your letters from me, there is no telling what else they did behind my back." I closed my eyes and slowly shook my head. "God knows I hope they didn't. I'm so sorry for all the hurt and pain I caused you over the years," I said and kissed the back of his hand because I meant it.

"I foot some of the blame too, I shouldn't have ever had them drugs and guns up in my crib anyway. Going to prison was a wakeup call for me. I'll never attempt to sell drugs again. That shit cost me our child and me asking you to marry me. Your last name is supposed to be Chambers instead of Blackmon. Wouldn't you agree?" He asked, showing a slight smile for the first time that night.

"Yes Jay." I returned the smile. "I probably would have married you. I wish you would have told me that when I found out I was pregnant. There's nothing my parents could have said to stop me from moving out then. A closed mouth can't get fed Jay."

For the next thirty minutes or so he and I talked about a little of everything. Sabrina and Dee included. He had even noticed the gold necklaces Dee had on were the same ones he'd bought for me when I was in high school. He was a man about it and didn't get mad. He told me he was more surprised that I still had the necklaces.

"Are you going to fire Sabrina?" He asked as he and I walked out of the restaurant.

"The way that heifer showed out on me tonight, she need not ever come near me or Dolly's again, but since I understand why she was so bitter towards me in the first place, we might be able to work something out. I hope she knows how to apologize first. She has my number."

"Alright Precious." He gave me a hug and a kiss on the cheek. "I'll tell her. You take care of yourself."

"I will."

He headed on back to his truck where Sabrina was sitting in the passenger seat, eyeing me with a hateful look. I smiled and waved at her out of spite, to let her know that what she'd done to me earlier didn't faze me and that I was alright. On the outside I might've looked like I was alright. However, I was devastated on the inside.

During my short drive home, Dee was all I thought about. Why did tonight have to happen? I probably should have told him about my relationship with Jay, but that was a skeleton I thought had already burned in hell. Boy was I wrong about that. Well Dee ever talk to me again? Will he answer my calls? Shit..., what will he think of me being his special now knowing that I'm not as pure as he thought? The best thing for me to do is not call him, he will think I'm pissed off at him for leaving me in that damn parking lot like that.

While unlocking my apartment door all I wanted to do at that point was kickoff my heels, take a shower and climb between my soft awaiting bed sheets.

"What's the matter with you girl?" I asked Monica nonchalantly as I made my way through the living room. I didn't notice the tears in her eyes until she looked up at me.

"It's Deavin..., he got shot."

"Shot! Where? When?" I shouted nervously, hoping she was only joking.

"Outside the club." She eyed me from the sofa without blinking. "You two left together. Where were you when it happened? I been trying to call you for the past hour. Why haven't you been answering your phone?"

Phone! Phone! Damn, I must've dropped it in that fucking parking lot when that bitch pushed me, but my Boo shot! "Dee and I got into a little argument out in the parking lot and he walked off leaving me. My God! I didn't know he'd been shot."

I ran to my room and changed clothes. Slipping on a T-shirt, jeans, tennis shoes and Dee's Tar Heel fitted cap. It didn't take me a hot five minutes and I was ready to go. The only problem I faced was finding out what hospital he'd been taken to, so I called Mark.

"Hurry up and get down here. Dee is gonna need all the love, prayer and support he can get," he told me before I hung up.

Monica drove me to Grady Hospital in the Lexus because I was in no shape to be driving. God please don't take away my Boo from me. Give him a second chance.

MR. WILLIS

I had never in my forty-seven years of living witnessed what I had seen happen outside the club. While Debra and I walked down Peachtree Street, heading to my truck, gunshots rang out. When she and I ducked beside a parked SUV, I saw a guy up ahead of us fall to the ground as he was getting hit. Immediately after the shooting stopped I heard the tires screeching on what I figured was the getaway car. Wanting to play things safe, we stayed hid beside the SUV for about another minute, making sure the coast was clear.

"Go straight to the truck and wait for me Deb," I instructed her before I ran down the sidewalk to where the lifeless looking body of Deavin laid. "My God!" I shouted, not wanting to believe it was really him. "Somebody call an ambulance!"

After checking and discovering that his pulse was weak, I started talking to him so he wouldn't die on me and used my shirt to slow down the bleeding until the paramedics arrived.

"Did anyone see what happened here?" The first arriving officer asked when he got to the scene.

"I didn't see a face, but the shots came from a late model Suburban," a guy in the crowd said.

"What about the color? Did anybody get a tag number?" The police asked.

"It was black with dark tinted windows!" Someone shouted.

I remembered Deavin telling me about a month ago, *"A black Suburban tried to run me into the median wall early this morning. I was driving home from work."* I hope he reported that incident to the cops, but knowing Deavin, he probably didn't. I'm hoping it didn't cost him his life.

When the paramedics arrived and took over, Mark popped up as I began telling one of the officers about the early morning incident Deavin had told me about. I told Mark to follow the paramedics while I finished giving the police a report.

Shortly afterwards, Debra and I were on our way to the hospital. Mark and Christine were already sitting in the waiting room when we arrived.

"What did they say Mark? Is he gonna make it?" I asked in an overexcited state.

The look on Mark's face told me what he had to say wasn't going to be good news. He dropped his head before he spoke. "It doesn't look good right now. They say he lost a lot of blood."

"Where they got him at?"

"They gotta give him some blood first. Then they're gonna take him to surgery. Bout all we can do now is wait and pray that he pulls through."

"I guess you're right."

"Have you seen his girlfriend?" Debra asked Mark.

Nah," he replied looking around. "I thought maybe she would be with y'all. I hope she's alright."

"I saw what happened. She was nowhere in sight."

"But they left out of the club together, didn't they?" Mark interjected.

"Yeah..., there's no telling what happened between them once they made it outside." I said.

"I got her number," Mark patted his pockets. "Damn! It's out there in Christine's car," he said before leaving to get it.

When Mark got the number and called Shante he had to leave a message because she wasn't home. He also called Deavin's family and told them what happened. They told Mark they would be on the next flight to Atlanta. Shante did eventually call Mark back to let him know she was on her way.

At 4:17 a.m., Shante and Monica entered the waiting room. When she spotted me she rushed into my arms.

"How is he? Is he gonna he alright?" She asked, hugging me tightly.

"Last we heard they were giving him blood so they could get him into surgery." I took a deep breath. "It's not looking good right now."

"It's that bad?" She asked, searching my eyes for answers.

"He was hit in the chest and his side."

"Oh, God!" She cried out, burying her head in my dried up blood stained shirt. "It's all my fault!"

"What's your fault?"

"We had a problem in the parking lot and he walked off. I thought maybe he would catch a ride with either you or Mark..., I guess he didn't see y'all before he was shot."

She stopped in mid-sentence when she finally noticed all the dried up blood on me. She stared at me in disbelief with her mouth wide open.

"I was there Shante..., I saw it happen."

"But why would someone wanna kill him?"

"I don't know. I was hoping you would be able to help me out with that question. Did he ever tell you that somebody had been threatening him?"

"No."

"What about the Suburban incident. Did he ever tell you about the black Suburban that tried running him off the road?"

"No, never."

"Let's all pray that God delivers Deavin back to us in full health. God is the almighty. He's the one we all should be talking to," Debra said, causing us all to gather in a circle and hold hands.

A couple of hours later a nurse stepped out and summoned Mark to her. I immediately had to grab Shante to hold her back while the nurse spoke with Mark. By reading their facial expression, I could at least tell that Deavin was still hanging in there with us. Soon as the nurse stepped off we all bomb rushed Mark to find out the update.

"I couldn't hardly understand those medical terms she was using. All I know is that surgery was a success and that Dee has been moved to the Intensive Care Unit."

"Can we see him yet?"

"Yeah, she said the visits must be brief and are for family members only. They got him in room 695."

Everybody's face showed a sign of relief after Mark filled us in on Deavin's status. Knowing that he was going to be alright for the time being, I decided to go home to get cleaned up.

"Shante, can I speak to you for a minute?" Debra asked her as Shante watched Mark head to Deavin's room with tears in her eyes. I could tell she didn't want Mark to visit first, but since they were so close, she sucked it up and waited her turn.

"Yes ma'am," she replied.

Debra pulled her to the side and they had a short conversation. Whatever it was they discussed, Debra didn't share it with me while I drove her home.

"I got a big surprise for you later on today baby," Debra said before she kissed me and got out of the truck.

SHANTE

I tried my best to hold back the tears as I entered Dee's room and saw the three tubes hooked to him. When I got close enough to see his face, his eyes were closed. The only movement from his body came from his chest area, due to his breathing.

"God, please don't take my Boo away from me," I prayed as I pulled a chair up close to the bed. I sat down and told him all about my past with Jay. I even told him about what happened after he left. I know he didn't likely hear or understand a word I was saying because he was heavily sedated, but I continued to talk anyway. "Why Boo? Why didn't you tell me you had somebody out to hurt you? Mr. Willis told me about it. I wished you would've shared your troubles with me. Do you realize how much I love and care for you Deavin James? I'd do anything to help you if I could Boo."

At that moment the black Suburban flashed across my mind. "Oh my God!" I said, standing up. "I think I might know who did this to you." I kissed him and dashed out of the room, looking for the detective that had been in the waiting room questioning Mark and Mr. Willis earlier.

"Excuse me sir!" I said urgently to the slim, light skinned detective who was talking to Mark, Christine, Monica and some pretty looking tatted up redbone I'd never seen before.

The detective quickly turned to face me. "Can I help you Ma'am?"

"Yes, I think I know who shot my boyfriend."

Mark, Christine, Monica, the tatted up redbone and the detective looked at me as if I had the answer to the million dollar question.

"Who?" They all asked simultaneously.

"A guy I use to date before I met Dee. His wife drives a black Suburban with tinted windows."

"Besides the Suburban Ma'am, what would give your ex a motive to kill Deavin?" The detective asked.

"After I broke our two year relationship off with him, he saw me and Dee out together one day. For the next couple of weeks that followed he constantly called me, but I wouldn't talk to him. He even came by my job one morning scaring me half to death. The last time I saw him was about three or four months ago when he popped up at my apartment unannounced. I remember him making a statement that I didn't take serious at the time."

"What did he say?" He asked as he scribbled on a small pad.

"That he'd never let another man have me."

"Do you actually think he would go as far as killing Deavin to get you back?"

I sighed and shook my head. "I honestly don't know."

"What's his name?"

"Julian O'Neal Patterson."

"Where does he live?"

"Cascade."

"Cascade," he repeated. "Be a little bit more specific. I'm going to need Mr. Patterson's full address if you know it?"

I gave him the address and told him everything I knew about Julian before he left the hospital.

"Would you mind picking Dee's parents up from the airport for me? Their flight is scheduled to arrive at eleven o'clock this morning. I'm beat Shante and I need to get some rest," Mark asked shortly after the detective left.

"I'll take care of that for you. Will you take Monica home for me? She needs some rest too."

"I'll do that," he said, handing me a folded piece of paper and giving me a hug.

Monica, Christine and the pretty tatted redbone also gave me sympathy hugs before they left. I watched as they exited the waiting room, trying to figure out who the tatted up redbone was and where she'd come from. Apparently she had to be a friend of Christine and Mark's.

I exhaled and sat down, unfolding the paper Mark had given me. It contained more information about Dee's parent's flight arrival.

Since I had several hours to burn, I went back into Dee's room to get a nap in the chair I had slid next to his bed, disobeying the nurse's order for a brief visit. Damn those nurses and their rules. My Boo needs me.

JULIAN

If Shante thought she could just up and kick me to the curb after all the time and money I'd invested in her, she had another thing coming. Even my marriage was on the brink of destruction because of her. Prior to me meeting Shante, I had never cheated on my wife. But once Shante and I laid eyes on each other I knew then that my marriage was doomed. She was everything I had ever dreamed of in a woman and it wasn't long after she and I started messing around that I fell madly in love with her. A few months into our relationship she told me she needed extra money to make ends meet and I gave her a thousand dollars. That eventually turned into a monthly thing. I would give her six hundred dollars a month to pay her car note. On top of the monthly stipends, I would buy her expensive gifts each time I bought for my wife. Tiffany's, Bloomingdales and Saks. You name it, I took Shante shopping there. However, I didn't mind spending money on her. I felt she was worth every penny of it.

The night she kicked me to the curb it crossed my mind to kill her as I drove home, but I realized that killing her would be a stupid thing to do. I didn't want her dead, I still wanted her as my beautiful mistress. So the thing for me to do was to kill her tall boyfriend. I set out to do just that.

I laid back in the cut and watched him for a while before I saw the perfect opportunity. Unfortunately, things didn't go as I had planned. After failing to kill him in what would have looked like he had fallen asleep behind the wheel of his truck and slammed into the concrete wall, I had to come up with another plan. I might as well shoot his ass and get it over with, I thought after the failed attempt early that morning.

With me having never fired a gun before, I started having second thoughts about shooting him. On the other hand, when my threatening phone calls failed to spook him enough to pack up his shit and leave town, it left me with no other alternative, I had to shoot him.

Again, I started laying back in the cut watching and waiting on my perfect chance to take him out. Finally that chance came and I was shocked when I spotted my target walking down the street by himself, especially after I had saw him and Shante come out of the club holding hands minutes earlier. Whatever it was that caused the two to part ways so quickly, I was glad it happened.

I had an adrenaline rush as I pulled up on my target, gripping my 9MM handgun. Seeing him out in the open with nowhere to hide, I didn't hesitate to pull the trigger and I didn't stop until he hit the ground. I stepped on the gas and peeled out then drove straight home, since I didn't see nobody following me. I didn't worry about anyone getting my license plate number, I had stolen the tag off another black Suburban. I was smart enough to park the truck inside my garage for precautionary measures. With my wife and kids down in South Georgia, visiting relatives, I had the house to myself and a lot of thinking room without having to worry about being bothered.

"Now that he's dead, I know you'll be needing a shoulder to cry on. I'm giving you forty-eight hours to mourn over him and then I'll be coming over to your apartment with a fifteen hundred dollar Valentino outfit. I know you'll forget all about him then. Material things have always jarred your memory. Remember the new Mercedes Benz you always wanted? I'm going to take you to the dealership next week and buy you a brand new one off the showroom floor," I thought while I stared at one of her pictures.

TRACY

The ringing of my phone in the middle of the night had awakened me. Who in the world is calling me at this time of night?

"Hello?" I answered.

"Get up and pack your bags girl! We 'bout to fly to Georgia! Somebody shot my brother!"

"Deavin? Shot!" I blurted on the brink of panicking.

"Yeah!" Tammy said sounding a bit hysterical. "Mark just called telling my parents! He's at the hospital with Deavin now! Get ready! We'll be over to pick you up soon!"

"Ok," I replied hanging up feeling numb.

From the moment we all boarded the plane until we arrived at Hartsfield-Jackson International Airport in Atlanta, there wasn't five words spoken amongst us. The only thing said was that Mark would be at the airport to pick us up.

Stepping off the plane into the large terminal in Atlanta, I couldn't believe how big the airport was compared to the one back home in Fayetteville. While my eyes scanned the thick crowd for Mark, this Halle Berry\Blu Cantrell looking sista approached Deavin's father, Darius.

"Hi Mr. James," the sista said, showing her pretty smile. "Mark couldn't make it so he sent me here to pick you all up instead.

"You are?" He asked.

"Shante..., Dee's girlfriend."

A big frown instantly appeared on my face when she said that.

"How is my son's condition?" Deavin's mother, Ms. Brenda asked, not showing any signs of warmth.

"I think he's gonna make it Ma'am. I've been at his bedside all morning."

"Good," Ms. Brenda said with an attitude. "What was the doctor's words?"

"They said his surgery was successful and that he appears to be out of danger right now. They moved him into Intensive Care around six o'clock this morning."

"Thanks for the update young lady, I'm Brenda. This is Deavin's sister Tammy and this is Tracy," she pointed at me. "She's a close friend of the family."

"Hi everybody," Shante said, eyeing my swollen belly.

"Now that we've all gotten acquainted, let's get to the hospital," Darius said.

About twenty minutes or so later, we were riding down I-85. Ms. Brenda had insisted that I ride in the front seat because of my pregnancy. The scenery along the way to the hospital was beautiful, the city's magnificent skyline had me in awe. We even rode past Turner Field where the Atlanta Braves played. It was also the site for the 1996 Olympic Games.

Even though I enjoyed taking in the city's nice sites, it all appeared to look gloomy to me in the end. My thoughts were focused on Deavin's health and Miss Thing who was driving. I didn't dare ask myself "what does he see in her?" It was obvious. She was gorgeous and appeared to have a lot of class. There was no doubt that she had my jealous meter at an all-time high. However, I wasn't going to let her know it.

When we got to the hospital Shante gave Darius her number and told him that she needed to go home for a while. "Please give me a call if anything new develops," she told him before she left.

I felt relieved when she left. Finally, I was able to exhale. I sat in the waiting room to give Deavin's family some private time to spend with him. For the next hour or so I sat tight with my fingers crossed and prayed that Deavin had a speedy recovery. All the anger I had built up inside me towards Deavin months ago, had vanished. Steven and Tammy both had helped me get over it. Though Steven and I were very close and had been that way for years, I knew that he could never be my man. He was more like a sister to me than anything. Steven was openly gay and had been that way as long as I'd known him.

"If I wasn't gay girl, I would wear that big ol' booty of yours out," he had told me a number of times when he saw me naked. 'Stephanie,' is what Steven liked to be called, moved in with me after he'd caught his lover of three years in bed with another man around the same time Deavin had broken my heart, so Steven and I used each other for healing. He and I did everything from discussing our personal problems and going grocery shopping, to getting our nails done together. We even slept together, but never did we go *there*. However, it felt good to have a warm body to cuddle with on a nightly basis.

Many of those late nights it had crossed my mind to *'free Willy'* when I felt it pressing up against my backside, but I couldn't do it. I was still hoping to woo Deavin back into my life. With Steven's plan it looked like it was possible. He was the one who came up with the idea of making Deavin jealous by telling him that we were a couple. To my surprise it worked better than I had ever expected. It was easy for me to detect the jealousy in Deavin's voice every time I mentioned Steven's name. It wasn't until Tammy called telling me how jealous Deavin was of Steven and I, that I actually realized he was still interested in me for me and not for me carrying his child.

"Tracy!" I looked up when I heard my name called. Darius, Ms. Brenda and Tammy were standing in front of me.

"Deavin's awake and he wants to see you."

"Not until he's moved to the recovery room, which shouldn't take longer than an hour," Darius added, holding his wife's hand.

"Did y'all get updated on his situation?"

"Yep," Tammy answered, taking a seat beside me.

"We're about to step outside to get some air," Darius said before he and Ms. Brenda headed for the elevator.

I turned to Tammy. "Fill me in on your brother's recovery?"

"The doctor said that my brother was shot in the chest and in the side. Neither of the bullets damaged any of his main arteries."

"Why was he unconscious laying up in ICU?"

"He'd went into shock after getting shot and losing so much blood. He told us he probably would have died on the scene from blood loss if it wasn't for some dude helping him."

"Thank God for sending that angel."

"The good news is that he's no longer in critical condition. That's why he's being moved to the recovery room only twelve hours after his surgery. My brother is a fighter," she grinned.

"Yes-yes!" I pumped my fist with a smile. "I knew God would answer my prayers."

"Now that we both are able to smile again, what do you think about Shante?"

"She seems to care a lot for Deavin," I replied.

"I don't want to hear the sugar coated version Tracy. I want the down and dirty version."

"I can't stand the prissy bitch and can't wait to tell her I'm carrying Deavin's baby."

"That's what I'm talking 'bout girl," she said, laughing as we gave each other high fives. "Fight for your man. Don't let her take my brother away from you without putting up a fight."

"Let's get real Tammy. That prissy bitch already got him."

"Deavin hasn't said a damn word about marrying her, so you still got a chance."

"I guess I gotta get in where I fit in."

"Mark!" Tammy blurted, jumping up and giving him a hug, disregarding our conversation.

Seeing Mark's face reminded me of Deavin because they were so close. I was glad to see him too and got up to give him a hug.

"I can't squeeze you like I did Tammy," he said looking at my big stomach, giving me a welcoming hug. "It's good to see some North Carolina faces. Where's Darius and Ms. Brenda?"

"They went outside," I answered as I sat back down.

"I don't see any long faces so I take it that Deavin is doing better?"

Mark sat down and Tammy began filling him in on Deavin's progress. Several minutes into the conversation a handsome looking man with hazel eyes approached us.

"Ladies," he acknowledged us and nodded before speaking to Mark.

"What's up Mr. Willis," Mark spoke, getting up to shake his hand. "This is the angel God sent to save Dee's life last night."

Tammy and I both got up and thanked him for being a Good Samaritan. We all sat around and talked about

Deavin. I was really surprised that Mr. Willis already knew who I was. He'd told me Deavin had talked with him about me a few times. Hearing that from him made me feel good. It also made me feel that I had a good shot a taking Deavin back from Miss Thing.

"Excuse me Ma'am," a nurse said, coming up to Tammy. She gave Tammy Deavin's new room number and disappeared back down the hall.

I looked myself over and took a deep breath before entering Deavin's room. I approached his bed with caution, not knowing how he was going to respond to me since he and I hadn't seen each other in six months.

"Stop creeping and get your fat bellied self over here," he said, startling me. "I ain't dead yet."

I excitedly rushed to his bedside, expecting to see a half ass smile on his face. However, what I saw was nothing close to a smile. He eyed me with a cold stare.

"Why you looking at me like that? I thought you wanted to see me."

"Where was your boyfriend last night?"

"What boyfriend? I don't..., oh..., you mean Steven. He's not my..."

"Where was he Tracy?" He demanded.

I hope he's not thinking Steven is the one who shot him. "When Tammy called, waking me up in the middle of the night, Steven was just coming in. He comes in late like that on Fridays because he be out partying with his friends, downtown at the club on Hillsborough Street."

"Hillsborough Street," he said, looking puzzled. "You mean..., Steven..."

"Is really my gay friend Stephanie. He didn't do this to you Deavin. Regardless of how bad you might treat me at times, I would never send somebody out to hurt you. I can't believe you would even think I'd stoop that low."

"I knew you wouldn't try to kill me, but I didn't put nothing past Steven. I thought he was your jealous boyfriend." He smiled. "You really had me going. You used sissy to make me jealous."

"Yep," I said and kissed him on the lips.

"You know I'm involved with someone."

I kissed him again. "When did you turn into Mr. Faithful?"

"When I got involved with Shante."

That comment hurt me all the way to the bone. "Why didn't you feel that way when you and I were together?"

"Let's just say I've really grown a lot since I left North Carolina," he said, cringing as he spoke.

"I see this really isn't a good time for us to be having this conversation. You look like you're in pain and need to get more rest."

"I'm gonna buzz the nurse in for some pain medication. It feels like my chest is about to explode."

"Rest baby. Don't say no more, I'll get the nurse for you. Just know that I still love you too Boo," I kissed him again and hurried out of the room because I was afraid to hear his response.

Feeling a little relieved being out of Deavin's presence, I told the nurse that he needed to be checked and headed back to the waiting room.

Mark, Mr. Willis, Tammy and Deavin's parents stood huddled around a slim light skinned guy with a thick mustache.

"We arrested a suspect in connection with the shooting of Mr. James about an hour ago," The man said.

I was thrilled to hear the good news and a smile appeared on my face. Then the elevator opened and out walked Miss Thing, carrying some flowers and stuffed animals. Damn I can't stand that pretty bitch!

SHANTE

Leaving the hospital after I had dropped off Dee's family and the pregnant girl, I went straight to Dee's condo and dropped off their luggage. Mark was home, but he didn't hear me come in. I heard him and Christine in his room, sounding like they were trying to tear the box springs out of the bed. Let me hurry on up and get out of here before I spoil their groove session.

I placed the luggage in the living room and dashed back out the door. As I headed home I couldn't shake the pregnant girl from my thoughts. She kept looking at me out of the corner of her eye like she wanted to ask me something. I didn't know what sista-girl's problem was and didn't care to find out.

As for Dee's mother, Stevie Wonder could see that she didn't like me. Why? I had no idea. I tried my best to be nice to her, but if she thought I was going to kiss her flat ass, she had me twisted. That applied for Tammy's tomboy looking ass too. It was obvious she didn't like me either. She was probably still mad at me for calling her a bitch over the phone a while back.

Dee's father was a different story. He liked me and I liked him. He was an easy going guy and you could tell that Dee got his height and looks from him. Whatever it was he saw in his evil ass wife, to stay with her for so long, I didn't see it. I felt he could have done much better than Ms. Brenda. Anyway, regardless of all the hate she and Tammy had for me, we all had one thing in common and that was Dee. We all loved and wanted him to get well.

By the time I pulled up in front of my apartment I had tears in my eyes as I thought about Dee and what had happened. I also had a guilty conscious about it because Julian may have been the shooter. If Julian was responsible for hurting my Boo, his ass needs to go to jail and rot.

I got in the tub and took a hot bath to relax and cleanse my body. I know I cleansed myself on the outside, but cleansing my inside was going to take a long time. I had hurt a lot of men over the years. From the men I did hurt, I know there were wives, girlfriends and even children affected by it as well. I was a devious bitch and being that, I knew I had to change.

The phone started ringing as I dried off. Monica would get it.

After the third ring it dawned on me that Monica had gone to work, so I rushed into my room and answered it. It was Detective Burns. He informed me that Julian had been arrested for shooting Dee.

"We recovered the alleged weapon we believe he used." I remembered him saying moments before he'd hung up.

"Damn!" Was all I could say as I flopped down on my bed. I felt like I had a thousand pound weight on my shoulders with all I had been through over the course of the last sixteen hours. My current boyfriend getting shot by my ex-boyfriend. The incident in the parking lot with Jay and Sabrina and Dee's mother and sister hating on me. Trying to cope with all of those issues at the same time was a little too much for me to deal with on my own. I needed to vent it all out to someone before I lost it.

I didn't want to discuss my personal problems with another woman, I felt a woman wouldn't be able to understand me. Calling my father was out of the question. Tim was a no, no. The only two men I had on my short list was Mark and Mr. Willis. Whichever one of them I see first, I'm going to pull him to the side and talk to him.

While working wonders on my bob with the curling iron, I thought about what Debra told me before she and Mr. Willis had left the hospital. She said that she knew my mother and remembered me. Debra had to be tipsy from all the glasses of champagne she'd consumed at the club. I was sure she had to be mistaken. I decided I would ask Mr. Willis about it the next time I saw him.

More drama, I thought as I saw Dee's family, Tracy included, staring me down when I stepped off the elevator into the hospital waiting room.

"Shante!" When I heard my name called I looked harder at the small gathering and was more than happy to see Mark, Mr. Willis and Detective Burns greeting me with warm smiles. I could also see that Dee's father wanted to greet me with a smile, but Ms. Brenda wasn't having it. She'd shot him one of those *'I dare you'* looks.

"If you don't mind, can I talk to you for a minute?" Tracy asked, stopping me in the middle of the waiting room.

"Would you mind if I drop this stuff off in Dee's room first?" I had flowers that I'd bought from the hospital gift shop and three of the stuffed animals Dee had won for me at Six Flags.

"No, I don't mind. Deavin's been moved to recovery. He's in room 633."

"Thanks," I said with a smile and headed on down the hallway to find Dee's new room.

I was glad he'd been moved to recovery. That told me he was doing a lot better. By the time I found room 633, a nurse stopped me at the door. She told me Dee had been sedated for pain and needed to get his rest. That was fine with me at the time, all I wanted to do was drop off the flowers and stuffed animals. He was asleep when I entered the room. I placed the flowers on the table, the stuffed animals in the bed with him and stole a kiss, leaving gloss on his lips.

Tracy was sitting at the far end of the waiting room when I got back. I went over to where she was and sat across from her.

"I couldn't help overhearing you at the airport when you introduced yourself as Deavin's girlfriend to his parents."

"Yes, I told them that," I responded, without catching an attitude.

"Well anyway," she said, sucking her teeth. "I'm Deavin's ex from North Carolina and I'm six months pregnant with his baby."

"Um-hmm..., I knew that already."

"You mean he told you about us?" She asked, looking surprised.

No, pot belly. Dee ain't told me shit about you or that crumb snatcher you're carrying. I'm not going to give you the satisfaction of seeing how hurt I am by finding out by you though.

"Yes Tracy," I nodded. "He told me everything."

Her hand instantly went up over her mouth. "Deavin must've really liked you because he used to be very secretive about his past and present relationships." She paused. "I guess he done changed. He never did tell me nothing about you."

"He's probably the same secretive Deavin then," I said, showing a weak smile, trying to conceal my anger.

She stood up. "Just wanted to let you know what was going on since I had no idea you even existed until today. Oh yeah, right before you got here the detective told us that the married man you been creeping around with was arrested for trying to kill Deavin. You home wrecker!" She spat and attempted to walk off.

"You black bitch!" I shot back, losing my cool, jumping up in her face with my fist balled. "Don't let the looks fool you wench! I'll whip your pregnant ass up in here!" I drew back to slap the shit out of her, but Mr. Willis caught my hand and pulled me back. Everybody in the waiting room was now staring at me like I was a Middle Eastern Suicide Bomber.

"Calm down Shante," Mr. Willis said. "Take a ride down the elevator with me. Everything is gonna be alright."

Since it appeared that he was my only friend for the moment, I got a grip on myself and listened to him. I got on the elevator with him and he took me down to the hospital cafeteria.

"Would you like anything to eat or drink?" He asked me after we sat at one of the tables.

"No thanks, I'm good sir."

"What caused that problem with you and Tracy up there?"

I sighed. "Everything. Everything that could have possibly gone wrong since Dee and I walked out of the club last night, has gone wrong."

"Sometimes things happen for a reason Shante."

"Yeah, like me finding out Dee's got a baby on the way. Explain that reason."

"Deavin and I are pretty close and we've talked about a lot of things. I told him to tell you about that situation at least a month ago."

"Well he didn't and it just killed me to hear it coming out of that wench's mouth. Dee should've told me something because I felt like a damn idiot sitting up there listening to Tracy run her mouth. It's a good thing you grabbed me, I was about to whip her pregnant ass."

"She must have said some pretty nasty things to you."

"Yes she did, but my problems go a lot deeper than her."

"Hey," he said, giving me that fatherly look. "I'm all ears Shante."

I looked into his hazel eyes for honesty before opening up the flood gates. I told him about my past relationships with Julian and why Dee walked off leaving me in the parking lot.

"The story about your ex, Jason Chambers."

Chambers. I didn't mention Jason's last name to him.

"Ja-son," I fumbled with his name. "You know him?"

"Met him in prison when he first entered the systems years ago. All he use talked about was his beautiful Precious."

"How long have you known that I was Jason's Precious?"

"After you told me about him. That young man really loved and cared the world about you."

"I know," I said with sorrow. "You must've worked as a prison guard back then?"

"No Shante, I was an inmate just like Jason."

My hands immediately went up over my mouth and I stared at him in disbelief. "You're kidding me, right?"

"That's one thing I don't kid about," he said with a serious expression on his face. "Not only did I spend twenty six years in prison. I lost my family too."

Twenty-six long years. Damn, that's my whole life. I wonder what he did to serve all that time. Now I know why he made the *since i come home'* statement.

"I'm not trying to be nosy or anything, but what did you do?"

"My past isn't good Shante."

"Who am I to judge? I'd like to hear your story."

He smiled. "Hell, why not? You've already opened up to me." He took a deep breath before speaking. "Twenty-six years, six months and twenty-three days ago, to be exact. I left the house early one morning to find some extra work to help make ends meet. Times were hard back then. My girlfriend was eight months pregnant with our child and she was unable to work." He closed his eyes. "God I loved that woman to death and would have done anything to make her happy."

He dug in his pocket and pulled out his wallet. He took out two pictures and handed them to me as he continued telling his story. I almost fainted when I looked at the pictures of my mother and my long lost sperm donor Mr. Willis. I couldn't believe it. I wanted to say something so bad, but I didn't interrupt him because I wanted to hear his full story before letting him know that I was the daughter he'd been searching for.

With the same skin complexion, hazel eyes, natural curly hair and same nose, I should have been able to figure it out the evening I first met him at the comedy club. Mr. Willis, Mr. Dennis Willis, is my biological father. Mama is really gonna be surprised when I tell her.

"If God is willing," he said with tears forming in the corner of his eyes. "He'll lead me to them one of these days."

He'd told me the whole story and it had me on the brink of tears too. "He already has," I said as I smiled, causing tears to roll down my cheeks. "Mama always told me how much you loved her, but I never believed her. Now I do. You're forgiven, Daddy. You've suffered long enough."

He stared at me, speechless, with tears coming out of his eyes as if he'd went into shock. "Carla Blackmon. Shante Blackmon," he mumbled just above a whisper and stood up.

I got up too. We hugged and cried in each other's arms for what seem like an eternity.

"Dad, you couldn't have come into my life at a better time. I need you now more than ever.

"My beautiful daughter." He smiled, holding my hands as we sat back down. "There's nothing in this world that could ever separate me from you again, but death itself. I'm gonna be there for you Shante and you know we got a lot to catch up on. What was it Deb said to you before we left the hospital this morning?"

"She said she knew my mama and remembered me from when I was a little girl."

"No wonder she told me she had a surprise for me later today. Deb and her sister Sarah has known Carla for years. We all lived in the same neighborhood together. That was a long time ago. How is your mother doing?"

"Let me use your phone? I'm about to call her and let you see for yourself."

He passed me his phone and I dialed my mother's number.

DEAVIN

"Life's a bitch and then you die, that's why we get high, cause you never know when you gonna go," I mumbled AZ's verse of "Life's A Bitch" on Nas Illmatic classic CD. The lyrics to that song were deep. I just didn't realize how deep they were until after I got shot. Waking up in a cold hospital bed with two gunshot wounds made me realize how lucky I was to be alive. My second chance at life.

The afternoon I first woke up, I had no idea how long I'd been out. I was just happy to see my family at my bedside. Even though my mother and sister had been angry with me about the way I handled my relationship with Tracy, they showed no signs of it while visiting me, it was all love. When my mother told me that Tracy was out in the waiting room I couldn't believe it. At the time, I thought she was responsible for me getting shot and I told my mother to send Tracy in to see me as they left my room. When Tracy did enter my room I wanted to jump up and slap her silly. However, I'm glad I was in no shape to do so, because after she explained the whole situation to me about Steven,

"Stephanie", I felt miserable. I didn't know that Tracy had it in her, but she played me and I silently gave her credit for it. She learned from the best.

Seeing her for the first time in six long months was a real reality check. It was easy for me to see that she was pregnant. She looked like she was carrying a WNBA basketball under her maternity shirt. Also, due to her being pregnant, I had expected for her to look all fat faced and ugly. I was certainly wrong about that. With her full lips, pretty coco brown skin and big brown eyes staring down at me, I couldn't help but have flashbacks about our past. As much as I hated to admit it, I still loved Tracy. When she kissed me that afternoon it felt so good I thought I'd died and gone to heaven.

On the other hand, the throbbing pain in my chest immediately reminded me that neither had happened. After the nurse had sedated me with pain medication, I dozed off thinking about Tracy and our unborn daughter.

I woke about six hours later to the smell of Hazel Eyes' Portfolio body spray. I peered around the room and didn't see her. What I did see was the stuffed animals I'd won her. The lingering scent from the body spray immediately made me think back to the parking lot incident. I couldn't believe that my Hazel Eyes, my Special, my Shante, was another man's Precious. To make matters worse, she just wasn't his Precious. She had been his pregnant Precious and aborted his child. Hazel Eyes might not have been the flawless woman I thought she was, but I still considered her my Special and loved everything about her.

While I laid there looking at the IV's that were hooked to me, I tried to figure out who it was trying to kill me and why? Bored to death, I was about to watch a few episodes of the web series "Damaged Goods" to see Patrice's fine ass, but something told me to check the news first. I did just that.

My eyes grew bigger and my heart began pounding when I saw the black Suburban with the dark tinted windows sitting on the back of a flatbed tow truck. I quickly turned up the volume to see what the news reporter had to say.

"A thirty-three year old Cascade man was arrested this afternoon at his home without incident, in connection with the early morning shooting outside of a Midtown night club off Peachtree Street. Julian Patterson, who is a married man, apparently shot his estrange ex mistress's new boyfriend over a lovers quarrel. The victim, a thirty year old North Carolina man, is hospitalized in stable condition. There was also another early morning shooting involving two rival gangs outside of a motel, off Metropolitan Parkway. No one was seriously injured."

I'd heard enough and flipped the TV off. After watching that news report I realized Julian was the married man Hazel Eyes had told me was her part-time boyfriend when she and I first started kicking it.

I heard my room door open and I looked up. Mr. Willis was coming in and I was glad to see him. He and I ended up talking for a while and he filled me in on almost every question I asked him. I was shocked to find out he was the person that saved my life and thanked him at least ten times before he left. Even though I was a little pissed at Hazel Eyes, I had asked him if she was out in the waiting room.

"No Deavin," he replied with a smile that lit up the room. "My daughter went home to get some sleep. She'll be back to see you in the morning."

"Huh?" I murmured, confused. "Hazel Eyes..., your daughter?"

"Yep. She's the one I've been looking for. Isn't it funny how the Lord works sometimes?"

"I guess so," I said, looking at him, realizing for the first time how much they resembled each other.

****

"Dee!" Hazel Eyes said, awakening me. "They just brought your breakfast in. Raise up so you can eat."

I'd been laying up in that cold ass hospital bed for four days and I was past ready to leave. Tracy and my family had left for North Carolina the night before and I wasn't too thrilled about seeing them go, especially Tracy. Watching her and Hazel Eyes pretending like they really liked each other for those couple of days gave me something to laugh and smile about. They both had told me how close they had come to fighting in the waiting room. They also talked about each other like dogs behind each other's backs. I kept all the hateful things they said about each other to myself. I didn't want to start World War 3 up in Grady Hospital and I definitely didn't want Tracy to miscarry our baby by fighting Hazel Eyes, or anyone else as far as I was concerned.

For three straight days Tracy greeted me with her soft juicy lips. I also enjoyed rubbing her stomach, feeling our baby girl move. I had sort of gotten use to her company and hated to see her go. Hazel Eyes had even walked in on us kissing right before Mark took her and my family to the airport. She'd got real mad at me, but I didn't trip it. I figured she would get over it.

However, the day before, Krushink came to the hospital to pay me a visit. I had no idea she was in Atlanta the night I was shot and had come to the hospital after Christine called, telling her what had happened to me. Kruskink and I would DM each other on Instagram every so often and I considered her a friend, even though she and I had only met once. There was really nothing sexual about the Instagram messages she and I exchanged over the months, even though I was sexually attracted to her. Hell, she was gorgeous, with a great personality. She was also tatted and had a booty that would make Nicki Minaj sit her ass down. With all those qualities, I couldn't understand why she wasn't married or at least in a steady relationship. I'd told her on more than one occasion that I would go down to Miami and snatch her up if Hazel Eyes wasn't in my life.

Every time I told her that she would always reply, "I'm not what you want." Well, I didn't find out what she actually meant by that statement until she told me that she wasn't born a female.

"Wow," was all I could say at the moment because there was nothing about her that appeared manly to me. Had it not been for Christine to verify it, I wouldn't have believed Krushink. It's all good though because we're all God's creation and I still consider her my friend.

"I'm sick and tired of eating this nasty ass hospital food. I thought you was supposed to be bringing me some eggs, cheese and ham croissants from Burger King this morning?"

"I thought I was too," Hazel Eyes said, standing over me with her arms folded. "Until I saw you kissing that pregnant wench last night."

"For the ump-teenth time, I told you it was nothing. And why are you calling her those names? I thought you two were trying to work out some kind of friendship."

"Some kind of friendship my ass. I only played that role because your family was all up in my face every time I came to see you. Back to that kiss Dee. You liked it didn't you? Is that why you didn't stop her?"

"Come on now," I said, getting serious. "It's been days now and you still haven't told me why you withheld the past about your abortion to me."

"Cause I never thought I'd ever see or hear from Jason again. I tried to bury it. I was ashamed to tell you about it. I thought you would look at me in a different way, knowing that I was damaged goods."

"You don't have to be ashamed to tell me anything. You're far from being damaged goods. You're still and will always be my Special and I love everything about you. Don't you ever forget that."

"I'm your Special again? She asked before giving me a long sensual kiss. "You know that was the first time you've called me Special since..., well you know."

"I know."

"The kiss Dee, I wanna know why it happened."

"She's about to become the mother of my child and I can't deny that I still have feelings for her. What you walked in and saw last night was more like a goodbye kiss. Tracy knows and understand that my heart is with you. I believe she accepted it after the long talk she and I had last night. I owe her a lot, Special and I'm planning on making it up to her by being the best father I can possibly be."

"A father is all you better be around her. If I catch you locking lips with her again you're gonna end up in worse shape than you are in now."

"Like I told you a minute ago. I still got feelings for Tracy, but you're my Special and I'm in love with you. I'll never cheat on you. Now I want you to answer a question for me"

"What?"

"Why am I your Dee again? I thought I was your Boo."

"I heard Tracy call you her Boo, so from here on out you're gonna be my Bae."

"That's what's up."

"There's one thing I can honestly say."

"What's that?"

"You are the love of my life Deavin 'Dee' James. I'm hoping our relationship will stand the test of time."

"We've already withstood one major test." I reached out grabbing her hand. "Anything else should be a cake walk."

"You know you never told me what the fifth stage of our twenty-seven hour date was."

"We fell in love with each other, right?"

"Yep."

"That sealed the fifth stage, Special."

SABRINA

EIGHT MONTHS LATER

After I graduated from college and received my degree in Journalism, my fiancé, Jason Chambers and I packed up and moved to Washington D.C. My Aunt Tina helped me get a job at the Washington Post as a staff writer. Moving to the original Chocolate City for me was all good and I felt that I would be able to adjust smoothly because I had a lot of family who lived in the South East part of the city.

Jay and I were both happy to be leaving Atlanta to make a new start. Even though he was no longer involved in the drug game, he felt that he was scarred living in Georgia and wanted to get away. Jay had inked a three book deal with Life After Death Publicationz for the book he'd written called "The Other Side Of The Hustle", which was based on his life. I had convinced him to write the book and I edited it to perfection before he submitted the manuscript to Katrina and Charles at Life After Death Publicationz.

As for my employment at Dolly's, after the incident Jay and I had with Shante outside the club, it ended abruptly. I couldn't see myself being in that saditty bitch's presence again. She had even called and told me the job was open to me if I still wanted it, but I declined. Going back to Dolly's would have brought back memories of me meeting the good looking and sweet talking Deavin. Those were memories that I wanted to forget about, since I was still recovering from the relationship Deavin and I had.

Some men are just hard to get over.

DEAVIN

With my hoop dreams being shattered once again after getting shot, I no longer considered playing professional basketball. It wasn't really that disappointing to me because other things in my life were going great. James' Janitorial Service was booming so good that I hired six new workers and appointed Mr. Willis and Mark to supervise the four men crews they worked with. That allowed me to sit back and take care of the paperwork and payroll checks.

I was also the proud father of five month old Nyisa Kenya James. I was at Cape Fear Valley Hospital when Tracy gave birth to our beautiful daughter. I even cut the umbilical cord.

"Thanks for being here for me and the baby," Tracy told me, hours after she'd had Nyisa. "But you could've left that hazel eyed bitch back down in Georgia."

"Come on Tracy. I thought you'd gotten over that shit by now."

"Never! You better not let that bitch touch Nyisa either. I'm warning you Deavin."

That was five months ago. Thank God things turned out to be a lot different.

TRACY

My boyfriend, Jaheem and I were getting ready to head out to the Fayetteville Coliseum to attend a concert. R & B newcomer Shante Miss Thing was performing as Fantasia's opening act. The local radio station, Foxy 99 had been playing Shante's hit single "Gotta Have You" at least ten times a day for a whole month. It was the most requested song for weeks.

Deavin, Shante and her small entourage had arrived in town the night before and they spent a couple hours at Deavin's parent's house. While there, Shante and I had a long woman to woman talk. It wasn't until then that I realized her love for Deavin was truly genuine. Since she loved and cared for him just as much as I did, I decided to stop being a bitch and made peace with her.

However, I was still willing to take Deavin back at the drop of a dime, but I wasn't going to continue holding out for him, thanks to Jaheem. All I wanted and expected out of Deavin was for him to be a good father to Nyisa.

SHANTE

A month after Deavin was released from the hospital, Tee Wiley signed me to his record label. He, along with a group of writers and producers, helped me complete my album in six weeks. My first single "Gotta Have You" had skyrocketed to number two on the R & B chart in a matter of weeks after its release. Overnight I had basically became the hottest R & B diva on the scene. Love 103 radio personality Missy E the Party Doll had even allowed me to co-host her Back In The Day Lunch Buffet. I was doing it big.

Besides the new found success, my life was going great. Deavin was there for me in every way possible and our relationship couldn't have been better. His mother and sister had finally stopped hating and accepted me into their family. Tracy had even let Deavin and I bring Nyisa back to Atlanta with us for a week after I performed in Fayetteville the night before. Nyisa was a pretty chocolate baby, with big brown eyes and I was crazy about her.

I carried Nyisa into my new Buckhead home when Deavin and I returned from North Carolina. She was asleep and I took her straight to my bed to lay her down. As soon as I left my bedroom, heading for the living room, my mother stepped out of my guestroom, looking like she'd saw a ghost. She had arrived in town the morning before I left for North Carolina. She'd came to Atlanta because she claimed she wanted to talk to my daddy, Mr. Willis, face to face. Why did it take her eight long months to get up the courage to finally see Mr. Willis? I don't know. I did know that she didn't tell her husband, Ricky, her real purpose for coming to the ATL. He thought she had come to visit me.

"What's wrong with you Mama?" I asked as she stood frozen in the doorway, wearing a silk spaghetti strap teddy.

"Oh..., nothing," she said suspiciously, looking over her shoulder. "I wasn't expecting you to be back so soon."

"For some crazy reason the promoters cancelled the Charlotte and Winston-Salem show. That's why I'm back early."

"I-I see," she stuttered nervously, backing into the room.

I smiled. "You ain't gotta act all nervous like a young teenage girl. I know Daddy is in the room with you."

"How did you know?"

"He called while I was in North Carolina and told me that you had invited him over. He just wanted to make sure it was ok with me first."

"It's not what you're thinking."

"You ain't gotta lie to me Mama." I smiled. "All I want to know is that you are happy again."

"Yes I am." She blushed. "I'm happy..., but Ricky isn't going to be when I tell him I had an affair with your father."

Other Books by
Life After death Publicationz

Visit us online at…
http://www.lifeafterdeathpublicationz.com/
https://www.facebook.com/groups/754362137964715/

Secretly Secured
by Kelvin Scott

After being abandoned by his father and thrown into the foster system following his mother's death, De' Angelo Smith -better known as Dezzy- finds himself drawn to the streets. His path crosses with Diamond, who is also a product of the foster system. But after a wild night in Tallahassee, Florida, Diamond and her friends become the focus of a very dangerous hunting game. Fate brings them together as they encounter true love for the first time, but just as quickly fate will tear them apart. Will they ever be reunited? Will Dezzy keep the promises he made?

Available on

Amazon

http://www.amazon.com/dp/B00SDIIHVU/ref=cm_sw_r_fa_dp_R7lfvb0EBRMKP

Barnes & Noble

http://www.barnesandnoble.com/w/secretly-secured-kelvin-scott/1121221054

Cable
By BornTrue Bethea

MONSTERS ARE NOT BORN…
THEY ARE MADE!!!

In the year 2015, the world is overrun by a terrorist group known as S.C.A.R. The last piece of freedom is a little part of the United States' west coast that has been renamed the Free World. The only thing that is stopping S.C.A.R. from overrunning the Free World is their super-soldier Cable. He is a half-man, half-machine who has found only one purpose in life, to kill any threat he sees, by any means possible. During one of their missions, Cable and his men come across a time machine made by the enemy. Knowing the location of one of their experiential sites, Cable volunteers himself to go back in time to stop the terrorist group before it starts. Before he can find what he's looking for, he discovers that the enemy also has a time machine along with vital information that can stop Cable. Will S.C.A.R. complete their mission of world domination, or will the terrorist group crumble by the hands of Cable?
Available on
Amazon
http://www.amazon.com/dp/B00ZYU507Y/ref=cm_sw_r_fa_dp_sI0Kv
b1VPT141

Barnes & Noble
http://www.barnesandnoble.com/w/cable-born-true-
bethea/1121213330?ean=2940150042261

The Next
by BornTrue Bethea

Meet Thomas Martin, a mechanic in Philadelphia who has a dream of one day opening his own garage. After breaking up with his fiancé Samantha, his primary goal is to go to school, work and take care of his kids. With that in mind and the lingering ache in his heart due to his ex's adultery, he plans on keeping to himself. As the saying goes; when you're not looking, love will find you and it did with not just one, but three women. Not to mention that his ex-fiancé is trying to slide her way back into Tommy's heart.

Will Tommy forgive Samantha and get back together with her? Or will one of the new girls steal his heart and become The Next?

Available on
Amazon
https://www.amazon.com/dp/B06XNKTN2R/ref=cm_sw_r_fa_dp_t2_apmYybZJXW6GP

Jack Boyz
By Charles Broadie

Malaki is a self-proclaimed Muslim on the outside, but on the inside he is a stone cold killer and a Jack Boy who is followed by his infamous crew, the Black Out Boyz. Their reign of terror is unstoppable and touches every dope boy with a sack. He has every girl around dropping to their knees before him and he greedily indulges himself. But Malaki's heart belongs to Jazmine, the good Muslim girl whose father thinks Malaki is evil. Everything is all good until one of the Black Out Boyz's enemies decides to hit back. Now Malaki and his crew will be forced into an all-out war or risk losing everything. Who can he trust and who must he get rid of? The loss will be great but the big question is, have the Jack Boyz bitten off more than they can chew?

Available on
Amazon
http://www.amazon.com/dp/B00ZMIOX6W/ref=cm_sw_r_fa_dp_Eoe Ovb14R4YZ3

Barnes & Noble
http://www.barnesandnoble.com/w/jack-boyz-charles-broadie/1123686013?ean=2940158323515

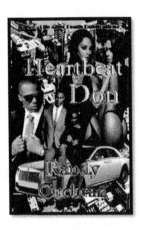

Heartbeat Don
By Randy Cochran

Heartbeat Don
By Randy Cochran

David was young, innately intelligent, charming, well dressed and filthy rich. He frequented posh clubs and hotels, owned posh houses, luxury cars, and anything anyone had a craving for. Women desired to be with him and men wanted to be like him. He was the Don of Hartford, Connecticut. A rogue, but a respected guy in the streets who had the money and power to demand that respect. He and his men were the objects of fear, they had a resolve to kill without mercy in order protect their own interests. The Don had come a far cry from the boy he was. Raised in Atlanta, Georgia by his grandmother, together with his two sisters, he was taught to be good and god-fearing. The gentle boy's life began to change abruptly when he, his sisters and his mother moved to Hartford, Connecticut to reunite with his stepfather and other siblings. Not only was he living with a stepfather who was an alcoholic and wife-beater, he also lived in a town where crime and belligerence ruled. Soon he surrounded himself with friends who, in one way or another, spent time in juvenile detention. Then one night he met his first Don. The don supplied the highest quality drugs known to the streets of Stowe Village, business was booming. David realized that he wanted to be the Don and to do that he would have to get rid of the reigning Don. In no time, he becomes the object of vengeance and hatred from the Under Lords of New York. What will David give up to achieve his dreams?

Available on
Amazon
http://www.amazon.com/dp/B00ZMJ8A2Y/ref=cm_sw_r_fa_dp_Oqe Ovb1N16KP5

Barnes & Noble

http://www.barnesandnoble.com/w/heartbeat-don-randy-cochran/1111592288?ean=2940158323577

2-Die-4
by Randy Cochran

David went off to prison to serve a long sentence but his son's Justin and Justice didn't stop doing business and they will do whatever it takes to keep the family name respected. Having a sister to look after makes the brothers work harder but when it's time to prove her position she turns out to be more dangerous than them all.

Tonya does something she can never be forgiven for while Lisa and Linda prove to be too much for each other. They run for their lives after breaking the code, 2 die 4.

Randy Cochran is the author of the bestselling family saga, "Heartbeat Don" He enjoys working with youth and is currently writing the sequel to this book and also the third part of another story he plans to publish.

Available on
Amazon
http://www.amazon.com/dp/B016SEPG1E/ref=cm_sw_r_fa_dp_s2Qi wb0Y17GJ0

4-Ever
by Randy Cochran

Justin is serving a prison term and while he is there Iesha talks him into converting to Muslim. But in prison Justin has to prove he can hold his own and be a man. He changes his name to Zulu Muhammad and he meets two brotha's who will change his life 4ever, Kabir and Ali.

David gets out of prison on an appeal bond, but his past just won't let him rest. Lucy is on a vengeance mission and won't stop until she gets David back for killing her best friend.

Will David escape death yet again? Or will someone close to him once again draw him into a death trap?

Find out who is 4-Ever Family.

Available on
Amazon
https://www.amazon.com/dp/B01GQFYBTI/ref=cm_sw_r_fa_dp_.9Uv
xbCYHQJ0Y

A Passion To Cry
by Randy Cochran

The gripping story of a family torn apart by murder, drugs and abuse. Stephanie comes from a nice upper-class family, how could she end up losing her three daughters to foster care? A nice, wealthy family takes the girls in, but all is not always as it seems in those big fancy houses on the hill. With trouble lurking around every corner it is up to Kayla to protect her family. When a serial killer goes on the loose, it is Kayla's responsibility to stop him as well. But, just like Kayla, Stan has been trained to kill. Will there be a final show down between Kayla and Stan Jones? It's just a matter of time.

Available on
Amazon
https://www.amazon.com/dp/B01M7U4FWY/ref=cm_s
w_r_fa_dp_t2_zxbeyb06Y8CFS

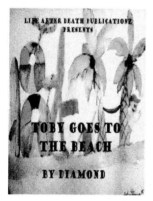

Toby Goes to the Beach
by Diamond

Meet Toby, the little boy who loves going to the beach. He loves playing in the sand and building sand castles. Come along on his beach adventure and meet some new friends.

Available on Amazon

http://www.amazon.com/dp/B014M085W8/ref=cm_sw_r_fa_dp_nCD4vb12T253W

Our Bench

This book is a collection of poetry written entirely by Life After Death Publicationz Authors and staff. It is a collection of our thoughts and feelings, but even more, it is a collection of our trials, our loves, our triumphs and yes, the things we believe in and the things we attest. Please sit back and relax, enjoy your read.

Available on Amazon
http://www.amazon.com/dp/B01A4CB2Z0/ref=cm_sw_r_fa_dp_daVJ wb1BMFB3P

The Streets or My Wife
By Shamica Gonzales and Kasam Hennix

Meet Kane. His reason for getting in the game was to get his money up, but he was romanced by fast cars and fast women. On one hand Kane wanted to open a business to take care of his family, but he got caught up in his old life style. Who can Kane trust? It seems everyone wants to take him down, or do they? Will Kane be able to stay alive and retire from the game or will he become another notch in its belt? Ride along with him as he decides between the streets or his wife.

Available on
Amazon
http://www.amazon.com/dp/B01AITIXSI/ref=cm_sw_r_fa_dp_vJNLwb0796QQ8
Barnes & Noble
http://www.barnesandnoble.com/w/the-streets-or-my-wife-katrina-breier/1124161888?ean=2940157059347#

Belly of the Beast: Book One
Inside Love Affair That Pays Off Big
By Knowledge Tauhid

This is the story of an inmate in a state's prison system who learned and put to use the gift of gab, proper articulation, a sincere charisma and a sophisticated, undetected, white collar scheme from the confines and restraints of the inside. Through his quest to manipulate the powers that be, on a level unlike EVER before, Maurice manages to seduce the African-American, female Warden that he works for as an aide within the prison. He works her into becoming a major participant in his fraudulent scam that he masterminded and into eventually becoming his 'lady friend' and the mother to be of their unborn child. He, being in need of a for sure way to raise some money to establish legitimate business ventures once he was free, and her, being in desperate need of love and male companionship that had the potential to grow into a marriage, had combined forces for the betterment and "good" of each other. Meeting one another in the facility and slowly but surely getting acquainted on a deep level, had paved the way for the pair to be a dynamic duo, a power couple like no one had ever thought to be possible. Their story begins here.

Available on
Amazon
http://www.amazon.com/dp/B01B1WSRIC/ref=cm_sw_r_fa_dp_ly9Q
wb1YYRD1Q

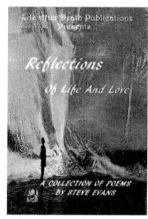

Reflections of Life and Love
By Steve Evans

My poems cover everyday issues that we all deal with. I write of pain and loss, of yearning and needing and of heartbreak and confusion.

When I write, I want the reader to be able to lose themselves in the story. I want them to see themselves in each word and to be able to relate.

I tend to go a little more to the darker side of life and love simply because I find it more interesting and easier to hold my attention and hopefully the reader's as well.

Steve

Available on
Amazon
http://www.amazon.com/dp/B01C7SF0FW/ref=cm_sw_r_fa_dp_EP4Z wb194F9JV

Savor the Darkness
Poetry By Steve Evans

CHAOS THEORY
(A Random Thought)

In the madness that is my
Reality, I tend to thrive on
Confusion and doubt.
I try to keep writing, hoping
The chaos will work itself
Out!

Available on
Amazon
https://www.amazon.com/dp/B01HKCDR3M/ref=cm_sw_r_fa_dp_.oZ
BxbNV7X8V5

Deceiving Eternity
by Steve Evans

Hidden in the darkness, is a special place. A place where a painted on smile is meant to cover internal agony. A place where pain and heartache drown out the sparkle of a once vibrant soul. It's a place reserved for those attempting to disguise their fears with fake emotions and timid dreams... A place designated for those lost souls who believe they are Deceiving Eternity!

Available on
Amazon
https://kdp.amazon.com/amazon-dp-action/us/dualbookshelf.marketplacelink/B06XRZF3QD

Bitter Sweet
By Jonas Brinkley
I composed this book of free verse poems from my life experiences and from what I see around me. Us as people and country have a lot of growing to do to reach that ideal dream we deeply crave. I don't expect to reach everybody through my words, but if I inspire one soul or ignite one smile then my job is done. So please, have fun exploring my thoughts.

Available on
Amazon
https://www.amazon.com/dp/B01IWTD7VO/ref=cm_sw_r_fa_dp_c_R
O5KxbYCJ1KAW

King of the Streetz Part 1&2

Fresh out of North Carolina's penitentiary after doing seven years for a robbery he didn't commit is TK, one of T-Ville's finest. TK wastes no time before he sets in motion a plan to take what he feels the streetz rightfully owe him. With adultery, murder and betrayal under his belt from the jump, TK fights to keep karma at bay. The only question is will he succeed???

Available on
Createspace
https://www.createspace.com/5922349

King of the Streetz 2&4

Fresh out of an eight month coma, TK seeks to get back to his old self as he deals with several baby mamas, enemies from his past, snitches in his own organization and an eager law enforcement who wants nothing more than to take him down. Then TK finds himself and his team locked up with very little chance of ever getting out. When he pulls off the impossible to get them free, he finds himself faced with a betrayal so unexpected that he makes emotional decisions. These decisions get him indicted by the FBI and this time they have a solid case. Everything he's worked so hard for is now in jeopardy. Can he pull off the impossible or is it finally his time to pay the price for the life he chose?

Available on
Createspace
https://www.createspace.com/6153284

KING OF THE STREETZ PART 1
http://www.amazon.com/gp/aw/d/B00NIC4TLI/ref=kina_tdp?ie=UTF8
KING OF THE STREETZ PART 2
http://www.amazon.com/dp/B00PM3D282/ref=cm_sw_r_fa_awdm_s
pr2vb1489116
KING OF THE STREETZ PART 3
http://www.amazon.com/dp/B00YJIEHJY/ref=cm_sw_r_fa_awdm_aKP
Svb1BPENRE
KING OF THE STREETZ PART 4
http://www.amazon.com/dp/B01BX1SBFA/ref=cm_sw_r_fa_dp_ZYMX
wb0TE5WHZ

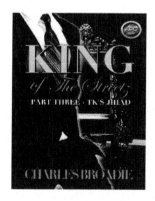
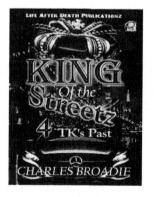

The Ghost
by H. Berkeley Rourke

H. BERKELEY ROURKE

WHAT NO ONE KNOWS, CAN'T HURT HIM...

A vicious rapist is loose on the Scalian University campus. He thinks he's invisible with campus authorities covering things up. He likes it that way. But she was not his first and she will not be his last.

UNTIL...

The Ghost accidently beats his victim to death and becomes a killer. Can he still hide from authorities?

WHAT WILL IT TAKE TO CATCH THE GHOST?

Detective Jeanne de Leon is on the case, wading through a campus cover up and the layers of lies that have followed. What will she uncover in this tangled web? How will it all end?

THE MANHUNT IS ON

Available on Amazon
https://www.amazon.com/dp/B06XPY4RJD/ref=cm_sw_r_fa_dp_t2_fZ73ybQQ5NXTT